TRIED
AS
SILVER

TRIED
AS
SILVER

A Historical Novel

Book Three of the Emily Alden Trilogy

SIDNEY S. STARK

Momentum Ink Press

New York

AUTHOR'S NOTE

This book is inspired by actual events. While the main characters and plots are all fictitious, some of the secondary characters and subplots are not. It is, therefore, a true composition of historical fiction.

Published in the United States by Momentum Ink Press, New York.

PUBLISHER'S CATALOGING IN PUBLICATION DATA
provided by Five Rainbows Cataloging Services
Names: Stark, Sidney S., author.
Title: Tried as silver / Sidney S. Stark.
Description: New York : Momentum Ink Press, 2022. | Series: Emily Alden trilogy, bk. 3.
Identifiers: ISBN 978-1-7358893-1-3 (paperback) | ISBN 978-1-7358893-2-0 (ebook)
Subjects: LCSH: Women musicians—Fiction. | England—19th century—Fiction. | Gossip—Fiction. | Family—Fiction. | Historical fiction. | BISAC: FICTION / Historical / General. | FICTION / Women. | FICTION / Family Life / General. | GSAFD: Historical fiction.
Classification: LCC PS3619.T3739 T75 2022 (print) | LCC PS3619.T3739 (ebook) | DDC 813/.6—dc23.

https://theunblockedwriter.com
https://momentuminkpress.com

For information about special discounts available for bulk purchases, sales promotions, fundraising, and educational needs, contact the author at sidney.s.stark@gmail.com

Book design by Kathryn Holeman

It seems equally true in Art and in Morals, that it is not by indulgence and favour, but by difficulty and trouble, that the spirit is formed; and in all ages of the world our Davids, Shakespeares, Dantes, Mozarts, and Beethovens must submit to processes which none but their great spirits could survive—to a fiery trial of poverty, ill health, neglect, and misunderstanding—and be "tried as silver is tried."

—Sir George Grove
A Dictionary of Music and Musicians (1877–1889)

BOOKS BY SIDNEY S. STARK

THE EMILY ALDEN TRILOGY

Certain Liberties

The Gilded Cage

Tried as Silver

Twilight Perspectives:
Essays of Life and Death

For more details, join us at
https://TheUnblockedWriter.com
where you'll find inspirational essays,
writing news, and event information.

PRAISE

Tried as Silver

"Stark's 19th-century violinist proceeds to London for her final act in this, the third in a trilogy of historical novels. After two decades in Paris, famed British-born American violinist Emily de Koningh (nee Alden) and her family are relocating to London ... There is a new energy in London's music scene ... where the Royal College of Music was recently founded to compete with the storied conservatories of the Continent. Are Emily's prospects about to experience a similar renaissance, or is her fragile ensemble of friends, relatives, and lovers about to disband for good? Stark's novel displays a depth of research and command of history."

—*Kirkus Reviews*

"Just finished your book. Really quite extraordinary. So grateful you wrote it."

—Virginia Stowe

"I'm loving it!! Emily is wonderful! Aunt Clara is perfectly annoying but I kinda like her..., [and] Professor Stanford! I'm really enjoying the book, it's excellent! It was a total compelling read for me! Bravo or is it Brava?"

—Eric Hensley

Emily Alden is a Nineteenth Century heroine battling the turbulence of society's demands. *Tried as Silver* roils with suspense as Emily, surrounded by actual and imagined characters from the Victorian age, redefines the meaning of family, parent, performer, and lover ... a page turner causing readers to examine how their own lives are "tried" by the pressures of modern society. Don't miss this third book in the trilogy."

—Paul Pitcoff, author of *Cold War Secrets* and *Beyond the Foster Care System*

PRAISE

"In *Tried as Silver*, Emily struggles with the universal themes of managing family and profession. The author invites a solution as elegant and crafted as her language, her historical figures, and her dealing with the restrictive sexual mores. Stark, like Emily, finds her forte in music and musicians of the times."

—**Denise B. Dailey**, author of *Listening to Pakistan: A Woman's Voice in a Veiled Land*, *Riko: Seductions of an Artist*, and *Leaving Guanabara*

"Sidney Stark writes with passion and elegance in this impeccably researched novel, full of rich details and nuanced descriptions of this historical era. It's a brilliant end to her superb trilogy as the wonderfully resilient Emily Alden discovers newfound joy and meaning in an art form most personal, intimate, and profound, called Chamber Music."

—**Jia Kim**, Artistic Director of Spruce Peak Chamber Music Society & Chamber Music Faculty at The Juilliard School and The Perlman Music Program

The Gilded Cage

"Stark follows the fortunes of a talented violinist and her family into the tumults of Reconstruction in this sequel to *Certain Liberties* . . . Stark weaves her characters' trajectories into the larger events of the time . . . Stark's detailed recreation of the time period—culturally, linguistically, and philosophically—should please those who like nothing better than escaping into previous eras . . . An unhurried and painterly novel of a musician finding her voice." —*Kirkus Reviews*

Certain Liberties

"The author masterfully sets the historical stage—the United States as it devolves into the Civil War—and she addresses the issue of slavery with nuance and rigor . . . a riveting storyline." —*Kirkus Reviews*

CONTENTS

1

On Stage

"A MOST CONGENIAL CROWD, I must say," a young man in a formal black dress coat commented to his similarly attired companion as they reviewed the audience milling about the Vienna State Opera House. "It's what I love about touring for the opera season. We could be almost anywhere, home in Paris, London, or even Berlin instead of Vienna. Music truly is a universal social connector, isn't it? But I assume you've caught sight of someone more interesting than me, my friend. I suppose we're all just musical tourists."

"Why would you say that?" the taller of the two muttered, continuing to focus past his companion.

"Because you haven't looked directly at me since we arrived," the shorter, stockier one said indignantly. "What lies over my right shoulder to intrigue you so?" He pouted over his friend's distraction, avoiding acknowledgment of it by turning to follow his line of sight.

"Apologies. I meant no insult," the taller of the two whispered to avoid any possibility his words might be overheard. He bent down slightly to lessen the discrepancy in their heights, though he was still able to see directly over his friend's shoulder. "I've just noted the arrival of the world-class violinist Madame Emily de Koningh with her family and male entourage." He picked an invisible piece of lint from his friend's black coat sleeve, paying far more attention to the unnecessary activity than his companion thought warranted. "Do you know of her? I know string instruments aren't your passion, but I saw her often in Paris, both on and off the stage. Don't look around," he ordered. "They're too close now."

"I can't see what you find so fascinating about a female violinist," his friend muttered. "That may have been unusual at one time, but no longer. And why are you ogling the people she's with when you have my most engaging company at hand." He knew his friend couldn't stop him from turning in place, so he did, slowing down a little to take in the group just behind him. His pique had been misplaced. The beauty of the dark-haired woman in a white-and-black closely fitted lace evening dress was enough of an attraction to create a stir, but the sophistication of the music aficionados at the Vienna Opera House ensured that the famous violinist from America would be recognized. And if her looks and fame were not enough, the group around her would have garnered attention anywhere.

"You always seem to be knowledgeable about those who make headlines in the newspapers these days. Who are they? I mean the men, of course." The friend in need of clarification chuckled, as if the idea of the woman being important enough to hold his attention was ridiculous. He sent another sidelong glance her way, however, obviously still fascinated by the spell she seemed to cast over her five male companions. She was clearly at the center of the group while the men stood quite close around her as if to catch her every nuance.

"The two young ones are her sons," his companion answered. "I've seen the darker one in Paris on other occasions with his grandfather." Pleased to be the primary source of information, he pulled himself up an imperceptible half inch. "They look alike . . . that same handsome, smooth charm. But the grandfather is a British lord and has the right to his imperious attitude, while the grandson tries to emulate it without the title, at least for the moment."

"What a waste," his friend murmured. "He's quite stunning, but obviously unapproachable. And the other one? He's a mess with all those blond curls, and his clothes are too artistic for my taste. Look at that tie—more of a scarf." He scanned the younger fair-haired brother slowly before turning back to his companion. "But he does have a sweet smile and cheerful way about him," he said. "Lovely dimples, too. I see he's not afraid to laugh in public!"

"Ah, always a good eye," the taller man exclaimed. "You mustn't say a single word about what I'm about to tell you. Promise?" The shorter man crossed his heart eagerly. "He's the one they say favors male company, as many artists do."

"They? Who says?" his companion asked, clearly tired of his friend's imperious arrogance.

"He's studying fashion design and has been part of the Parisian avant-garde for a while. Do you pay no attention to the flow of other artistic disciplines? You know how people opposed to modernism fan the gossip around realist artists. I'm surprised you hadn't heard it. He should have stayed in France instead of moving back to England with his family, as they plan to do soon. He'd have enjoyed a better environment for his career and his social preferences."

"Quite so. We French are so enlightened. Victorian England is no place for a young, pretty one like that to grow up the way he wants to. What a shame." The young man winked at his companion and undid the bottom button of his waistcoat. He pulled a white silk handkerchief from his pocket and patted his temples, apparently uncomfortable with the rise in temperature due to the crush of opera patrons inside the vestibule. "And who are the others? One of them looks familiar, and the exceedingly tall, blond gentleman cannot be ignored. He's pretty as the boy, in a mature sort of way."

"He should be. That is Madame de Koningh's husband and the boys' father. He's an American folk musician, whatever that is. And the other two are his wife's . . . 'friends.' " The companion lowered his voice again. "The fit-looking gentleman with the mustache is the Silver King John Mackay, an industrialist from America—possibly the richest man in the world, they say, even though he's of Irish origins. And the rakish-looking dark one—too informally dressed for this opera house, I might note—is the newspaper editor J. R. Dunne. I believe he wrote the society column for the *New-York Times*, among other things. You know how I love talk," he added.

His friend rolled his eyes. "Gossip, pure and simple. But it does keep you in the ebb and flow of society," he acknowledged, grudgingly. The informant continued as if he hadn't been interrupted at all and had been mesmerized by the sound of his own voice.

"I think he lives in Paris now, which is probably where they got to know him." He looked quite satisfied with himself, having given a full account of the vivacious party passing behind them, all apparently enthralled with their own companions and disinterested in the opera crowd around them.

"Truly? I had no idea," the man identified as the Silver King was saying to the woman, his lilting Irish brogue rising above the heads of the others. "I didn't know you and Johnny met originally in Vienna. I'd always assumed it was in New York."

The two young gossipers tried to stall their departure from the vestibule to take their seats, but the crush of opera patrons flowed relentlessly toward the auditorium, taking everyone in its wake; all except the group of six in the de Koningh party who seemed to resist the flow, as a mid-river dam causes eddies with obstacles swept around it. And so it was that the young men lost sight and sound of the de Koninghs, feeling they were going to miss out on a much more interesting performance than the one offered on stage.

⊱✦⊰

"So, you met when Emily started touring?" The Silver King's slight stutter as he paused before the word "started" was no longer noticed by his friends after so many years of closeness, and Emily jumped in quickly, intuiting the question's direction.

"Good heavens, no. I was still a music student under Professor Haussmann's tutelage."

"Ah, but at this opera house," Mackay continued. She shook her head emphatically, as Johnny Dunne interrupted.

"This place didn't exist then. It was just a hole in the ground and the building only partially completed. We ran into each other, literally, and entirely by chance in St. Stephen's Square. I had no idea she was a musician at the time." He and Emily looked at each other and laughed, both remembering the haphazard nature of their initial meeting, which had been more of a collision as she chased a child's runaway hoop into oncoming traffic. Racing like the wind to retrieve the toy with her skirts hiked up to her knees had made a wild and free-spirited vision neither one could forget.

"Sounds as if Mother was her impulsive self even in those days," Emily's fair-haired younger son pronounced with a wink. She smiled and nodded, a clear affection between them.

"There has never been a time your mother didn't mutiny against something," her husband added. "I've known her longer than any of you, and I can confirm that her revolutionary soul was in full glory even in her childhood."

Looking taller than his six-foot-four height in his long, black formal dress coat, Corey de Koningh offered his arm to his wife, smiling down at her as he did so. "We were two adventurers together at the age of twelve, and if she tries to tell you I led her astray in any way, I'll deny it and lay much of the blame and intrigue on her shoulders." Emily smiled distractedly back up at him, obviously less taken with the memory of her youthful escapades than her husband had been. Her childhood seemed so far back in her past as to be almost invisible now, while his had never ended. They'd agreed to allow each other the freedom to live in whatever moment they chose for themselves, even if the other had moved far away. Each one being comfortable with their choices, they were remarkably accepting of the other, yet Emily found much less to share with and admire in her childish, aging husband than she had in her youth.

"Speaking of adventure," she said, a lilt lifting her voice as she turned to Mackay, "you're just back from the Middle East, John. Was it Turkey? Wherever you were, I imagine you have some rich tales to tell. I'd love to see that part of the world someday. It's just such a long trip and I have no performances to take me there. You men who enjoy work demanding continuous exciting travel are luckier than you can appreciate."

"How so?" Emily's elder son William finally spoke up. He looked dissatisfied. "I never want to go to Turkey, or experience any distant travel, for that matter."

"That's an unusual attitude for a young man of your age and means," Mackay said, not unkindly. "Why would you not want to see the part of the world where civilization was born?"

"Smallpox," William answered. "I have no intention of exposing myself to that killer affliction or any of the side effects of avoiding it, like being quarantined on board ship for weeks before disembarking at one's destination." Intent on informing the older world-traveler of his opinion born of inexperience, he continued, "I've read the accounts of those horrible trips. Not for me, no thank you."

His mother stared at him and shook her head slightly in disbelief that William could be as impolite as he was closed-minded. "You can get inoculated against smallpox, William. This is the 1880s, remember. The vaccine has been in use successfully for decades! I'm sure John wouldn't have risked the trip himself without being inoculated." She turned a questioning eye in Mackay's direction. "John, would you even have risked the trip here unless you'd been vaccinated?"

"Of course not," her friend assured her. "The effort to eradicate the sickness has been extremely successful, thanks to the efforts of your own countryman, Dr. Jenner. And many British noble*women* champion the cause, inoculating their own families very publicly to help reassure the populace."

"Oh please, Mr. Mackay," William sneered. "British nobility is always game for some attention or advantage. I hardly think they're self-sacrificing, and I won't give them the satisfaction of killing me with their experiments."

"Not so, young man." The Silver King flushed as his Irish skin gave away his emotion. "Their motivations and politics are not the issue. Trust is the key to vaccination, and the women and doctors of your mother's homeland have been instrumental in gaining that trust for everyone in England and throughout the Middle East."

"Trust! Why would anyone trust anything so dangerous, or the government, for that matter?" William scoffed.

"Because they have faith in the individuals championing it. And then others trust them, take the vaccine, and avoid the pox, continuing the messaging around the world about the importance of helping children and adults to be vaccinated."

"Mr. Lincoln spoke of how important trust is in a kind of self-perpetuating ladder. I find that an interesting concept, John," Emily broke in, looking directly at the man at least fifteen years her senior.

"But it's time we all moved from affairs of the intellect to matters of the heart, and that's what music and the opera have. Let's be seated now or we'll miss the whole first scene!" She slipped her other arm easily through the Silver King's, walking between him and her husband while her sons and the newspaper editor walked together behind them. That evening, as Emily moved with her husband, sons, and friends down the aisle to take their opera seats in the fourth row, center, many in the audience nearby looked up to study the faces they'd seen only in newspapers or on stage. Some in the audience continued to stare at the famous American violinist while she worked hard to let her frustration over her eldest son's odd aggression go.

She took deep breaths to relax her tension building since he'd launched his verbal attack, seemingly on Mackay, but truly on her. William had always been her antagonist almost since the day he was born, long before any personality trait or transgression could have affected his opinion of her. The years of living together had done nothing to improve their relationship, try as she might to strike a fair and even balance between good parenting and good cheer. He'd always been a darkly handsome boy, yet so uncomfortable with himself that he'd found it too difficult to learn in the traditional ways in school. He'd felt he knew more than any of his teachers, and she'd grown tired of fighting with him to see the acquisition of knowledge differently. Private tutors (none of them adequate, he'd felt) had started him on the path to superiority he now felt he'd completed, and his own time spent learning a multitude of languages was something she no longer questioned. When asked about his motivation he'd explained language was the quickest route to control and power. There could be no doubt why he no longer listened to those he might learn from. It was clear he was training himself to run the world.

But she was a trained performer, after all, and what was a night at the opera if not a performance? There was usually more going on in the audience than there was on stage, which was one of the reasons she preferred an evening of chamber music, where the intimacy between the musicians and their audience didn't allow for thoughtless egos to interrupt. Her husband squeezed her hand gently, perhaps a reassurance that he understood how disquieting her son William could be for her, and how important her friendships were as well. William had never presented the same challenge to his father, but she assumed that was because he discounted the importance of a man who had no interest in controlling his own life's direction or the people around him. She knew William had always been jealous of her success; a performer's somewhat hypnotic effect on people through music was a strength her son could neither compete with nor fully understand.

She knew her struggle to balance her reaction to William over the years had become severely strained lately and worried that an eruption might well be near at hand. But tucked comfortably next to

Mackay, whose strong, fit body filled the entire seat between her and her elder son, and her husband on the other side, whose height forced him to angle his legs sideways against hers, Emily felt well cared for while the orchestra began to warm up in preparation for the overture. She knew the next couple of hours of music and dramatic mayhem would take all concern for the real world completely out of her mind. It was a lovely way to spend an evening, and realism had no place in it.

⚘⚘⚘

"We should walk back to the hotel," Johnny said as they left the opera house, motioning William away from the carriage he seemed intent on summoning. "That's why one stays at the Hotel Sacher these days. It's central. In addition, the food is incomparable . . . to say nothing of the port and cigars," he added with a grin, sliding his arm around the young man's shoulders and giving him a squeeze. William glowered at him and shook the embrace off crossly, something the newspaper editor wasn't used to. "Ah, too old for such affection, William?" Johnny glanced back at Emily as she walked with the others. She shrugged and shook her head, as if there was no good explanation for her older son's insolence, at least not one she was aware of. Johnny had been as close to William as an uncle at one time, and so this rejection seemed sudden and thoughtless, another rebuff of William's childhood mentors and Emily's friends. Two decades spent mostly in France had pushed memories of living in New York so far down it was hard to believe her family had ever grown up together in the de Koningh mansion.

"Mama, what did you think of the music tonight?" Emily's younger son Connie always seemed to know how to break up a bad exchange with a good question. He popped around in front of Emily and his father as they strolled back to the Hotel Sacher.

"I think your young son needs movement," Mackay chuckled. "He and I may share the same opinion of the value of opera after sitting for a few hours." Connie turned and bounced backward, flashing his dimpled smile at the family behind him.

"Well, I don't hear an answer, Mama. What did you think of the tenor? I assume the soprano was doing no more than her job, by your standards, if that." Emily burst out with a peal of laughter that stopped her dead in her tracks.

"Yes, my artistic son, you have it. The soprano was fine, but the tenor had a lot more to offer, musically speaking."

"Even with those occasional voice cracks and missed high notes?" Connie asked, goading his mother into a deeper disclosure of the weaknesses of that evening's performance.

"Even so. They've pushed him too far too fast, expecting too much of him without letting him gather himself between performances. What really upset me was the ongoing battle for control between him and the conductor." Everyone in the family group walking together looked surprised except Corey, who nodded. They all watched her intently to see what would come next.

"You mean when the tenor would slow a section down and the conductor would try to speed him up again?" Connie asked.

"Exactly," his father replied. His years of leading singers and choral works lent his opinion the weight of expertise. "He should have let his star soloist go his own way and simply followed him for support. They should have worked the timing out well before the performance. Once on stage, trying to manhandle the tenor stood about as much chance of success as forcing a child to do what you want him to. It's impossible and only makes everyone else miserable as they get drawn into the battle. Wouldn't you agree?" he added, looking down at his wife where she stood next to him. For a moment traffic seemed to stop and the only sound was a horse's hooves echoing somewhere in the distance.

Finally, Emily nodded, taking a deep breath and letting it out slowly. "Had the conductor given the tenor his head, the audience would have been spared the tug of war. No matter who was correct, faster or slower was the right of the singer to determine on stage, and we would have been better off either way for his personal triumph." Looking pointedly at William, she started off fast enough to keep up with his brother out in front.

"Come on, people," Corey called, cheerfully. "A rich Sacher torte awaits us all."

"I don't like them," William muttered. "But I'll try some of that port and a cigar at the lounge," he added. His mother glanced at her friend Johnny, putting him in charge of limiting the damage to her twenty-year-old son's health and reputation in the lounge at the Hotel Sacher.

"I'd like to join you two," Connie said to his brother. "Would I be interrupting anything? The lounge sounds a little more modern, and that appeals to me, too."

"Do you trust your friend Johnny with our precious sons?" Corey asked, smiling over Emily's head at Mackay as he held the door for her at the top of the stairs to the hotel.

"Implicitly," Emily replied. "Didn't our dear President Lincoln once say that people, when rightly and fully trusted, will return the trust?" She nodded to Mackay as she passed him in the hotel. "Where did Mr. Lincoln get all that wisdom?" she asked. "Trust your friends, your family, and your soloist, or risk ruin."

⁕⊰⟨Ｗ⟩⊱⁕

"What a wonderful evening that was," Corey said, "full of good music and companionship." Smiling as he stretched and yawned while removing his coat and laying it on the back of a chair in their hotel suite, he went on dreamily, "I've been wondering if we might not benefit from a detour to the Leipzig Conservatory before moving on to England. We'll not get an opportunity to hear such great music again in a long time."

"Leipzig? Why Leipzig? England's not a total wasteland, you know," Emily replied, sinking down on a red damask love seat without removing her gloves and waist-length cape. She had an air of tension seemingly inappropriate to the late hour in such an appealing place. The night at the opera appeared to have been less pleasant for her than for her husband. "I'd agree that London is a great deal more parochial and conservative in its current musical tastes than any of the other major cities of Europe, but Leipzig is no longer in its ascendancy, musically speaking. I think of it more as a university town than a cultural capital now."

"True . . ." Corey ran both his hands through his graying blond hair as if to release all that remained of the evening just behind him. "The traditions of Mendelssohn died out over a decade ago, but the music school's reputation is still in a major orbit, I think. I'd like to have a look at it even if it's not what it once was." He yanked off his tie and tossed it down, unbuttoning his waistcoat and sinking into another large, overstuffed chaise longue where he could stretch his legs out fully. He let out a contented sigh, resting his head on the back of the chaise and shutting his eyes. "Don't you want to see how the Germans are training the next generation of musicians?" he asked, without opening his eyes.

"No, as a matter of fact." Emily smiled a little at her husband's disingenuous appreciation for German classical music. "And I think you're just putting off a final rendezvous with my father in England," she added, unable to hide a small annoyance in her voice. The overcontrolling conductor and her son William's pretentious tirade about Middle East travel and the dangers of vaccination may have seeded it, but there was also the letter from her father, Lord William Alden, that had arrived just before they'd left for the opera. Which reminded her, maybe she was the one avoiding her first return in decades to London and her father's home.

When he'd dumped her on his best friend's doorstep in New York after her mother died, she'd built a new family there with Corey and his father, Klaas de Koningh. Their eventual departure for France, precipitated by Klaas's remarriage twenty years ago, had convinced her that family was vital, but not always made of the blood of one's ancestors. She'd missed Klaas terribly though he was totally unrelated to her, and cursed her father even more for abandoning her to the de Koningh household in the first place. Now she'd built her own family around her, Corey, and her children after two decades of adjusting to their new lives in France, and this sojourn in Austria on the way back to visit her father for a while brought all the bad feelings unleashed by her original departure from his home swirling around inside her as if she were thirteen again.

"I think I'm just worn out now for some reason," she said quietly. "Or possibly I've reached a dead end in my life and performance career." She heard the silence around her as if it held its breath, waiting for something to happen. Corey hadn't moved or made a comment or sound, so she assumed he was giving her enough rope to tie around her own neck.

"Yes," she said, a look of grim acceptance on her face, turning her once warm brown eyes dark and unfathomable. "I no longer get the lift of joy from playing before an audience, no matter how beautiful the music is. Something is missing for me, and I suppose I'm afraid if I go to England now, I'll never find it again." Corey remained quiet, she assumed not interrupting the vital revelation she seemed intent on disclosing unexpectedly.

"It's not my age," she said, looking into space as if to find an answer not obvious in the everyday world. "I've adjusted to the physical changes of being forty, and the ways to play something differently than I have before. And it's not the pressure becoming too much, especially now that I no longer worry about bringing up two small boys. If anything I have more time than ever to prepare and practice with fewer personal demands on me. And yet I feel as if I'm just politely going through the motions without really caring . . ."

Her voice died out as if lost. "Does any of that make sense?" she asked quietly, finally glancing at Corey in the dim light to get a feel for his reaction. After all, he'd known her musical soul longer than anyone else in her life—since she'd first come to visit at his home in New York when he was only twelve. He'd found her reading a score in bed and insisted from then on that she join his music lessons. He was very much responsible for starting her on this journey in the first place. The stillness was suddenly broken by slow, shallow breathing, and she realized he was asleep. Undoubtedly, he'd missed everything she'd said.

Why had she expected him to share her inner musings with her tonight? They'd agreed long ago that they had little in common other than their nostalgic connection through their youthful bonding to ward off similar loneliness. But they liked each other, perhaps even loved each other as siblings sometimes do if they're lucky. And they had their shared appreciation of music, even though their dissimilar tastes had taken them in opposing directions. Corey's preference for modernism had led to the café music halls and cabarets of Paris, while her classicism had taken her all over the major cities of Europe. But their shared music training from Robert Haussmann at the de Koningh mansion throughout their youth had given them the unique, almost intuitive understanding between two people who've learned the same language the same way at the same time.

She took no objection to Corey's friends, mostly very different from hers, or the women he played for and with in the cabarets. Sometimes she even enjoyed an evening with them at the Folies Bergère because the easy, improvisational atmosphere made her feel happy and relaxed. Then his friends sometimes became hers, just as her male friends were family of a sort, as well. It was not a marriage society would champion for the perpetuation of its accepted structure. But the arrangement between them had satisfied them both and, she thought, hurt no one else. But what had brought these thoughts on tonight, right before their move into another change for their lives? Maybe that's exactly what had produced her musings about a life gone by. Or maybe it had been Corey's unusual supportiveness at a time when she seemed to need it most.

"Oh Lord," she murmured, glancing over at his long frame stretched out on the chaise. She was experiencing the strange sense of rejection sharpened by someone's physical presence without their intellectual connection. She couldn't end her evening with emptiness. Rising quietly, and still in her evening dress, gloves, and cape, she moved silently across the plush carpet to open the door to their suite and exit softly. She didn't bother to look back at her sleeping husband, knowing he was exactly where he wanted to be.

2

THE ROYAL COLLEGE

WATCHING ROW upon row of red brick and terra-cotta town houses with bow windows and iron balconies pass his carriage window, Lord Alden imagined the open farmland and markets of his childhood they'd replaced. He wondered if the sights would be as appealing now to his daughter Emily, and his grandsons William and Connie, as they would have been then. But of course, they were all city people, brought up first in New York and then Paris. Bringing Emily's family to live with him in London for the first time in their lives worried him more than he'd have thought. He wanted everything to be perfect. He wanted them to stay.

South Kensington's suburban fields and proximity to midtown had presented an irresistible temptation to the developers of nineteenth-century London. Deals struck with the Crown and parliamentary politicians finalized the transformation of rural agricultural neighborhoods making a few architects and developers unconscionably wealthy. It was a saving grace, perhaps, that some of the land had been held for "the people" of England via the Crown's transformative edifices such as the Royal Albert Hall and the Victoria and Albert Museum. As the coach slowed, he could tell that his coachman was preparing to deliver him to the Royal Albert. It was his fault for having only identified his destination as South Kensington.

Lord William Alden signaled his driver to continue on, tapping on the door with his cane to indicate his destination a little farther west. His longtime servant was seldom surprised, but the lift of a corner of his left eyebrow suggested this was one of those times. Lord Alden looked up at the strange little building across from the Albert Hall before stepping from the carriage. His own expression of dismay said everything his coachman had tried not to. There were good reasons that critics of the time identified the building as "having strayed from Istanbul." The mixture of decorative floral designs and scrollwork certainly reminded one of a Middle Eastern art form. Scores of half-dressed overfed cherubs marched in a musical band across the first-floor windows, with others grouped on the lintel above the front door, engaged in some undetectable activity when viewed from ground level. Whatever the motivating aesthetic, it was far from the neat red brick and terra-cotta of its South Kensington neighbors.

"Oh dear, Brody," he breathed to his aging servant, holding on to the coach door before climbing down. "What an odd concoction it is. This does not augur well."

"Perhaps a mistake, sir?" Brody queried, glancing again at the double-story building with red, gold, and brown plaster decorations framing all the windows and side pillars. There were no plain walls, just huge panes of glass surrounded by dark wood and ornate plaster trim giving the building an air of decadence.

"I wonder what the architect was thinking," Lord Alden muttered, shaking his head in disbelief as he stepped to the pavement. "What do you think, Brody? Is this indicative of a preference for modernism? I think Sir Charles Freake outdid his usual bent for self-promotion on this one." The handsome silver-haired gentleman replaced his silk top hat and tightened his gloved hand over the carved metal head of his cane. His coachman reached out to assist instinctively but withdrew quickly when he saw the help wasn't necessary.

"I've read that the builder made this at his own expense," the coachman said. "Perhaps the structure reflects his origins as a carpenter. But where did he get so much money?"

"Well, carpenter at one time or not, he ended up a very wealthy man with ties to royalty and philanthropy all over the city. I think the building shows there were too many cooks spoiling this broth while the builder was busy elsewhere with domestic architecture for his wealthy clients." Sir William's expression had taken on a grim edge, resigned as he was to complete his business in the odd structure contrasting so garishly with its neighbors.

"I'll probably be about an hour, Brody," he said, nodding to the coachman with a small smile. The acknowledgment brought a bow from his servant, who watched as his employer moved to the front door of the strange building. The coachman waited until he saw one side of the black wooden double door open, and Lord Alden disappear inside. Deciding to wait in full view of the unusual house in case he was needed, he got back up on the carriage and moved it slightly forward. Experience told him that there might well be a reason to leave earlier than planned from such a strange place. It was his job to be prepared.

"Good day," Lord Alden said with a slight tilt of his head to the handsome young man who closed the door behind him. His smooth, well-kept appearance seemed in stark contrast with the hodgepodge of the building's exterior. Perfectly trimmed short dark hair and a mustache augmented the three-piece pinstripe suit of fine dark wool. A pair of gold-rimmed pince-nez glasses attached to a gold chain completed the look of a most proper British gentleman. "I'm here to meet . . ." Lord Alden smiled weakly, a doubtful greeting exposing his discomfort. "I am William Alden, and Mr. Grove is expecting me."

"Indeed he was," the young man announced. "Director Grove is devastated to be delayed, but I am honored to take his place to meet someone who has done so much for our country." The young man's eyes shone with such pleasure that his sincerity could not be questioned. "I'm Charles Villiers Stanford, professor of composition and conductor of the college orchestra," he said, extending a graceful hand with the longest fingers Lord Alden had ever seen. "His Royal Highness, the Prince of Wales, also informed us of your visit. He's eager to have you see what we've accomplished, as well as what we intend to achieve in the future. If you'll join me in my office first, I can give you a little history of the school, which might help you understand its evolution. We're delighted to have you with us today."

He bowed slightly and motioned toward the almost empty middle of the building. Lord Alden followed in the direction of his gesture. The surroundings and even the young man who greeted him were unexpected, but he had a pleasant sense of the energetic young gentleman, which helped to erase his misgivings. He knew how fortunate he was to have been a diplomat who'd traveled extensively all his life, as there was now very little about any social situation that upset him for long.

Moving through the central foyer leading from the entrance, he was struck by the plainness of the halls and rooms he could see spread around the building's perimeter. They were completely unadorned to the point of bleakness, in sharp contrast with the ornate decor of the building's façade. "May we talk first?" he asked, unsure whether his attractive young host understood the purpose of his visit. There was nothing casual about his interest in the college and he wanted his goal to be perfectly clear. "There's a lot I need to learn about this place. The prince was enthusiastic but . . . unspecific about his vision of it. Its metamorphosis is somewhat . . . baffling," he added, after searching for just the right word. They stopped at a sign next to a plain door much like all the rest.

PROFESSOR C. VILLIERS STANFORD
THE ROYAL COLLEGE OF MUSIC

"Tortuous its path most certainly has been," the professor said, turning to face Lord Alden. "Even to the directors and supporters involved with its many births and deaths along the way." He motioned toward one of the simple wooden chairs placed around his sparsely furnished workspace. Lord Alden removed his hat and gloves, placing them on another chair with his cane. "I apologize for the lack of comfort," the young professor offered with a sheepish smile. "But the college is fashioned as all our British institutions of learning are, austere to the point of being punitive. Can I take your coat, sir?" he asked.

"No, thank you. I doubt that will be necessary," Lord Alden replied.

"Oh, if you're going to learn anything about this place, I'm sure it will be," Professor Stanford responded with a grin. He touched the gold watch in his vest pocket as if reaching for an old friend's hand. "We have plenty of time together, and I intend to fill it with enough information to clear up all your confusion. If you change your mind about your coat along the way, I'd be happy to hang it up for you." He smiled fully, adjusting his pince-nez glasses attached to his vest by a gold chain.

What an unusual person. Lord Alden was used to full deference from those he met other than within the royal family, so the young professor's easy attitude was remarkable, yet not as irritating as might be expected. He seemed to possess an understanding of his own intelligence that one could see in his face. That was the kind of person Lord Alden most enjoyed sharing a dialogue with. He sensed that whatever it was the professor actually did, he felt he did it well.

If Professor Stanford hadn't been adorned with all the accoutrements of sophistication, including a full dark mustache under his straight, perfectly proportioned nose, Lord Alden would have suspected he was in the presence of a school friend of one of his grandsons. Yet the professor's bearing suggested maturity. Lord Alden caught sight of a handsomely tailored wool coat much like his own hanging in the closet. The professor was clearly a man of means if his garments and accessories were any indication.

Lord Alden was suddenly stunned by the thought that even though the professor was unquestionably younger than his daughter he would have made a most acceptable partner for her through life. He chuckled at the realization that he was applying his own personal inclinations to the choice of his daughter's romantic associates, regardless of her actual preferences. He acknowledged to himself having made that mistake more than once in the past. But that was because her husband had been such an unsatisfactory choice, in Lord Alden's opinion. Apparently she did not agree, as they'd been married over two decades.

Corey was Lord Alden's best friend's son, and therefore heir to the lineage and fortune of one of the first Dutch families in America. But there was no weight to his legacy and never had been. Corey had always seemed unconcerned with the responsibilities of his inheritance, too quick to squander the talent he'd been gifted as a musician, and undependable as an accompanist for his daughter—as either a life or musical partner. Lord Alden had learned early on when he'd tried to maneuver his daughter's relationships that he must give that up or lose her. She'd seemed to him to be cheerfully blind to her husband's faults.

Lord Alden had seen more of the family when they moved to France from America, and he'd continued to sense that his daughter's life was unfulfilled in many ways, while the burden of being mother and father to her boys was becoming very heavy. He thought perhaps it was time to lighten her load and therefore keep her by his side, as she'd once been in her youth. This young professor with the assurance of support from British royalty and the greatest artists of his day was an exact embodiment of the partner Lord Alden had imagined for his daughter for a very long time. "Please enlighten me," he said, removing his coat and passing it to the professor. "I'm ready for my lessons."

Professor Stanford pulled a chair over next to his guest, looking like the teacher he was as he prepared to impart information of importance to his new pupil. "Can you tell me, Lord Alden, why your interest in the arts, of which I am aware, brings you to the Royal College of Music today? If I understand your motivation, I may well be able to avoid boring you with facts you have no interest in, an accomplishment much to be desired, you'll agree."

Lord Alden burst out laughing. "How I wish I'd had teachers with your sensibilities, young man. I'm sure I would have absorbed a great deal more from my music lessons if I had. But why do you question my interest in your institution, Professor Stanford? If you know of my patronage of the arts, then surely you recognize my enthusiasm for learning more about the college."

"Ah, but you'd have been here long ago if an interest in music education filled your spare time, yet this is the first we've seen of you. I sense you have a more specific reason for your involvement with us." The directness startled Lord Alden momentarily, yet why not get on with his business? He felt perfectly comfortable revealing the truth about his mission. He smiled back at his audacious new acquaintance.

"You're right, Professor. It originates in this institution's rejection of my daughter's application to attend as the first female in its history. It was a terrible blow both to her and to me at the time, as I was working with Her Majesty and had been assured my connections would secure my daughter a place (even though female violinists were a rarity back then). But the timing wasn't right." He watched the professor's face carefully to see his reaction.

"This story is not unfamiliar," Professor Stanford said, frowning gently. His response was not what Lord Alden expected.

"You've heard of my daughter's dilemma, then?"

"No, not your daughter's directly," the young man answered. "But I too have experienced the stultifying discrimination against female musicians in our supposedly modern nineteenth-century society."

"How so?" Lord Alden looked perplexed. "You could not possibly have a daughter old enough to participate in a career in music!"

The professor shook his head. "I was the conductor of the Musical Society as an undergraduate at Cambridge and tried to convince them their refusal to admit women singers greatly hindered the quality and breadth of their performances." He shook his head slightly again and sighed, obviously disgusted. "They refused, and so I had to stage what *The Musical Times* termed a 'bloodless revolution' by creating a competitive and vastly superior mixed choir." His eyes sparkled and crinkled at the corners with the pleasure of the memory. "The Society eventually had to merge with us. But how did you and your daughter adjust to your shared disappointment?" he asked his guest.

Lord Alden chuckled. "Much as you did, Professor. Recovered quickly and effectively." He smiled, remembering Emily's continuing musical education under the tutelage of Robert Haussmann in Europe, and recounted to the professor how fast her solo violin career had gained momentum once she started performing in Europe again as well as America. The experience acquired in front of sophisticated audiences had lifted her to a higher level. Naturally, his thoughts were affected by the changes humans always make to their own stories, and his current pride in Emily's successes as a world-class performer, as well as a wife and mother, went a long way to sculpting the account of her early career he gave the young man sitting with him now.

"A satisfying outcome to a disappointing start," Professor Stanford said, when his guest had finished. "Did she eventually move on to teaching as well as solo performance? Often these detours in life become the best paths to success after all."

"Not to my knowledge," Emily's father responded with a pensive look. "But I know she's talked of her pleasure in helping other chamber musicians learn some of the things she's discovered during her career, so teaching figuratively more than literally."

"And how does that bring you to us now? You applied in your daughter's youth to the National Training School of Music, which, thank heaven, we've moved a long way from today. The failures of administration and financial management have been rectified, and what we have now is known as the Royal College of Music." Professor Stanford smiled almost sheepishly, apparently neither comfortable with nor proud of the college's past. "Why would you want to reflect on that wound from your daughter's previous experience?"

Sir William, a diplomat entering old age with a lifetime of strategic negotiating skills, knew enough not to reveal his entire hand at once, no matter how much trust had lowered his usual defenses. He understood that Britain had a long history of failure in its arts institutions. It was no secret and was truly an embarrassment when compared to the other capitals of Europe, and the financial straits the National Training School had found itself in were well known to have caused its eventual demise. Now the new college needed him more than he needed it, and so he would play out his tactics slowly, saving the most important for last. He wasn't going to risk another embarrassment at the hands of the British government. "Tell me about the college today," he said firmly, "and then I'll tell you why it matters to me."

"I'd be happy to," the young professor answered. "Happy to!" he repeated. Clearly he saw his responsibilities included promoting the school in the circles most likely to support it financially, a distinct possibility in Lord Alden's case, as the Prince of Wales had suggested. "But would you tell me the name your daughter performs under today? I assume she uses a stage name, and I should know it, but the director has kept me too busy lately to expand my research in current affairs as I would like to, and I haven't had time off in Europe for my own listening pleasure for a while." He had the distinct air of a young student caught without his homework done as he looked guiltily at his guest.

"Understandable, Professor," Lord Alden said, evenly. "She uses her married name for performance, as her husband is also a musician, and the name is well known in New York as one of the oldest Dutch families. Women must use every advantage since they start so far behind," he added ruefully, though he need not have. The professor had made his sympathies quite clear. "She's Madame Emily de Koningh, and her teacher was Professor Robert Haussmann, foremost proponent of the pianoforte in New York." The professor sat up straighter in his chair, reminding Lord Alden of a lithe greyhound suddenly aware of a new scent on the wind. "Have you heard of her or her mentor?" he asked, casually, as if it meant little to him either way.

"I have," Stanford said, without elaborating. "The community of world-class musicians is exceedingly small. And where has her career taken her since she began it?" he asked. There was an air of expectation in the room, which was just as Lord Alden wanted it. This was his favorite story, and he enjoyed telling it to new ears.

"Her solo performances began right after the Civil War in America. She and her husband lived in his family home in New York and raised their two young sons there. Are you married, Professor?" Lord Alden asked, offhandedly. The professor nodded. "And have you children?" He nodded again. "Ah, then you understand the pressures a young family exerts on an early career. They moved to France after a few years and she performed all over Europe, while her husband made quite a name for himself in the new cabaret circles in Paris. He's a classically trained pianist, but he's never performed except as his wife's accompanist, or to entertain the patrons of the café-concert halls in Europe." Lord Alden didn't hide his distaste for what he obviously considered a waste of his son-in-law's talents and advantages.

"All music that gives pleasure is of value," Professor Stanford said, openly refusing to be sucked into the downgrading of Emily's husband. "I've never approved of the fashion to constrain musical tastes in the classical or modernist camp. I've developed a passion for the music of Brahms and Schumann, branding me a classicist when tastes are moving distinctly to the modernism of Liszt or Wagner. I have a dislike for both, yet I immensely admire *Die Meistersinger*. Art abhors constraint, which is why it should never be limited by cultural restrictions." He smiled gently at his guest, clearly comfortable sharing his views with certainty.

Lord Alden looked back at him a little longer than either one felt entirely comfortable with. He was not used to being chastised, even surreptitiously. "Well, yes, I suppose," he finally said, breaking the silence as if it hadn't existed at all. "But now they're both tired of the Paris music life and intend to come here to introduce my grandsons to their mother's ancestral roots and to see if her husband can find work in the British choral movement. I neglected to mention he's an accomplished vocalist and choral master, so that might be a more worthwhile connection than the world of cabaret music." He shifted uncomfortably in his chair, remembering the scolding he'd just received from the professor about prioritizing music by social taste. Pulling himself up straighter, he went on.

"And now we come to my interest in the college." He leaned forward to signal they had reached the crux of the matter, adjusting himself as if he needed a new platform for a fresh beginning. The professor remained in his alert posture, giving no indication of a similar need, however, not having allowed his attentions to wander. He was clearly a practiced listener.

"I want my daughter to make this her permanent home for a purely selfish reason." Professor Stanford smiled and nodded. "Her career has been remarkable for a female violinist," Lord Alden continued, "but I'm afraid she'll tire quickly of redecorating my house in London, and I think if she had steadier creative motivation here now, she'd stay."

Lord Alden looked very directly at the professor, as if they could not possibly misunderstand each other. He leaned forward a little, resting both elbows on the arms of his chair, while his hands were grasped quietly in his lap almost in a form of polite supplication. "It sounds as if the United Kingdom is finally moving towards a music college worthy of its great traditions," he went on with the same level of intimacy he'd implied since the discussion had turned to his disclosure of purpose. "Clearly the Royal College is on the cusp of change." He noted that Professor Stanford nodded ever so slightly, just enough to convince him he understood.

"I'm hoping my daughter will find this new direction for classical performance education exciting and join in the mission to teach a broader base of students," he continued. "I want to hear more about the purpose of the college as you plan for its future." Emily's father leaned forward in his chair again, but more purposefully this time, as if to send his message directly through Professor Stanford's body. "I can't be convincing unless I understand what you hope to do here." He took a breath and sat back, inviting the professor into his space at last.

There was a quiet pause, a place for both men to gather their thoughts. Lord Alden watched the intelligent young man's hands, one resting open on his knee and the other relaxed and hanging off the rounded scroll at the end of the chair's worn wooden arm. He found himself mesmerized by the length of the graceful fingers with a small gold signet ring on the fifth one. The slim wrists were set off by two silk-covered buttons starting up the sleeve topping white shirt cuffs that had been fastened with small, knotted gold cuff links. The forearms were incredibly graceful. He hadn't ever considered the importance of a body built to handle the require- ments of an artistic craft before and found himself wondering how his daughter had managed to meet the demands made of her small hands by the violin. Would her interest in the instrument wane with age as her capabilities shrank? Would she look for another life altogether, perhaps with him?

"Doesn't your daughter resent your involvement in planning for her future?" the professor was saying. His question startled Lord

Alden out of his reverie of a future imagined to fulfill his own desires. "I certainly know I did when my father objected to my tastes in living and sought to inflict his on me." The professor was entirely serious, suggesting he clearly felt he'd found a weakness in his guest's plan.

"Never," Lord Alden exclaimed. "We understand each other perfectly and she knows I'm trying to give her every advantage available through my personal connections. She has a healthy respect for my position with the royal family."

Professor Stanford showed no reaction on his face. "Then let me try to summarize," he said. "You want to know if the Royal College of Music would offer your daughter (whom I gather has never taught) a teaching position, and if so, if she would be inspired enough by our mission to accept it. Does that describe your concerns accurately?"

"Yes . . . yes, precisely, entirely," Lord Alden stammered, caught off guard by the succinct analysis of his goals. He noticed the professor smiling gently, more as if pleased he'd understood his guest's purpose than at Lord Alden's lack of attention.

"Well, that is quite easily answered. To the first half, yes, your daughter is just the kind of teacher we are engaging now to carry the college's changed mission forward. She has the professional skill and performance expertise as well as the celebrity we want for the British music student of tomorrow. And as for the rest of your concerns, the changes to the quality of the music education offered at the Royal College will be monumental. The forerunners of the college were abject failures. They left us well behind the music conservatories all over the rest of Europe. There is finally a consensus in Britain that we need to train young people to have professional careers in music rather than simply amateur appreciation of the art form."

Lord Alden chuckled a little. "That's the new thrust of progress during our sovereign's reign, is it not? Everything is professionalized, creating a kind of 'smoothing out' of society, one might say. It isn't enough to simply enjoy something for its own sake anymore."

The young professor grimaced. "I understand your discomfort, not being a musician yourself," he said. "But sometimes we must push the pendulum all the way. I would agree that our era tends to form professional bodies to adjust and systematize the activities of each vocation, but there is a reason for that call to excellence." His eyes narrowed as if he was dealing with a painful thought before he continued. "The demeaning tradition of treating musicians and teachers as servants should be affected positively by the inclusion of all classes of students, thereby raising the level of importance of both art forms. Mr. Liszt, to say nothing of the great Mozart himself, worked tirelessly to shut down that practice of degrading those who perform and teach in the arts."

Lord Alden nodded. "I have heard of Mr. Liszt's contributions and of Mozart's frustrations in that regard. But there's no more convincing argument than that championed by a parent of a beloved daughter who might have been overlooked in the past. I fully defend the importance of supporting the arts at an elevated commitment in this country. The time has come, and I'm sure my daughter would welcome such a mission. It lifts the teaching to an even broader purpose."

The professor's eyes seemed to take on a light of their own as he listened to Lord Alden. "Do you know, sir," he said, leaning forward in his chair, "that fewer than ten percent of our orchestral players in this country have attended our own music schools?" He raised his eyebrows as if shocked by the fact all over again. "The prince consort wanted to change this dismal reality and was trying to do so before he died. He wanted to offer scholarships to those with the skill but no means to participate in private music education, so we would have a broader base of students to work with in this country. He wanted to ensure success by including a different level of teaching, as well. It has taken more than two decades for us to put his vision into practice."

"A very Germanic approach," Sir William muttered. He didn't seem disturbed but more in recognition of the continental shift confirming the change in British attitudes since Prince Albert introduced many of his concepts to British society. Professor Stanford nodded in total agreement with his guest.

"I would be happy to show you a list of those we already have joining our teaching faculty, as well as those whom we intend to approach in the future. I think your daughter would be inspired by the opportunity to work with such a distinguished faculty. And Director Grove is as dynamic a leader as anyone could ever hope to follow."

"Could I take a copy of the list with me?" Lord Alden asked. "There's no enticement as convincing as written proof." Professor Stanford nodded, pushing up from his chair quickly and heading for his desk. The energy that had been so evident from the beginning of their meeting seemed to have grown exponentially since their talk had turned to teaching.

"We're especially keen on training musicians for orchestra," the professor said, seemingly out of nowhere.

What would his daughter know of or care for that? She'd never even been in one herself. "I'm not sure I understand the need," Lord Alden added, as he watched the professor open his desk drawer to remove a large ledger.

"Oh, it's so important," the professor said, pausing with both hands resting on the closed ledger in front of him. "Not only does it train many young people for jobs they'd not have access to if solo performance were the only route open to them, but it also gives aspiring composers a chance to hear their own work performed before they've grown up. Without an extremely musical family or unlimited financial reserves, a budding composer has no access to the sound he's heard only inside his head."

Lord Alden looked pensive. "I hadn't thought of it," he said, quietly. "But then, how about those unusually gifted few who wish to pursue a solo career? Would someone like my daughter have been able to benefit from that level of training had this college existed when she applied?"

The professor beamed, as if his prize student had just asked the question he'd been waiting for all along. He opened the ledger, turned it around and slid it across the desk toward Lord Alden, who pulled his chair close enough to read what was on the page in front of him. He read aloud:

"Jenny Lind (singing), Hubert Parry (composition), Ernst Pauer (piano), Arabella Goddard (piano), Walter Parratt (organ), Henry Holmes (violin) . . . my goodness," he exclaimed, looking up at the professor with a smile. "This is very impressive. And what is this listing here?" He pointed partway down the page, turning it back toward the professor.

"It's a record of the musicians who have already committed to play with our orchestra. Some will be reprising past performances with us. Joseph Joachim and Hans Richter, August Manns, and Eugène Ysaÿe . . . As you can see, Lord Alden, our students will have access to the best soloists and conductors the world can offer."

"And so I therefore have one more question about the students who will attend the college. Can you explain how they will differ from those who've been included in music institutions of the past? It sounds as if more than just the space housing them has changed."

Professor Stanford closed his drawer, leaving the large ledger out on his desk like the main platform of a structure still to be built on. As he leaned forward over it toward Lord Alden, his eyes flashed again with the same pleasure they'd shown at his success in including a mixed chorus during his tenure at Cambridge. "You've come to the most important part of our plan, Lord Alden. You seem to have an affinity for the heart of an issue." Pointing to a tall oak filing cabinet standing almost floor to ceiling in the far corner of the bare office, he smiled again as if its very presence gave him the utmost pleasure. "There are the records," he stated with assurance, as if Lord Alden had asked for them, which he clearly felt he hadn't from the look of uncertainty on his face.

"Records . . . ?" he asked, staring at the professor as if he might find an answer written on his face. ". . . of the students?" he added, looking more doubtful than he had at first.

"Not the current students," Professor Stanford said, almost gleefully. "No, that filing cabinet contains records of hundreds of potential students!" He adjusted the glasses on his nose as they slipped a little in his excitement. "Potential is what the new Royal College is about. We want the student body to be national in scope, sustained by a vast scholarship net rather than only a few wealthy private pupils. The old academy was resistant to that change, but the prince consort had always wanted it and his supporters have, too. The Duke of Edinburgh formed a committee to break with the academy, and that's why we're here now." He seemed almost out of breath with excitement, waving one of his hands with the elegant, long fingers to encompass the air around him. "You've understood all along without knowing it, Lord Alden, that the college is about the students and the music, not the building." His eyes shone with a light Lord Alden suspected was usually reserved for his pupils and their music.

"And the money . . . ?" Lord Alden asked. "Where will that come from?"

"Also nationwide," the professor answered. "Director Grove has prodigious fundraising talents, and the Prince of Wales is also, shall we say, extremely well connected." He finished with an easy smile.

Sir William felt a clash of emotions governing his facial expressions. He was unsure how to react and how much to disclose. He was doubtful about the success of an institution reliant on the under-classes and likely to be shunned by England's privileged society. He knew for a fact the cultural elite abhorred anything embracing modernism, at least in the short term, and that's all it would take to sink yet another experiment in British music education. But this young man had such energy and enthusiasm, as well as the social aplomb and connections to carry it off, making Lord Alden suspect that a thaw of the petrified upper crust restricting the culture of the United Kingdom had already begun.

"I hope you're not being overly naïve in your plans for future success," he said, worried about the irrepressible enthusiasm he'd been swept up in since he'd first entered the professor's company. "It seems to me as if there are many obstacles to instructing students who come from deprived backgrounds with none of the refinements needed for a classical education."

"Refinements! Just the right word, Lord Alden. But possibly not for the reasons you choose it," the professor exclaimed. "Are you familiar with Director Grove's *Dictionary of Music and Musicians*?"

Sir William nodded. "It would be hard not to know of that gentleman's contribution to the layman's musical vocabulary, especially after his commitment to the prince consort and his amazing work at the Crystal Palace concerts. The dictionary is required reading in my household overrun by professional musicians—the only way I can understand them, at times!"

"Well, in that case you might remember his comments on the necessity to test an artist the way silver is refined, as almost a trial by fire, in order to find the very best of what the artist has inside." Sir William nodded again. "It is a simple concept proven true repeatedly. Not only do we find those who have grown in the harshest environment the most inspired, but we also have a better chance of finding the most valuable ore when we can mine the broadest segments of society."

"That concept sounds arduous and costly," Sir William said, remembering the ill-run and poorly financed former training school. "I worry that your plans will be too expansive, not giving attention to those who deserve it most."

"Ah, Lord Alden," Professor Stanford said, smiling a little. "You of all people should know there are no restrictions in art's fertile soil. It isn't true that women cannot excel in music, or that only the affluent and well educated can benefit from classical training. Art knows no such limits, and so it is time here in England to profit from that expansiveness." Lord Alden nodded slowly, clearly allowing the truth of the young professor's proof to sink in. He continued to keep nodding without realizing he was doing so.

Professor Stanford understood the truths he lived with every day might not be as obvious to his guest. It was time to slow his flow of information down. "Would you like to have a look around, Lord Alden?" he asked. "The building is very straightforward." He motioned toward the door to his office with a small bend forward, and Lord Alden nodded thoughtfully. He was still considering the complexities of a school composed of mostly needy students and was also growing weary. Projects like these were better approached by the young, which was why he hoped his daughter would be intrigued.

"We could also postpone our walkthrough for another day if you'd prefer to digest this more slowly," Professor Stanford offered.

"Most thoughtful of you," Lord Alden answered. "But this is important to my daughter, and so to me. If successful, it will mark the turning point for musical training in Britain. It will be part of the modernization and innovation of the Victorian era. Let us continue." And leaving his belongings on the chair in Professor Stanford's office, he moved determinedly to open the door to the rest of the odd little building, realizing his adventures at the Royal College of Music were about to begin.

3

VIENNA

"Now, just who do you think this is trespassing on our peace?" the disheveled young man muttered into his cat's fur, holding her against his face so only she could hear. The sleek black-and-white feline offered a stark contrast to his rumpled appearance. The hair at the top of his head was already thinning despite his youth, and what was left on the sides surely hadn't been combed for days. His baggy, wrinkled cotton shirt had the distinct air of being worked and slept in for just as long. He held the cat resting in the crook of his arm, cradling her as if she could shield him from whatever threat might be on its way up the stairs to his garret. He despised uninvited guests breaking in on his work, and since he seldom asked anyone to the studio, everyone who came was assumed to be an intruder.

"Connie, could this be for you?" he called out to the young man arranging paints and art materials on one of the huge tables along the far wall. Connie looked up from his efforts quizzically, glancing at the entrance to the garret. He realized the intrusion was most definitely connected to him as his mother and older brother appeared in the stair doorway. He was even more surprised than his friend. His look of disbelief moved quickly into one of pleasure as his mother took two final steps into the room, clearly out of breath from the challenge of scaling the five stories to the Klimt studio. Dressed in a simple charcoal-gray ankle-length wool coat trimmed with black silk braid and leather buttons, she looked very modern in a small fur hat covering her dark hair twisted close to her head. Little curls escaped to frame her face in a becoming contrast to the simple, elegant lines of her outfit. Her large dark eyes shone with the pleasure of her discovery of and arrival in the garret, and her two dimples in full evidence flashed with one of her deepest smiles.

"Mother," Connie exclaimed. "What a nice surprise! But how did you find me here?" He put the brushes he'd been holding down on the table and took three large strides across the floor to fold his mother in a hug. His own dimples, much like hers, were sparked by his warm greeting and embrace.

"Your brother," she answered, still struggling to regain her breath as she pulled back to look at her blond, somewhat tousled son wearing a wrinkled artist's smock, and turning to the tall, dark, uncommonly handsome young man standing just behind her. "We were at a luthier nearby so I could have some work done on my violin, and when we left, William mentioned that the studio you enjoyed spending time in was nearby. I suggested we visit you while we were in the neighborhood."

"Wonderful!" Connie exclaimed. "Come and meet the studio's incomparable owner." He turned to face the artist, still holding his black-and-white cat. "Mother, this is Gustav Klimt and his cat Sisi." Klimt still preserved the space between himself and his uninvited guests, and Connie wondered if the intrusion would create an irrevocable breach with his friend, but looking at Klimt more closely, he saw fascination on his face rather than the confrontation he'd feared.

"Your mother," Gustav breathed. "What a pleasure. So you are ..."

"Emily de Koningh," she answered, moving forward to fill the emptiness between them as she removed her right kid glove, which Connie took to hold for her. She reached out to the artist, and he readjusted the cat to his left arm to shake her hand.

"Gustav Klimt," he responded, never taking his appraising gaze from her face. "I'm honored to have you here in the studio," he continued, with mounting excitement. "I've heard of your career, of course. My mother was a hopeful amateur musician, always desirous of a career but never up to the task. But you were quite an inspiration to women who wanted things our culture denies." She smiled warmly at him, reaching out toward the cat with her bare hand.

"May I?" she asked, pausing before touching it. He nodded, continuing to soak up her presence by memorizing her face. "It's a lovely compliment to be told one's made a difference in the attitudes of other women and the culture we must maneuver together," she said, stroking the cat's head and ears as it closed its eyes in pleasure. "Even more so than hearing praise for my violin. I'm sorry your mother didn't follow her passion for music, but perhaps it wasn't her calling. It's most definitely not for everyone. Do you have a large family, Herr Klimt?"

"Indeed," he chuckled. "I have many siblings and a demanding father to keep my mother busy. There was no room for her music, and she gave it up easily. So as you say, the passion wasn't hot enough. Would you come in and have a seat? Or look around if you'd prefer. Connie has made this a second home since visiting Vienna." He moved backward and nodded at Connie, suggesting he bring his mother into the room and get a chair for her. Emily followed her son across to the big double windows, which let in enough light to fill every corner of the garret without any additional illumination.

"How did you two come to meet?" she asked, as Connie moved a chair at the table over near one of the windows. She removed her other glove and gave it to him so she could unbutton her coat with both hands from the neck to the top of her chest. The artist watched attentively.

"I knew one of Gustav's friends when we were in Paris," Connie said, running a hand with some dried blue paint on it through his curly hair to push it out of his eyes. "He and Gustav's brother have joined together for a number of art projects here in Austria. The three of them have already won many prizes, and there's no question that Klimt will be a famous name in the art world going forward. It already is!" He grinned, flashing his dimples at the artist again in full recognition of the truth of what he was saying.

"Connie, there's no place in art for competition," Gustav said with a slight frown, waving his hand as if wiping away the notoriety his protégé was heaping on him. But Connie was aware of the remarkable circumstances of the moment, with two people of world-class talent meeting because of him. It made him feel he was part of the art world in a way he never had before. The artist asked Emily, "Would you mind turning toward the window and then back to look at me again?" Emily turned slightly, then looked over her shoulder at her son.

"Have you been taking lessons from Herr Klimt?" she asked.

"Not as such," he answered. "But just being around these three geniuses when they're working is enough to inspire a stone! There's nothing they can't do. One minute they're architects and the next, painters. They can design inside and outside and even work metal. Gustav's father worked in gold—"

"And sadly, I find myself following in my father's footsteps. We'd all prefer to create in our own unique ways," Gustav chuckled with a wink at Connie, who put his mother's gloves down, grabbing a stool beside the art table and sliding it over next to her. Perching on it in his usual energetic way as if only to alight for a moment, Connie leaned toward Emily, propping himself up on both knees with his arms straight. "All the Klimt collaborators are fascinated by the changes in art and culture they can feel coming. Gustav has talked a lot with me about joining the art revolution in Vienna now. There are illustrators involved in the fashion industry, and he sees them as becoming very influential in the future."

Connie turned back to the artist, who had lowered his cat Sisi to the floor before moving over next to Emily's chair. "My mother has long been part of the fashion revolution. She fought against the unhealthy styles and corsets enslaving women in her youth," he announced proudly, suddenly noticing his friend wasn't listening to him but remained fixated on his mother's face with the light falling behind it from the window.

"Would there be a chance I might sketch you for a portrait while you're in Vienna?" Klimt asked, almost under his breath. He continued to stare at Emily, moving very slightly from side to side, and up and down to see her from different angles and reflections. She laughed easily, neither a dismissive nor a deprecating tone but just one of simple pleasure.

"I'm flattered you should ask," she said, turning back to face him and Connie. "But we're leaving Vienna soon and still have much to accomplish before we go. I do thank you for your support of my son's work, though. I've often wondered if he should have more formal training, but I question the usefulness of conservatory learning now. Did you have a classical education in the arts, Herr Klimt?"

He nodded. "I did, yes. But to be honest, there's nothing like jumping into the work and living it directly. Herzmansky's department store is employing artists to advertise their ready-made clothing now. I think Connie could benefit greatly from being around other artists specifically involved in the industry of fashion. He has talent, and particularly with fabric and texture." He lowered himself to the stool Connie had just vacated to be at Emily's eye level. "Understanding his upbringing by a mother who participated in the fashion revolution herself, I now see why he has such an acutely developed sense of style. Connie should come to work with us," he said. "We'd take good care of him."

"I have no doubt," Emily agreed. "I can see how happy he is here with you. But both boys . . ." she looked to William now, standing back near the stairs as if in preparation for immediate flight, ". . . they're returning for the first time with me to my birthplace in England. I want them to spend time getting to know their grandfather and their ancestral roots. It's a trip I've put off for a long while and can delay no more. But we won't be staying forever, so if Connie decides to return here on his own, then that will be his decision to make for himself, later."

"Surely we've taken up enough of Herr Klimt's time, Mother," William interrupted, clearly hoping for a departure sooner rather than later. He nodded grudgingly in the artist's direction, holding his hand out to his mother and opening the garret door to the stairs with his other. Connie frowned slightly but moved also as if to assist in the leave-taking figuratively, if not literally.

"Indeed we have, Herr Klimt." Emily moved smoothly toward William to cover the awkwardness of his interruption. "All your best light will be gone if we don't leave you to your work. I thank you both for putting up with our intrusion and look forward to seeing more of your efforts in the future."

"The pleasure was mine," the artist said, bowing slightly. His loose, wrinkled tunic and disheveled appearance made the gallantry somewhat incongruous. "I hope your concert schedule brings you back to Vienna soon." Emily also smiled and inclined her head.

"We'll see you later, Connie." She gently squeezed his hand as he gave her back her gloves. "Will you be joining us for dinner?"

"I think not," he answered quickly. "I have friends to say goodbye to before we depart, so after work is the only time I can see them." She nodded and turned to leave through the door William was still holding open. He shook his head slightly in disapproval, either over Connie's declined dinner invitation or his mother's freedom of speech with a man she didn't know, or both. Emily's annoyance at her elder son had stayed hidden for a while, an accomplishment she'd hoped might extend well into the evening or even the next day to follow. They were too often at odds.

✦⚶ ⚶✦

"What was that all about?" Emily asked William, looking back up the curved marble staircase as she stood on the bottom floor. She noticed the buildings housing artists' studios in Vienna were made of sturdier, prettier stone than the rickety wooden ones in Paris. She'd visited many of those over the past decade to play chamber music with friends and colleagues. "Could you not have tried a bit harder to be civil to Connie's new friend?" William eyed her with an unswerving glare that held no likelihood of an apology for something he'd had every intention of doing. "I don't claim to understand you, William, but there's no excuse for rudeness, no matter what ails you."

Emily shook her head about the carriage William had started to hail, unable to imagine herself riding in the confined space with her son when he infuriated her. "Let's walk," she said, as if the thought had just come to her. "I need some air and it's not far to the hotel. Now that I'm not carrying the violin, I feel less vulnerable in the street." Her elder son glowered at her, not because he was averse to the exercise but because he understood she was angry with him. Truly it was time to find a way for her family to coexist in a communal support system. Was it her fault they all wanted to live separate lives without care or sacrifice of any kind for each other's welfare? Had her focus on her own career battles taught them all to attend only to their own needs without concern for anyone else in the family? Neither her sons nor her husband shared any of their private thoughts with her, or perhaps even each other anymore. Even though she'd been so close to her sons when they were children, it was understandable that they identified with their father and each other as young men. But they hadn't gotten any closer, and the worst of it was that no one seemed to mind. Except her. Certainly her frequent trips to perform over the past twenty years could have taken a toll on them she'd never acknowledged. Taking Corey with her as her accompanist so often might have also reduced her sons' chances to relate to their father, and the family to correlate to itself.

So there it was, the unattractive irony that wanting a family just as much as a career, she was probably the sole reason they had no unity. "Come along," she ordered, "you can explain your disapproval of Herr Klimt to me as we go." She struck up a fast pace made more possible by her ankle-length coat and low-heeled boots with laces. Gratefully acknowledging her freedom to move even faster than her son, she gave thanks to the newer, non-confining fashions they'd mentioned during her visit to the Klimt studio.

Moving quickly along the streets of Vienna together, the silence between William and Emily stretched out long and loud, until William finally said, "I don't disapprove of Gustav Klimt, per se. I just worry that Connie isn't demonstrating enough restraint in his relationships, Mother. He's very free to advertise his loose connections, and that reflects on not only him, but also on us." Emily looked at her son sideways without slowing her pace.

"What do you mean by 'loose connections,' William?" She purposely gave him no time to think, fearing without fully admitting it that he would say something she didn't want to hear. She'd worked not to limit her sons' freedom to express their opinions, yet she found William's jealousy and negativity confining, and diametrically opposed to her own optimistic views of life's opportunities. She knew his struggle to control everything and everyone in the world around him mirrored her own father, but Lord Alden had found ways to moderate his effort to govern with a natural charm that appealed to those who knew him. It was a skill William did not possess. She had possibly tried to emulate it in her own life, but it was less feasible for a woman held somewhat at arm's length by a society that didn't understand or trust her entirely.

"Mother, you can't be so blind to the quality of Connie's friend-ships as to think them acceptable. If you do, I can assure you no one else does."

Emily fought to let go of the rising resentment in her throat. "William, don't scold me as if I was the child and you were the parent. You've been doing that since you were four years old, and I couldn't stand it then!" William had the imperious tone of a self-ap-pointed arbiter on the family's morals and manners, and she knew her bitterness had more to do with her innate resistance to authority than it did to him, although he seemed to elicit the same response from everyone else he spoke to that way. The revolution always brewing in her soul, even in her forties, couldn't be dominated. It exploded now before she could contain it. Stopping short and spinning around, she purposely flashed a warning with her taut body and angry eyes that her son couldn't miss.

"I have no idea what you're talking about, William. If you disapprove of Connie's artist friends and find them inappropriate for both your brother and this family, you'll need to be a lot more direct. Innuendos and snide comments don't communicate plainly enough." She stamped her foot before she could stop herself, feeling childish and guilty as she did it, her old mutinies coming clearly and embar-rassingly to mind. Yet she needed to be in control of her family and her life now, and it was time to take a stand.

"I, for one, don't find anything objectionable about artists like Herr Klimt," Emily announced firmly. "As a matter of fact," she spat out in staccato, "I find him an unusual and attractive intellectual." She stood her ground, challenging William to deal with their differ-ent values and opinions, a confrontation impossible to avoid. Fighting for her beliefs face-to-face with another adult, even a twenty-year-old one, was still uncomfortable for her. She had to remind herself that he was indeed grown up now, even if one whose opinions she disagreed with and disliked. "So, tell me, William, what's so offensive about Herr Klimt and the others? I'm listening."

But William stood his ground as well, a tall, handsome replica of his English grandfather, with generations of upper-class arrogance arming his self-righteousness.

"Mother, you can't possibly be as naïve and blind as you pretend!" He stared at her as if seeing her for the first time, as one might a child in need of guidance and censure. She stared right back at him in defiance of his disapproval. William narrowed his eyes, drawing himself up to look down at her. He took a deep breath.

"I believe Connie is a sodomite, Mother. His flagrant relationships with artists and others are dangerous. Someone needs to caution him." Emily stood frozen in place. "Sodomy is a sin, Mother, and an allegation and subsequent trial could ruin a man's life, to say nothing of those connected to him." He pulled the collar of his coat up around the back of his neck as if to protect himself from indictments stirred up in his brother's wake. Emily shook herself slightly, opening her eyes wide as if to invite in all charges William might let fly.

"That's detestable, William," she spat out. "Connie's life and how he lives it are his own business but assisting in the criminalization of your own brother is truly immoral. I'd better not hear you discuss this again with anyone or you'll find yourself ostracized from this family in ways you can't even imagine. Do you understand me . . . perfectly?"

She spun around and took off again at top speed in the direction of their hotel, never looking to see if William was following or had chosen another way back. The fact that a son of hers could be so consumed by the malignancy of jealousy that he would accuse his own brother overwhelmed her with nausea. Of course Connie could rise above it, and probably wouldn't even hold it against William because that was his way. But Emily could not, because it was not hers. Disloyalty was a black sin to her with no nuance or shading. She knew William well enough to know he'd never drop his assertions now that he'd begun them. Maybe Corey could help, or possibly one of her male friends, or maybe all of them. She had no idea how other men would react to William's claims, but she knew instinctively that the boys' father would automatically sense the right direction, because that was his way. *But what if . . .* She stopped her thoughts from advancing any further.

The discussion must come immediately, before leaving for London. Possibly such a criminal allegation delivered less of a blow in Austria than it would in England, but that wasn't something Emily wanted to risk. She would talk with Corey as soon as she returned to the hotel and would spend some time later that evening with John Mackay, although not offering the kind of evening he no doubt would prefer. She felt instinctively it would be best to steer clear of Johnny Dunne. An exposé leaked to the newspaper would be the worst of all possible outcomes, and much as she delighted in his company, his professional proximity couldn't be risked.

As bad as William's accusations were, the pleasure he took in them was of far greater significance. Had they exposed something vile in William possibly always there but now to be handled carefully before it destroyed him and all of them as well? Could her son have been born completely amoral, or were his values somehow her fault? That was something she had no idea how to deal with.

4

FAMILY AND FRIENDS

COREY LOOKED UP from his newspaper when the editor from *Le Figaro* wished him a good morning and farewell in the same breath, asking if his wife was nearby so he could bid her goodbye as well. The friends' vacation in Vienna had come to an end, and each would be returning to their current homes, with the de Koninghs on their way to London for the first time in many years. The move and separations were unsettling, and Corey couldn't tell if the discomfort had to do with the prospect of living under his father-in-law's roof for the first time since his marriage to Emily, or just the suggestion of a fresh start to a new life. Either way, he wanted to begin the journey, and having tired of the cabaret scene in Paris and hungering for more conducting and vocal work, the move to something new could be just what he needed. He knew his wife had always been uncomfortable waiting in the space between the present and future, and that made him uneasy, too.

Corey smiled at Johnny Dunne, the longtime acquaintance who'd become as much his friend as his wife's over the past years living in France. An agreement without words at the start of his marriage to Emily had given them room to form alliances of their own. And for the most part, they understood each other past and present, usually approving of the people they brought into their relationship from the outside. His unfaithful liaison at the beginning of their marriage had naturally started the momentum toward the arrangement, yet he could tell soon after that Emily had been unsure herself about marriage and the parameters it set, feeling it robbed her of independence. Ultimately, he knew they were both perfectly happy with the way they'd lived apart while together, and even though their musical tastes differed, their mutual admiration for each other's work and skills made more of a bond than a division between them.

"I'm sorry you missed her, Johnny," Corey said. "I don't think she was aware of your departure today. She'd never have taken off to see the princess without connecting with you first had she known."

"Good heavens, the Princess von Metternich is vastly more interesting than I am. Who could blame Emily for preferring her company to mine! She's even better connected to the social and political tides than our newspaper is."

Corey nodded with a broad grin. "It's amazing how she rises to the top of any culture she circulates in, isn't it? Who would have thought she'd be just as effective in Vienna as she was in Paris."

"We should have," Johnny said. "Her husband may have lost his job as Austrian Ambassador to France after the Franco-Prussian War, but Pauline retained hers as the head of European culture. Whether in Paris or Vienna, she sets the standards by which society grades itself."

"Well, as you know, she was very kind to Emily when we first arrived in Paris, promoting her work and supporting her entrance to the European music world. She's such a passionate patron of the arts, to say nothing of women who challenge male-dominated fields, that there was never a doubt they'd be attracted to each other." He was apparently reviewing one of the princess's audacious moves in his mind and comparing it to Emily's own, so evident in her years growing up in the de Koningh mansion in New York. "But you are quite wrong, Johnny, if you think Pauline could ever take your place in Emily's affections," he said with a shake of his head. "You're family; she's just an intriguing acquaintance." The two men smiled at each other warmly, their connection clear and evident.

Johnny had an uncanny ability to fit in with almost anyone, anywhere, and that made him both the perfect choice to be the newspaper's culture editor as well as everyone's easy confidant. He and Emily had been remarkably close since they'd met twenty years ago, and he'd always shown up just when she'd needed him most. He'd even been a guide and counsel to her sons over the years, taking the place of a caring uncle providing that kind of unbiased advice so difficult for parents to offer. Corey had found Johnny's relationship with his wife too close for comfort at one time, but eventually he became a help that Corey, too, could rely on. He pointed to the wing chair next to his, and folded his paper, preferring to talk than bury himself in the news. He doubted any of it was important, anyway. He had very little curiosity about other people's affairs and so his use of the papers was limited.

Taking a seat, Johnny said, "I know she didn't want to leave out seeing any of her friends on this trip. But putting Pauline von Metternich last on her list might have been a mistake." He grinned at Corey, who'd already started to laugh in appreciation of the truth of what Johnny was saying. "Can you imagine," he continued, dropping his voice surreptitiously, "how long it will take for Pauline to expose Emily to her latest social experiments, extract all Emily's gossip from Paris, and immerse her in the rumors circulating around Vienna!" He groaned a little, resting his head back between the upholstered wings of his chair and closing his eyes as if to shut out visions of Emily and Pauline von Metternich endlessly tangled up together in trouble. "You'd best be careful, Corey," Johnny warned. "Emily may come back smoking cigars and refusing to play all music but Bedřich Smetana's in an attempt to support the princess in one of her disputes."

Corey threw his head back and laughed. "Doubtful," he said. "She's still more of a classicist than she'd like to admit, and no more interested in gossip and other people's business than I am. She's very much a laissez-faire kind of woman and always has been. But that reminds me," he added, adjusting himself in his chair a little as if the thought he'd just had made him physically uncomfortable. "What do you make of her continuous quarreling with William? That doesn't seem like her, do you think?" He watched Johnny carefully, truly hoping their friend would settle this mysterious tension that Corey was so completely at a loss to understand. But Johnny shook his head and shrugged.

"Oh, I don't know," he said, wondering why the stress between Emily and William had never been mentioned before. It had been there since the boy's early childhood, but Corey hadn't seemed to notice or care. Perhaps that was why father and son had gotten along. There was never much judgment between them. He glanced out the ornate hotel window at the gray Vienna sky to avoid Corey's eyes. "I think she's on edge with the move to England, and it's probably also hard to accept that her boys are no longer children."

"No harder than for their father," Corey said. "Every time I see them going off to some appointment of their own making I wonder how they could go without inviting me to come along. Then I realize that I'm truly too old to be of any interest to them, and it's an unpleasant shock, I can tell you, while I wonder if I shouldn't go anyway to keep an eye on them."

Johnny laughed and pushed himself up out of his deep chair. "Well, I must be on my way." Corey, too, rose as Johnny added, "Please tell Emily I'm sorry we didn't get a chance to say goodbye, and that I enjoyed this little vacation with the family immensely. Write to me when you get settled in London, my friend." He shook Corey's hand and then reached out with his other arm to embrace him. A few people around the hotel parlor glanced over, unused to the expression of affection between two well-dressed gentlemen of obvious means.

"As I said, I'm sorry to see you go before she's back, but we didn't speak after dinner last night. We didn't talk during dinner, either. We often get lost in our own thoughts these days, I'm sorry to say." Corey moved to pick up his coffee cup to cover his discomfort with his statement that sounded just as empty as it was. He saw the cup had been drained long ago and put it quickly down again. "She didn't feel well after her outing with William yesterday and went right to bed, and she left early this morning." He was surprised to find his disclosure of the lack of connection with his wife had embarrassed him. "So I had no idea she was visiting the princess today until I saw her note after she was off," Corey added, hoping to deflect some of Johnny's disapproval from himself to Emily. But he quickly felt guilty for that, too, and forced himself to end with the comment that he'd had little control over what Emily did for a very long time.

"We'll both write you as soon as we're in Lord Alden's home," he said, as warmly as he could. "But hopefully not in his grasp." Johnny turned away, disappearing through the hotel parlor door, leaving Corey to feel the anxiety of inertia as he glanced at the space Johnny had once filled in the chair next to his. The fact remained with him that he was lonely, a truth he'd not been aware of until now.

⁕✹⁕

Emily and Pauline von Metternich kissed each other on both cheeks, first right, then left. The greeting was automatic between European women, but the squeeze they gave each other's arms afterward was not. "I had hoped your trip might coincide with Franz Liszt's visit," Pauline said, motioning to Emily to sit next to her on the settee in front of the tea table. "But you're too late. He left last month for London. He's gotten terribly infirm, and I was quite relieved to see him go. I didn't like being responsible for him in that condition."

Emily watched her pour the tea with a firm assurance she found more attractive than any of the decorative feminine maneuvers many women of society worked to display. Pauline was no beauty, but there was something solid about her that Emily had been drawn to instantly when they'd first met in Paris. Learning of her strong patronage of music and contemporary arts, Emily had found something very unusual and unexpected in the princess: someone who cared as deeply for music as she did, even though she was a non-professional. Pauline's social connections to composers whose careers she backed and advanced were legion, and her substantial support in the music circles of Vienna and Paris could bring a musician or composer forward when they'd spent their whole careers in the shadows. And she and Emily sought out each other's opinions. For Emily, it was a rare relationship of equals of differing backgrounds, and she valued it highly as the special and unusual connection it was. Other than Pauline, all her friends were men.

"You also barely missed running into the reviled Empress Elisabeth," Pauline groaned, feigning the pain such a meeting would bring any who experienced it. But Emily smiled and shook her head a little, aware that the Empress Elisabeth, wife of the Austrian Emperor Franz Joseph, was a foe of Pauline's more from jealousy than just cause. She was famed as the most beautiful princess in Europe and obsessed over her looks and weight, exercising excessively to drop any extra ounce that might have found its way onto her body. But her annoyance over the rigid protocols of court life reminded Emily of Pauline's own sentiments, making her wonder at the strength of her friend's bias against the stunning Elisabeth.

"Oh for heaven's sake, Pauline. Haven't you moved past that enmity yet? I don't know her well, but she appears to me a sweet lady and strong supporter of the common people, and her simplicity of fashion I find appealing. In fact, I had my son, who's an artist, design me a dress for the opera in her elegant style—just an ankle-length black and white lace gown free of decoration. It was beautiful and comfortable. I think of her as an innovator of trends."

"Naturally! Sisi has nothing else to be concerned with but her body and beauty, though I'll admit both are highly developed. I do admire her in those regards."

"Sisi . . . is that what they call her? I'd forgotten if I ever knew. I just met a Sisi who's a cat, so named by her owner Gustav Klimt. She too is sleek and black-and-white, so I see the connection is apt."

"Gustav! You met him? He is one of Austria's brightest stars. I know what I'm talking about!"

"Yes, I was extremely impressed with him, though I'm not sure why. I had little time to see any of his work, but there's some air about him and an intensity anyone would be fascinated with. My younger son Cornelius has been working with him, and I went to visit him in Herr Klimt's studio. You think him to be a valuable mentor, Pauline?" Emily sat rigid, her teacup frozen in place as if fixed in stone for posterity. The princess took note.

"If Gustav has chosen your son as a protégé, then his future in art, as well as Viennese society, is assured," she said, smiling easily at Emily. "Is that what's worrying you? I can't help but think there's something disturbing you, though, that remains unmentioned."

Replacing her cup on the tray before her, Emily took a deep breath. "Somewhat, but not exactly," Emily said, wanting more than anything to appear calm. Much of Paris feared how widely the princess could spread a rumor. But Emily had always considered her to be from a different cloth. Her talk was about real people and issues of true concern. She neither fabricated events nor related only that which supported her own preferences, as she'd just demonstrated when talking about her archenemy, Empress Elisabeth. She admitted to truths she found uncomfortable and omitted facts she couldn't verify. Emily had found her more an intellectually curious, highly sociable woman than a purveyor of lies or innuendos to support her own fantasies. Somewhere in the middle of her sleepless night Emily had decided Pauline was in the best position to know the truth about Gustav Klimt and his colleagues.

"I have been extremely worried, Pauline, it's true, since I heard . . . suggestions that my son's relationships are perhaps . . . unhealthy for both himself and society as a whole." Emily was proud of the way she was able to hold her body, voice, and thoughts together. "There have been allegations that Herr Klimt might be attracted to other men, and therefore that my son is implicated in that crime by association. I have no such evidence, but I know a mother is sometimes the last to hear painful truths. Do you know of Herr Klimt's and his brother's private lives, Pauline? If anyone does, I'm sure it's you."

The Princess von Metternich stared at Emily in disbelief, just long enough to make Emily wonder if she'd made a terrible mistake, exposing such a crime to the woman responsible for a social network extending throughout the societies of much of Europe. Had she given the princess the power to ruin Connie before there could even be evidence gathered to exonerate him? She noticed Pauline's thick but kindly features were beaming with pleasure she found hard to make sense of. Suddenly the princess burst out with a peal of laughter that shook her, so she had to put her cup carefully down next to Emily's, holding her other hand over the top of it to stop it from careening off the saucer and into her lap.

"Emily," she fairly choked with hilarity, "Gustav Klimt is one of the lustiest, most admittedly erotic appreciators of the female body I have ever known. As you've seen, he's only in his early twenties, but he's already fathered several children with different women, and I have no doubt will be doing so well into his eighties!"

Emily stared at the princess. Pauline reached over to squeeze one of Emily's small, strong hands gripped in her lap. "If your son has befriended the Klimt artists, I can guarantee you he's no sodomite, dear Emily. The discomfort he would feel in such a group of colleagues would be too much for either side to bear. I don't know who told you this, but I can assure you it isn't true. I assume it might have been to that person's advantage to implicate your son in a crime somehow, but it's what I would call false information. Society can be vicious, and such a savage assault certainly could ruin someone's career or reputation. If you want me to try to find out how such a rumor got started, I'll listen in some of the right places and let you know. But I would worry no more about it."

She watched Emily's grip loosen a little in her lap. "I see it's very hard for you to be a mother," she added. "I understand that too well, having daughters of my own. It's even harder than to be a world-class musician who plays an instrument society would prefer she didn't."

Emily laughed quietly for the first time since she'd arrived. "Well, the problem with the rumor's origin still exists," she said, almost under her breath. Her friend assumed she was recovering slowly but hadn't found a way to let go of her fear yet. She assumed a change of topic might help. Princess Pauline had an instinct for the passions of utmost importance, and she had always greatly admired Emily's commitment to her violin and the art of performance.

"My dear, how has your career been going? Tell me of your musical exploits and let me pour you some more hot tea to take the edge off your terror." She reached for the porcelain teapot without waiting for a nod from Emily. "I know Wagner and Liszt have never been your favorites, though they are mine and I forgive you, but have you performed Saint-Saëns and Gounod lately? I correspond with them both regularly. I also became highly enamored of the Czech musician Bedřich Smetana. Have you heard of him?" She leaned forward to hand Emily back her teacup. "Ah, wait," she said, putting it down and raising a small carafe of pale gold liquid. "A little sherry would soften the blow of the false information you've been dealing with for the past few days. Yes?" Emily nodded and Pauline poured some into the teacup and handed it to her.

"Honestly, Pauline, you amaze me. Your connection to the musicians moving about the world today positively vibrates like the strings of their instruments. In a way, you are a composer in your own right. Your work is their work, and yours is just as vital as theirs. But mine . . . well, it's lost some of its luster for me. I feel as if I've made my point as a woman in performance, and I've conquered as much of the technique as I ever will. I feel as if there's little left to surprise me, challenge me, or give me the lift I used to get from the discovery of a new composer or performance. My music feels . . . stale," she said, taking a big sip from her teacup. The sherry warmed her chest just as the tea had warmed the sherry. The princess watched her carefully, assessing where the weight of her thoughts had come from. "Actually," Emily went on, "I can't decide whether I should continue to play or just retire quietly. When I return to London, I could become the housekeeper my father hasn't had since my mother died. Maybe family duties would be enough for me now. Certainly they would be a change since they've never been the center of my life before."

She drained her cup and returned it to the tray in front of the settee. The princess stayed silent, viewing her guest and friend through narrowed eyes as if to focus on her better. The silence in the room suddenly became noticeable, and Emily shifted in her seat uncomfortably, not sure if she should say her goodbyes or wait until her hostess gave her a sign.

Finally Pauline spoke. "I have no experience like yours to go on," she said, pushing a few loose strands of hair back off her homely face, "but I sense you need to see your life from a different perspective, to shed some new light on it, and possibly to involve new people."

"Pauline, what in heaven's name do you mean?" Emily gasped, smiling with embarrassment at her lack of preparation for her friend's comment. Had John Mackay's notoriety finally caught up with her? His likeness was centered in almost every newspaper and periodical of the day. Had her name been linked with his in some of her performance venues around the world and noted by Pauline, the gossip queen? Or maybe Johnny Dunne's bachelor status had attracted more attention lately, with their rare trysts in Paris becoming nourishment for the speculation Pauline controlled so deftly. What would the point of those disclosures be? That her public persona jeopardized her children? That she was, in fact, a bad mother? Emily pulled herself up to sit straighter. She had to head right into that wind. "Are you suggesting I need new lovers in some different settings?" she asked, laughing softly and attempting to appear comfortable and sophisticated without any hint of crudeness.

The princess chuckled along with her. "Possibly, if that's the first thought that comes to mind," she said, "but I actually meant that you might want to find a way to share music with others now, bring it to the future with a very personal point of view, as a great educator would."

Emily let her breath out, greatly relieved that the subject was music rather than meetings with her male friends. "You mean, I might do some teaching?" Emily said, looking past Pauline to the huge casement windows behind her and into the clearing sky beyond. "Oddly enough, I've thought of that before," Emily whispered, almost inaudibly. Then she lifted her voice to share her thoughts with the woman most likely to understand her feelings about work, and love, and family. "I've found playing chamber music brings me much more pleasure than performing solo lately," she said, loud enough to include her friend this time. "Maybe I've outgrown the need to shine, to have all the light on me," she added.

"Who knows?" Pauline replied. "But there's only one way to find out. And when you take a new direction, there will be new people and new challenges. Aren't those the bells you need to wake you up now?" she asked.

"Maybe," Emily replied. "I don't know. But one thing I do know is that the isolation of the solo career isn't good for me anymore." She rose to say goodbye to her friend, hugging her close in a decidedly unladylike show of affection.

John Mackay sat on the window seat in his hotel room, one of the largest and best the Hotel Sacher had to offer. Not because he'd asked for it, but as usual, because they wanted him to have it. They needed men like him to promote their fine reputation. With one of his strong, muscular legs hanging down and the other bent to act as a brace, he viewed the architecture of Vienna with a frank appreciation. Even though he was familiar with most of Europe's capital cities, this was perhaps the most beautiful. Every building he could see from his window had some charming trait of architecture, set off by the cobblestones, fountains, and greenery softening all the stone.

None of the ugly streets of his early impoverished childhood in either Dublin or New York reminded him of what he saw now. But he sensed those early horrors had contributed to his appreciation for blessings like these in his later life. Though he might now be the richest self-made man in the world, there was an unpretentiousness about him, ironically coupled with an unquestioned sense of leadership, a combination that made those above and below him equally at ease with him. A man of his wealth would undoubtedly have employed a servant at the hotel to assist with his wardrobe, but as John was more comfortable taking care of himself, he glanced around now for his vest and collar, which he'd left somewhere last night on his way to bed after Emily arrived unexpectedly.

They'd been together so long now, a marriage of sorts over almost two decades. It was not unusual for a man of his wealth and connections to live more than one life, with more than one wife, so to speak. But he was very much in the public eye, and therefore his lawful family was, too. He and his wife could not possibly have been cut from more different cloth, and her pretensions and criticisms of the American way of life had left him no alternative but to set up two different homes, one for himself in New York or wherever he was working, and one in Paris for her, where her social life could match her needs.

Emily, as a woman, could not expect the kind of acceptance for her inventive lifestyle as he could for his, but her silver lining came in the form of lowered social expectations for a female performer, regardless of her background. And so they had enjoyed each other's company and support, living together occasionally while she performed in Europe, a relationship that had started when they met in New York and Emily was very newly and most unhappily married. Neither his wife nor her husband seemed to care if the lives they wanted for themselves went on uninterrupted, and he could even argue that both of their lawful marriages had benefited greatly from the alternate relationships keeping everyone satisfied and fulfilled.

"Is this what you're looking for?" Emily asked, cradling two silver cuff links cupped in her hand as she walked across the room to his side.

"No," he answered, getting up from the window seat with a wry smile under his prodigious blond mustache, "but they'll help. I need my collar and vest," he said, slipping an arm around her waist and kissing her bare shoulder where she stood beside him.

"In the bedroom," she said, "right where you left them."

"No surprise, then," John said, slipping his other arm around her waist and turning her to face him. "How are you feeling this morning?"

"A little calmer," Emily said. "But I sense the worry for Connie's welfare won't disappear in one afternoon with the Princess von Metternich, or one night with John Mackay, either." She dropped her forehead to his shoulder as he pulled her closer.

"I thought we'd been through all of that and moved on, and you were comfortable with what you heard yesterday," he said, resting his chin on her head to help her feel totally safe. She didn't move or speak, and he couldn't tell if she was thinking or trying not to cry.

"What is it?" he asked, pulling back to look at the obvious distress in her huge dark eyes swimming with tears.

"Oh, it's foolish, I know, but I can't help but think that either Connie's brother is right and he's in serious trouble, or if not, then William is for his lack of loyalty. Either way, I feel I'm somehow responsible though I'm not sure how. I feel a failure, as if I've reneged on the only contract I needed to fulfill." She couldn't seem to stop the tears from overflowing and running down her cheeks now, and John let her cry, realizing that she'd already spent too much time and effort trying not to. She took a breath and started to talk again.

"I've never missed a performance or let any one of my music colleagues down," she choked, looking into his clear blue eyes and knowing instinctively he'd understand her need to deliver on a promise she'd made to herself. "But my own boys have missed out on every perquisite a child of a caring parent has a right to expect. And their father, who used to keep them so happily engaged when they were children when I couldn't be there as much, has washed his hands of any responsibility to them in their older years, and I fear that's my fault as well. Maybe I've pushed them all away," she added, straightening up and wiping her eyes with the back of her hand. "What was wrong with me? Why wasn't I more motivated by my home than my music?" She pushed herself away from John with a slight sigh, running her hand over her bathrobe to be sure it was up around her neck and closed. "What's wrong?" she whispered. "Am I embarrassing you? Can't you deal with any human struggles other than those of a bunch of men in a silver mine?"

"My dear, beautiful, and talented Emily," he said quietly, "you know perfectly well I don't judge anyone for their choices in life, as long as they're honest in dealing with themselves and their fellow human beings and keep a core of kindness in their souls. I don't see how that judgment should differ between a man or a woman, and I appreciate that you have always done your best to follow that voice within yourself. I have no doubt your boys have benefited from your example, and their father's as well, and I think you must have a bit more faith in what this world will bring you." They both looked at each other long and deeply before he stirred himself, opened her hand, and took the silver cuff links in his own. But she held on to his arm as if to stop his leaving.

"You had an exceedingly difficult childhood, didn't you, John? As did I. Don't you think we've earned some peace and . . . happiness now, after all we've been through?"

"Oh, I have no idea," he said. "But I admit to being not only used to the toil, privation, and hardship life can bring, but actually enjoying it! I'm happy taking on any challenges—aware they stimulate me and tell me I'm alive. Perhaps that's different from being a mother, but also, perhaps not." He slid his arm around her shoulders and steered her back toward the bedroom where the vest and collar still waited on a chair.

"We're both about to leave for London soon, I to rejoin my wife and children, and you your father and original home. We both return to former lives, but in a new way. The 'new' and 'life' should tell us all we need to know. Perhaps we both must find different ways of doing the same things as we grow older. Granted, I'm almost fifteen years your senior, but as a result, the changes are even harder for me."

"It's difficult to believe you find anything hard," Emily said. "But how would you think of Connie—or of me, for that matter—if William's allegations turn out to be true?"

"You know me well enough to know the answer to that," John said to her, leaving plenty of space between them to give her some room for discretion. "But do you know how you'd feel about yourself?" he asked, watching her quizzically with his head to one side. "I wonder."

5

LONDON

THE LIBRARY in Lord Alden's Grosvenor Square home offered a warm, cheerful contrast to the chill gray of the London day. His grandsons faced each other on the window seat with plenty of room left for books and newspapers. "Do you know where we are, literally?" Connie asked, studying an older couple across the street dressed in dour clothing. They looked almost identical to most of the other London pedestrians, no matter their ages. "It's certainly not Paris or Vienna," he said to his brother, who in turn simply gazed out the window without comment. "I can see London won't be the stimulating fashion center I'd hoped for," Connie added. "But I don't think we'll be staying too long, so best make the most of it."

Propped up against cushions at each end of the bay window, the young adult de Koningh brothers seemed to be reprising an early childhood spent in their other grandfather's music room in New York. One might have expected the window seats and plenty of time to relax to bring out their sibling solidarity, but it hadn't then and now it seemed more of a civilized truce than a camaraderie. They looked out occasionally, pointing and commenting on the people walking by below the window, and carriages moving purposefully toward destinations the young men knew nothing of. Connie had been particularly reluctant to leave both Paris and Vienna, feeling he was finally on a more direct path to begin a bohemian career in fashion design. But William seemed pleased to be heading for the clearly stratified class structures of London, knowing full well he would be at the top of that ranking.

"This is a more homogeneous population," William said, watching the traffic distractedly. "Paris was like a giant stage show with everyone in costume, and Vienna had so many different nationalities mingling with each other . . . the dress reflected many bits of different cultures. But I rather like the uniformity of these people," he added. "They're neither as flashy as the Parisians nor as unpredictable as the Viennese . . ."

"Nor as interesting as either," Connie chimed in to finish the thought, shaking his head and smiling at his brother as if he appreciated his sibling's contrariness despite a taste in fashion and life Connie didn't share. He couldn't resist a small tease when William was in a better mood than usual as he seemed now. "So, you know something about Grosvenor Square, do you?" Connie looked out at the street again before turning back to pay better attention to William. "Is this not considered a 'fashionable' address, then?" A small smile that William missed pulled at the corners of Connie's mouth. It acknowledged something almost resembling an understanding between them. His tall, dark, smooth, and exceptionally handsome brother had always been an uncooperative ally, but Connie had not given up on the possibility that someday they would come together to find some connection missing in childhood, yet making them happier and stronger adults.

"Grosvenor Square is much better than fashionable," William said, looking seriously into Connie's eyes. "It's *exclusive!*" Connie couldn't decide whether to laugh or cry. Clearly his hope for a companion of his own age to share his values and good humor seemed unlikely where William was concerned. Never one to befriend the servants when they were growing up in New York, William had missed some of the wonderful and intriguing friendships Connie had enjoyed; the laundress and his mother's seamstress came quickly to mind. He well remembered William lecturing him at the age of six on the "usefulness" of friendships to advance one's social standing, rather than to enjoy for the sake of the fun of human connection.

"So you're saying we live at an *important* address?" Connie queried.

"I've heard that if one means to be in society in London, the most valued asset is the proper address; it's a matter of life and—"

"Ha! Now I know you're toying with me—"

"Not at all!" William blurted out, angrily. "Obviously, Grandfather Alden has chosen wisely with his connections to the royal family in mind."

"What's all this?" Lord Alden interrupted, coming into the room as his grandsons' raised voices suggested disagreement. "What did I do wisely, William? It's always nice to get a commendation so early in the morning." He noted how the room had changed, brightened with the addition of the two young men in the window. Everywhere around the house felt better, warmer, and fuller since his grandsons had arrived.

"You chose your London address scrupulously," William answered, flashing his most charming expression meant to connect conclusively with its recipient. His grandfather looked perplexed. Remembering how his father had bought the house from the land agent without even seeing it, he wondered if his grandsons had somehow found that out and were chastising their ancestor for his lack of care. So few people of means had settled in the city in that generation it hadn't seemed to matter much where one went.

"You're not serious, are you?" he asked, glancing from William to Connie and then back again. Sensing an instant discomfort coming from William, he moved on into the room to pick up a cup and saucer from the side table nearest the window and pour himself some tea. "Your great-grandfather chose this address, William, so I must defer to his good taste. I was merely a lucky recipient. But to be honest, Grosvenor Square has long been a magnet for Americans in London, starting over a century ago when John Adams set up the first American mission to the Court of St. James. He lived in a house that still stands on the corner of Brook and Duke. I'll take you to see it," he offered, noting Connie's grin and enthusiastic nod coupled with William's look of surprise.

"And you're right about the square's aristocratic connections," he said, not wanting to leave William dangling for too long. "It's the centerpiece of the Mayfair property of the Duke of Westminster, named for Sir Richard Grosvenor who developed it and the surrounding streets at the turn of the century. It's been one of the city's most fashionable residences since then, with many members of the aristocracy as neighbors." He smiled at William, who looked much brighter than he had just minutes ago.

"Sounds a little stiff and dull, Grandfather," Connie chimed in.

"Oh, like most places these days, Connie, the square has also been invaded by modern-day royalty of a different sort." Lord Alden grinned cheerfully at his artistic grandson. "Oscar Wilde had a house here until last year. I'm sorry you missed him. He made quite a sight sashaying out every day in his creative costumes."

"Now that I would have enjoyed!"

"You would!" William snorted in disgust.

Connie laughed, paying no attention to William's disdain. "And Grandfather Alden, what lies behind the houses?" he asked. "Are there more streets where I see an occasional roof, or is that still part of the square's property?"

"All of those small buildings behind the houses are mews, serving as stables for the horses and carriages . . . and other things," Lord Alden added, almost under his breath. Neither boy picked up on his shift of mood, so intent were they at figuring out where the houses' perimeters started and stopped. "Your mother liked to run back and forth between the square and the mews as a small child. She felt as if she had the best of the country and the city that way ..." He looked off back in time somewhere, apparently caught in nostalgia. "But she may not remember any of it. She hasn't been here for any length of time since she was thirteen."

"That may be all to the good," Connie said, suddenly feeling the drop in mood and a need to cheer his grandfather up. "If she doesn't have too many memories to honor, then she can do something new and creative with her renovations of the house. I think she'll enjoy that, Grandfather, and we can help her."

"I agree," Emily's father said, nodding emphatically as his grandsons conspired with him to engage their mother in the running of the household more fully than she ever had before.

"But how long will she stay enthralled with Grosvenor Square?" Connie asked no one in particular. He was hoping the stay would be short so he could return to his apprenticeship with the Klimts in Vienna or one of the designers he'd met in Paris.

"Long enough to become committed," Lord Alden said, "and if not, then I have other plans afoot. Don't anyone doubt my intent to get my daughter back here in London permanently. She's already been gone a lifetime." Connie's eyes widened.

"No, not that long, Grandfather," William said, looking at him more closely. "I heard my father saying we might all start a new life here, so I guess that other half doesn't count."

"I hardly think your mother would agree with you, nor should she," Lord Alden replied, glancing at Connie over his cup as he lifted and drained it.

Connie looked back at him and gave a slight nod. "Her performances have been amazing—"

"Unless she was forced into a vaudeville act or fundraising event to educate American Indians in the West," William added.

"Or to inaugurate a new music hall someplace no one else wanted to go to," Connie said thoughtfully. "Remember her battle with the Chicago fire, William?" His brother nodded grimly and shook his head as if he wanted to rid himself of the pictures in his mind. "But here she is now, established, acknowledged, and sought after all over the world," Connie said, proudly.

"Maybe a little too established," his grandfather interjected. "We must keep her involved in projects that can only be worked on here in London. I hope you boys will help me with that; at least if you feel it's in her best interest, of course, and yours as well. I've missed you all, and there's nothing I'd like better than to have you with me going forward."

"We understand, Grandfather," William said, in his most congenial manner. He was beginning to feel very comfortable in his handsome grandparent's presence and his elegant house, as well. And there was no way he could miss the family resemblance between the two of them, something his mother had often commented on, but he'd paid little attention to, until now. Naturally, some had picked up on the fact that the likeness made his mother very uncomfortable, but William now chose to believe that was because Lord Alden was the patriarch, putting his eldest grandson in the direct line to inherit his grandfather's most valuable assets, both financial and social.

"Grandfather, if you let us know how we can further your plans, we'll do all we can to help make them reality, won't we, Connie?" William smiled magnanimously at his brother as if to say he'd already decided for them both.

⛭ ⚜ ⛭

Brody glanced around the butler's pantry one more time before taking off for the mews. The midmorning tea service was already washed and put away, and it was time to make sure his equine charges were as well cared for as his human ones. At another time long ago, when carriages were one of the first symbols of wealth, Brody's job had revolved only around the stables. As a young groom, he'd wanted nothing more than to spend the day with the matched pairs and the two lovely coaches owned by the Alden family before Lord Alden had moved away because of his work for the queen. Eventually, less time spent at the Grosvenor Square house meant fewer servants were necessary, and Brody's commitment to Lady Alden had become so great that he could no longer bear to think about it. After her death and Lady Emily's move to New York, Lord Alden had never spent more than a few weeks at a time in London. Was it his wife's death, or his work that kept him away? Brody didn't know and no longer cared. He was there to care for his master whenever he came to Grosvenor Square and to tend to the house and mews when he didn't. This was his life.

Moving methodically from the back door of the house, across the little lane, and through the mews' entrance, Brody stopped briefly to take a deep breath of horse. It was his favorite smell. It meant life, and health, and strength. Connection with a horse made a friend unnecessary. He was just about to start checking on the feed when he was caught up short by a competing scent. He knew his surroundings just as the animals did, but the unmistakable fragrance of fine perfume distracted him, reminding him of something like the flutter of unseen silk. Deep in the first stall, Emily turned around, a hand resting on the neck of one of the matched fillies.

"Good morning, Brody," she said, her large dark eyes a reflection of the horse she now stroked. "I always think of you with your charges, so I feel much more comfortable knowing they're still your primary concern."

Brody bowed his head slightly. "They always have been my concern and will be, Madame de Koningh, though perhaps not primary." It felt odd to be here with the young mistress in the mews where she'd been only a child when last he saw her.

"Why no longer primary?" she asked.

"Because your father is now my first duty," Brody answered. He couldn't conquer the feeling of disorientation with her as an adult, which she most surely was now. Her vibrant dark hair swept up off her neck, she stood tall as if she had her father's height, which she clearly did not. He assumed her years of performance training gave her some of the Alden eminence of bearing usually reserved for the males of the lineage.

"Please, Brody, call me Emily if you would. I'm having enough trouble adjusting to this house again without feeling a stranger."

"Very well," the groomsman nodded, dropping his large head of profuse white hair peppered with dark flecks left over from his middle age. "Madame Emily it is, if you prefer."

"That will have to do," she said, her dark eyes gleaming as she looked up at him. "Tell me, Brody, how have you been over all these years, and how is my father faring?"

"Well, on both counts," he said.

"I see you're as efficient with your descriptions as ever." She laughed, turning slightly away as if she and the horse shared a personal joke. "There's something about you Scots that simply cannot be corrupted. Nothing, and certainly no words, are ever wasted."

"I'm glad you recognize me and my tendencies after so long," Brody said. "And now, I'm here to check the fillies' feed, and as there's no room for us both in that wee stall, you'd best change places with me, Madame."

"And have I changed much, Brody?" she asked, patting the horse's muzzle as she moved back out of the stall. "It must be just as strange for you to have me here as it is for me to be here."

"Not so much," he answered with his typical few words. But instead of stopping there as usual, he added, "You remind me of your mother."

An hour after Emily left the mews house Brody was just finishing up in the fillies' stalls. None of the work was overly taxing for someone who understood the economies of effort possible in a job made almost reflexive over many years of practice. He'd call in the man for coach repair, no longer capable of that work on his own, to prevent breakdowns now that they'd be in steady use by the whole family.

Fully satisfied that his stable duties were done, and preparing to return to the kitchen, Brody was surprised to hear footsteps approach the door again. Assuming Emily had returned for some misplaced item of clothing—a glove, her purse, a hat—he opened the door quickly and said, "Forget something?" His breath caught when he found himself face-to-face with her father instead. The two men stood within inches, both startled and looking oddly like actors re-creating a scene they'd played before.

They stared at each other, a chasm of understanding between them that was obvious, yet totally private. "Who were you expecting?" Lord Alden finally asked.

"Certainly not you, sir," Brody answered. "You haven't been to the mews in many, many years."

"Yes, I know, Brody. But who might be here instead of me?" Lord Alden looked and sounded pained, as if the strain of asking his question caused him unusual effort.

"Your daughter came to see the horses, sir. She's always liked them, and I think she was trying to recall her previous connections to things about this home she remembered." The two men continued to look at each other, Lord Alden with the narrow gaze of one who continues to assess an unsteady situation, and Brody as one who maintains an even course.

"Just so long as she doesn't recall something she never knew, Brody." He stepped back, turning quickly, and disappearing down the walk to the rear of the main house.

Emily knew her violin practice was essential to her peace of mind, yet she'd had trouble finding the motivation for it at Grosvenor Square. After a lifetime of practice, she'd come to know what she absolutely must do to stay in good musical shape and what she could get away with not doing. Even the bruise mark from holding the violin under the left side of her chin had faded somewhat, proving her lessening level of engagement either through practice or performance. She opened the case now but stood staring at the instrument while her thoughts strayed. How odd that Brody should have remembered her mother when he looked at Emily. There was so little similarity between them. The portrait hanging in the dining room showed a young woman in a gauzy white silk evening gown with a minuscule waist that was either a creative fiction of the artist's eye or the unhealthy result of a very tight corset. Either way, it accentuated the femininity of the portrait's beautiful young subject. Emily's waist was not her best feature, especially after having two large sons. And of course she'd discarded the painful undergarments women of the nineteenth century had worn, which hadn't assisted in the reshaping of her waist as the young woman in the portrait had benefited from.

In the portrait of Lady Alden, one arm supported her on a wall of some kind while the other ended in a delicate and seemingly boneless hand with long, tapered fingers resting lightly at her jawline. The gesture was thoughtless, as if she were reflecting about nothing at all. But the delicate hand had clearly never worked at anything very difficult, and certainly not to hold a bow or create a vibrato on steel strings. Blond hair hung in ringlets from a gathering at the back of her mother's head, and a long strand of pearls wove its way through the ringlets and finally draped over her white shoulders. Emily's dark hair had left ringlets behind at the age of thirteen, as soon as she'd arrived at the de Koninghs' home in New York, and she'd long avoided jewelry and anything decorative that might get in the way of her playing the violin.

The huge blue eyes of the girl in the painting were most unlike Emily's own, though according to the portrait, two small dimples at each corner of her nicely formed mouth copied those on Emily's own face. There was something vaguely familiar in the spirit of pleasure about her, possibly a reminder of Connie's easy temperament and joyful attitude, though the blond hair and blue eyes could have been her excuse to draw such a parallel. It made Emily feel guiltier than she had in a long time. What kind of mother tars one child with ignominy and glorifies the other simply from a preference for certain personality traits?

There were no physical features in her mother's portrait suggesting a similarity to Emily—except something in the frankness of the gaze. The artist had captured the fact that this young woman had known who she was, and Emily understood that confidence at such a vulnerable age stood as a challenge to the world. Instinctively she knew that any resemblance between her mother and herself was suggestive rather than real, but perhaps those psychological traits were more authentic than physical ones, anyway.

You remind me of your mother, Brody had said, nonetheless. *In what way?* she'd wanted to ask. She'd yearned to remind people of Lady Alden for years after her mother died, but now she wondered why. Why was she becoming so uncomfortable with who she was? Naturally, as she'd grown up and mastered the violin, she'd gained confidence in her own place in the world that the young Lady Alden in the portrait seemed to have been born with. But *who was her mother really?* Emily had always wanted to ask her father, but he'd been unable or unwilling to tell her. It wasn't something he'd expressed; she'd just understood it. So the only person left who would have known her mother was the once-young Brody, stablemaster to Lord and Lady Alden at the very beginning of the Victorian era and start of her father's career in the world of British diplomacy.

She stared at her violin. *You'll get nowhere with your practice just looking at the instrument and bow enshrined in their blue velvet case.* Now an accomplished soloist, Emily approached middle age knowing that only music could settle her mind, but there were still private secrets she needed to solve. Here in her childhood home at Grosvenor Square with children of her own she wanted enlightened about their grandmother, she might become braver and start asking the questions about the past she'd instinctively put off long ago. If her father had purposely lost his memory, then clearly Brody had not.

Feeling somewhat calmer, Emily picked up her instrument and placed it under her chin. She looked out of her bedroom window across the garden of the square. Feeling the focus of the music in her head beginning to take her over, she picked up the bow from its case and adjusted it in her right hand. *Your magic wand,* Corey had called it when they were children. Poised just above the strings as she took her deepest breath, she froze with it and the violin held high when she saw William dashing down one of the side streets. As he was new to London and had neither acquaintances nor appointments, she found his flight and disappearance oddly disturbing. Everything in Grosvenor Square seemed out of step since she'd arrived, a fact that left her feeling decidedly wrong-footed and peculiarly off balance. But at this moment, she had two choices: put the violin and bow down again and give in to the continuous distractions of questions in need of answers. Or put the bow to the strings and push the mysteries off for another time. Considering her years of discipline and commitment to her music, she chose the latter, but just for the moment.

6

OUTSIDE THE HOME

EMILY PUT THE NOTE from John Mackay back in her skirt pocket, delighted to read he'd be staying at the Langham Hotel for two months, when her father came into the room and surprised her with questions about hiring new servants, a distraction she had no interest in.

"I'm not sure I understand the problem." William Alden looked at his daughter through narrowed eyes, ostensibly to improve his focus. "You're saying you can't hire and organize the additional household staff?"

"Well, not exactly." Emily chose her words carefully.

"Then, what?"

"I don't think I'm the *best* person to do the hiring and directing of the new staff." Emily tried not to drop her eyes to avoid her father's penetrating gaze. It was all she could do not to smile. His expression implied the question, *then what are women for?*

"Then, whom do you suggest?" her father asked.

"Well," she began brightly, "I rather think Corey would do a better job than I."

"Corey! Your husband? He would be better at running this home than you?"

"Oh, yes," she exclaimed, even more cheerfully than before. "He and his father ran the household in the mansion in New York. He's

73

very experienced at it!" She smiled at her father and took a breath as if to move to another subject, but he was not so easily deterred.

"And you were and are comfortable with that arrangement?" He stared at her with a small, unaccustomed frown on his fine-boned face.

"Oh, quite!" she exclaimed. "As a matter of fact, I much prefer it. In America, the men always control the running and administration of property."

"And since when have you ever been comfortable with men always running anything?" her father asked. He'd found the weakest link in her argument and Emily knew it. She looked at him in dismay, shaking her head and glancing out the window for a second.

"Since I had to do it myself when he and his father went down south on business. I'm quite sure it's not my calling. In my estimation, the true liberation of woman is to free her from the home. Oh, Father, you know I'm not afraid of hard work. As a matter of fact, I revel in it. But that all depends on the nature of it. Working inside the home is not for me."

Her father watched her carefully, but the frown was gone. She sat quietly, waiting for whatever he wanted to say to her. At this point in his life, it really didn't matter. She wanted him to be happy. Finally he said, "So, the chambermaids, general housemaids, between maids to run errands in and out to the mews, to say nothing of the house-keeper and cook, are all to be entrusted to Corey. Is that right?" She nodded with a smile, wondering if he was actually toying with her now. "And even the first and second footman, gardener, groom, and stable boy will all report to Corey?"

She tossed her head as if to rid herself of an annoyance. *Well, two could play at this game.* "Oh good heavens, Father. We already have a butler who is our groom and stable boy all rolled into one. And surely Brody could hire a cook he felt comfortable with. It's likely a housekeeper would be better off chosen by him as well." She noted her father was working to put an uncommonly severe look on his face. "And we can do without chambermaids and all the footmen.

This is 1885, Father, and servants aren't as easy to come by as they once were. Maybe you've been away too long to know that. But I certainly have no interest in running a traditional household when I could be employed in a more interesting and useful task. I mean no disrespect," she added, somewhat sheepishly. "I only offer you the truth as I see it, and as I live it myself." The dark-haired woman and her silver-haired father looked at each other, eye-to-eye. Suddenly, his frown disappeared, and he burst out laughing.

"I feared it," he chuckled. "You never wanted to run a home in the first place. Your energies are otherwise directed." She thought it too easy a victory. He rose from his chair and moved over to his desk, opening the shallow middle drawer and searching through it. Quickly finding what he was looking for, he pulled out a sheet of paper still folded to fit his inside breast pocket. He opened it and pressed the seams back before walking over to hand it to his daughter. "Have a look at this," he said, sitting back down at his desk and waiting silently while she read at her own pace. He could tell nothing from her face. Finally she looked up.

"Jenny Lind, Hubert Parry, Henry Holmes . . . ," she recited, looking at him with a raised eyebrow. "Joseph Joachim, Hans Richter, August Manns, and Eugène Ysaÿe," she read out loud, looking at him again. "What do they mean to you?"

"It's more what they'll mean to you that matters," he said. "You undoubtedly know some of them yourself, and others by reputation. But would you say they represent the best in music today?" He'd begun to look like a parent with a special gift hidden behind his back.

She laughed gently, happy to play along with his game of cat and mouse. "Of course. There could be no disagreement about that."

"And would you say your energy would be better directed working with them than with my household staff?"

Now, what did her father have up his beautifully tailored sleeve? "Certainly, Father," she answered carefully. "But I don't recall any new performance contracts of late, more's the pity. Are you aware of something I'm not?" She was beginning to feel like the battered mouse.

"I am," he answered. "Though not performance contracts, exactly." She looked at him questioningly, but instead of responding he said, "Let's go reassure Brody the running of this house will remain his responsibility with the occasional assist from Corey, and then we'll move on to the Joachims and Holmeses of the world instead of the parlor maids." Did her father know she was holding her breath, fully prepared for one of his schemes that would complicate her life and maneuver it onto a different path to a place she couldn't imagine now?

Escorted out of the upstairs study, Emily considered how often this had happened in the past—the trip to Europe when she was only nineteen, ostensibly to attend college in England when they had no intention of admitting a woman; the plan to get her family to France when her father-in-law announced his marriage and intention of taking over the house in New York for his new wife and her niece. That trip had been meant to encompass a year of transition through European performances, but here she was twenty years later, her boys grown up and as much French as American, and she herself with a fading European career and Corey possibly as bored with his as she was with hers.

And the move to keep her family together seemed to have forced them further apart. Now, for many reasons that had seemed important once, they were supposedly enjoying a brief stay in London to close the family history circle. She still hoped that a deeper understanding of those who'd come before them and endured so much in the past might bring them all closer to each other in the future. But what did her father have in mind for her here? He couldn't possibly expect them to adopt the house at Grosvenor Square and the life within it as their own forever. Or could he?

Emily was startled when her father called out, "Corey, how fortunate. Emily and I are on our way now to meet with Brody. I'm hoping you won't mind assisting him with the hiring of the new household staff. Emily tells me you've had a lot of involvement with that in the past at the de Koningh mansion." He smiled warmly as they caught up with Corey in the hall. Emily closed her eyes briefly behind her father's back, indicating a continuing need for restraint that Corey couldn't possibly miss. His expression gave nothing away as he connected with hers.

"I . . . could certainly take that on if it would help while our family is living here," he said. "I know there are a lot of us for Brody to handle alone now. But is there a reason why Emily has been passed over for this honor?"

"Because she doesn't want it!" her father exclaimed, almost joyously.

Corey raised his eyebrows, and a tiny smile brushed the corners of his mouth. "Really," he said, never moving his gaze from her face to her father's. "And what will my dear wife be doing while I'm administering to the needs of the household?" Emily took a breath as if to respond, but her father interrupted.

"We're just about to discuss that, and it's important that you join us, if you can." He took Corey's forearm in a firm grasp, as if to tie them together. "We're going to find Brody first to let him know he can count on you when in need. But then I'd like to tell you both about a discovery I made that I think you'll be most interested in. It won't take long. Join us?" he asked Corey, as if he was giving him a choice.

"I suppose so, Lord Alden," Corey said, a small sigh indicating he had in fact had other plans before they were interrupted. "This is after all your home, and we must help in any way we can while we're here."

"Oh no, no, no indeed," Lord Alden exclaimed. "That's not it at all. I want you to be exceedingly happy and comfortable." He hooked his other arm through Emily's and started toward the back kitchen stairs, guiding them all in a most congenial manner as if they were of one mind and purpose.

It took longer than expected to complete the meeting with Brody in the kitchen, as he naturally had questions about staffing and the timing of their hiring, and Corey hadn't been informed yet of Lord Alden's wishes. But as neither Brody nor Corey felt they understood the importance of this new assignment fully, they found it simplest to agree with Lord Alden and each other, planning to meet again later to finalize everything. That left Emily's father in a jubilant mood, and eager to accompany them back to the study to discuss his proposal, yet undisclosed. Corey noted a rising tension in Emily, and rightly considered it to have been triggered by her father's suggestion to free her up for "something more appropriate" than working "inside the home." They both knew enough of his penchant for controlling people and events around him firsthand to be wary of his triumphant mood.

"Just a few minutes, that's all I ask," he was saying, ushering them upstairs and then back to the study. Emily steeled herself, knowing her father couldn't see her expression. Lord Alden entered last, reaching to shut the door behind him. For some reason, that put Corey in a heightened state of alertness, and he made an involuntary move toward it as if to secure his escape before it was too late. "Really, this won't take long," Emily's father reassured them.

"Why don't you both sit for a moment," he suggested, punctuating the directive by sitting himself and leaving them no alternative. They both lowered themselves beside each other on one of the settees by the fireplace, more perched than seated. Lord Alden pretended not to notice their hesitancy.

"I had an interesting visit to an unusual place a few weeks ago," he said, "and I think you'll want to hear about it." Emily and Corey passed questioning looks between them, but both clearly saw no alternative to listening. *What was the harm?*

"Why all the mystery?" Emily asked. She was clearly beginning to lose patience and interest. She'd been aware of a hidden agenda for over an hour and had decided she could be satisfied never learning her father's "secret" at this point. She wanted to go find her sons and see if she could figure out why William had been running off somewhere as if he knew where he was going. She wanted to be sure both he and Connie were planning interesting days and making the most of their time. She also wondered why her father was involving Corey today, who no doubt had plans of his own before they were hijacked. She felt responsible for involving him in the first place. But in what? "Tell us, Father. We all have other commitments calling us this morning." She was instantly sorry for her words and tone, feeling they were there to pay attention to her aging father, for once, and she quickly apologized. "We're listening," she added in reassurance. "Please, go ahead."

"I'll be brief," he assured them, looking from one to the other with eagerness. "A well-positioned friend of mine asked me to visit one of his latest projects, probably in hopes of a financial donation. But he's connected to interesting cultural ventures, and I felt I had little to lose. To condense a full morning, I'll simply say I found myself fascinated by England's newest initiative to launch a world-class music college at last, one to rival the best Europe has to offer. The building itself left a little to be desired, but the contents of the program excelled in a way I could not have imagined."

He looked back and forth from Emily to Corey, and they stayed fixed on him as he spoke. "I know you'll both remember the fiasco of Emily's first connection with the Royal Academy. That is a blight not easily forgotten. Well, the academy is no more, and the Royal College has taken its place. That list of musicians I showed you," he said, gesturing to the piece of paper Emily still held in her hand, "comprises some of the world-class teachers and performers working with the college today." Corey finally noticed the paper and Emily handed it to him, although he still didn't look at it.

"There's much, much more that's groundbreaking about the new college, but the better man to tell you about it is its director, Sir George Grove, or the professor most involved in the teaching there, Charles Stanford. He was the man I met with. Knowing what dedicated musicians you both are, I paid better attention than I might have in other circumstances." He smiled a winning grin. "Look; look at that list, Corey. You'll see the quality of teaching already in place. And for you, my boy, I assure you Professor Stanford had much to say about choral music and the need for conductors and piano accompanists, as well as teachers." He seemed to instinctively catch a flash of interest behind Corey's eyes and jumped up to stand in front of him.

"I also remember your interest in public education," he went on. "Well, I'm told our former prince consort shared that with you, as do others, and this college will make a thrust deep into that pool of talent. It's understood by these men that classical music cannot advance here without offering the education to all, instead of only the few who can afford it." His eyes flashed with excitement, and he bowed forward to be closer to Corey. "I tell you," he said, sitting on the edge of one of the chairs next to the settee, "I have never seen anything more impressive, nor heard a more dedicated intention than that of this college. They are seeking teachers just such as the two of you, and I hope you'll join me to go back and meet with Director Grove and Professor Stanford soon. I think they'd be worthy colleagues for you both!" Emily and Corey stared at Lord Alden. They made no effort to fill the silence, but finally turned to look at each other. Their expressions of skepticism said more than either one of them could have articulated. Finally, they turned back to look at Lord Alden and Emily took a deep breath.

"I'm at a loss to understand, Father. I've really never taught professionally, and Corey hasn't taken pupils in years. What made you think we were looking for a way to do that here in London?"

Lord Alden sat forward eagerly. "Come now," he said, "I know how committed you've always been, Corey, to the idea of public education of all kinds, and especially for the arts." His eyes seemed to glow with intensity as he caught and held Corey's gaze. "I well remember how excited you were when I came to see you both after you were just married, and President Lincoln had thought public education so vital that he pushed through that Land-Grant Act to establish new agricultural colleges." Emily adjusted herself on the settee, turning to watch Corey more closely.

"You even spoke of how important the investment in public education in the South was for Reconstruction, and how you wished music education had been included at the top of that list," Lord Alden said. "I've never forgotten your enthusiasm when you talked about it and mentioned how singing, in particular, brought people together." He glanced pointedly at his daughter, perhaps having sensed her interest in what he was saying, and as if he sought her assistance in engaging her husband in the conversation. The fact that she wasn't yet a part of it didn't seem to bother him, and in fact, Emily had begun to nod slightly, as if recalling the very scene from the past her father was now describing. Corey, however, watched his father-in-law quizzically, as if he still didn't fully understand why he was being included in the hypothetical plans.

"I haven't thought of those days for many years, Lord Alden. And although I took some private piano students in Paris, I've not given institutional music education any consideration for a couple of decades. I'm amazed you even recall my earlier interest in it." He turned to catch Emily's eye, a look of consternation on his face.

Emily was used to observing events unfold in front of her as if watching an intriguing and complex plot on stage. She often kept quiet to let the group emotions play out, exposing whatever the real agenda might be. Whether a family discussion, a dinner party of her favorite friends, or a quartet rehearsing a new chamber music piece, she'd always felt she learned so much more by listening and observing. Often there was a catalyst in the form of a family member, one of her friends or a musician who served to supply the heat and stir the blend. But today there were only the three of them, and only one of those was in control of the conversation. The lack of balance made her force her own will on the group, and so she blurted out in unusually blunt language, hoping to unnerve her father enough to shake his mysterious motivation free.

"Father, whatever you're getting at, neither Corey nor I have expressed any interest in teaching while we're here. We intend a short but pleasant visit before we take the boys back to America to visit Corey's father, and we don't anticipate having enough time to do anything but show them around London and enjoy some of the sights with them and you. Whatever else you may have in mind, if it doesn't fit that itinerary, it probably won't work." She felt that her look was rather more severe than necessary as she sat with her back ramrod straight and her shiny dark head tilted slightly up. But her father often had trouble hearing messages not to his liking, and so she wanted no extra room for him to misunderstand her. Even the slightest slip in her resolve could be mistaken for capitulation. Her father's pleasant expression never changed as he smiled at her, gently. He looked at Corey as well, before looking back at her.

"I'm not asking you to change your plans, Emily, just to enjoy an afternoon with me visiting the wonderful new music college in Kensington. I think you and Corey will be intrigued and delighted with it, and one cannot care about classical music without being enthralled by the plans being put into action there." He moved over to his desk to close the drawer left open before their visit to the kitchen, never indicating he wanted Corey to return the list of instructors.

"At the very least, I think you'll both be delighted with the new direction music is taking here in Great Britain in Sir George Grove's school. We could even meet him if you'd like. But I also think you'll find this young man who runs it with him unique. I know how you enjoy connecting with musicians around the world, and Charles Villiers Stanford is clearly a connection worth making." Emily knew her father had saved the personal relationships for last. He knew her too well to think there was anything about the school's royal bene-factors that would appeal to her, but everything about the musicians who ran it would draw her in. She glanced over at Corey, who was also paying better attention to Lord Alden than he had earlier.

"The young professor was educated here and in Leipzig and Berlin, he told me. He had extremely eclectic tastes in music that are entirely his own. He's keen to express a dislike for musicians who seek only to please popular tastes, and he champions female musi-cians, taking on the Cambridge chorus to turn it into a mixed group against the university's preferences." He moved the pen on his desk and straightened a small pad of paper as if his attention wasn't entirely focused on his conversation. But Emily's interest was now piqued, just as he'd known it would be. Timing being a skill he'd long ago perfected, he now prepared to finish their talk and leave the room.

"I don't see why we couldn't—" Corey began, looking again at Emily to read her thoughts if they showed on her face.

"Nor do I," she jumped in. "It sounds like a fascinating project, Father. Why don't you see if you can set up some time for us there? We'll fit to your schedule and that of the college, of course." Her father beamed with apparently innocent pleasure.

⁕❦ ⚹ ❦⁕

"What was that all about?" William asked as he came into the study just as his grandfather was leaving. "I haven't seen Grandfather Alden that cheerful in a long time."

"Oh, he's been examining the new Royal College of Music and wanted our opinion on its viability. I think he's considering giving them a large contribution under pressure from the Prince of Wales," Corey answered, sighing a little and stretching out his back from sitting too long. His height was proving an uncomfortable challenge as he approached middle age. "Your grandfather wants to feel he's making a wise investment, I suppose, and we should be flattered that he considers us to be his expert advisers."

"Understandable." William nodded, the all-knowing look on his face that Emily had never been fond of. "The future king of England is not easy to deny, but I've heard his business acumen is not always insightful."

"True," Emily said, thoughtfully. "But is that really what he was after, Corey? I'm not so sure."

"Then what?"

"Father wants to get us so involved with the school that we can't get loose." She shook her head and stood up. "I thought it easiest to agree to a preliminary meeting and then reject the idea later," she sighed, looking more closely at William. "Where are you going?" she asked, taking in his formal morning outfit: a single-breasted cutaway of a dark blue, somewhere between navy and royal, topping beige striped pants and a gray silk ascot over a white shirt. He held in his hands light brown kid gloves along with a black silk top hat.

William's smooth, shiny black hair, so like her own, had been paired with a small, manicured black mustache ever since he'd passed his eighteenth birthday in Paris. His striking resemblance to Prince Albert's younger portraits would no doubt win him appreciative glances in London as it had in Vienna. William had always been very precise about his looks, even as a small boy, so Emily realized she'd stopped noticing the way he dressed a long time ago. But for some reason she was more sensitive lately to everything her boys did. Was it her lessening pleasure in her performance career that shifted her focus solely to her family, or possibly William's shocking disclosure about his brother in Vienna that had caused her heightened awareness? Either way, she felt a strong need to connect with

William's plans for himself now that they were in London. She had possibly spent too little time worrying about both boys in the past when her music had been more prominent.

"You look very handsome, dear," she said, smiling at William as he stood in his finery before them.

"I'm off to see friends for lunch at their club," William said, squaring his shoulders in a movement meant to show off his cutaway to its best advantage.

"What friends? I didn't know you had any here in London," Emily said, quizzically.

William tightened the grip on his hat and started to back toward the door. "Oh, friends of friends from France. You don't know them, Mother. I must be off," he added, nodding to both his parents and turning to go out the door as Brody stepped in, almost running him over.

"Excuse me, sir," Brody said with a slight bow, even though the fault had clearly not been his. William returned it absently and took off quickly down the hall and out of sight.

"Good heavens, everybody's in such a hurry around here," Connie said cheerily as he also stepped into the study just behind Brody.

"Yes, your mother and I are the only people satisfied with where we are, apparently," Corey answered, grinning at his youngest son and bringing him into a quick bear hug. No one could resist Connie's warmth and good spirits. "I guess he's off for an afternoon with his Parisian crowd, or one of those lovely young ladies attached to it like flotsam in a foaming sea."

"I doubt that," Connie said.

"Why?" Emily asked.

"Oh, just because William isn't interested in . . . that crowd," Connie announced, stopping himself, as if he'd almost made the wrong turn at a crossroads. "And I'm off now myself to meet one of the Klimts' patrons. Gustav referred me to her as a potential client for a new fashion design. The work would be perfect for me," he said, "but the young lady is also delectable looking, if Gustav's portrait of her is at all accurate. One never knows . . ." He grinned openly at his father before waving to both parents and leaving the room.

"Now I wonder what 'one never knows,'" Emily muttered. "And what sort of 'crowd' isn't William interested in? Do one's children ever speak plainly enough to be understood?"

"What is there to wonder about?" Corey asked. "If they wanted us to know they'd make sure we did. Brody, forgive the intrusions. What can we do for you? I'd all but forgotten you were there. That's what interruptions can do."

Brody seemed unperturbed and continued standing quietly at attention, waiting to be included in the conversation when he was needed. "I wondered about timing for dinner tonight," he said, "and as I saw you were all preparing to go your separate ways, thought I'd best check now. And will you be needing the carriage?" he added.

"I have no idea what my father's plans are or what he's up to," Emily said. "But it appears the boys are off on their own, though how they've both suddenly become so busy is beyond my understanding."

"I'm going in search of a number of friends from America who've written me, Brody, but I'd rather walk," Corey said. "And I'll be back for dinner whenever it is." He planted a light kiss on the top of Emily's head and followed Connie to the front hall. Emily looked toward them.

Without turning toward him, she said to Brody behind her, "How quickly one can become obsolete in this world, Brody. Is that what family is all about?" It was clear she didn't expect an answer. But as he wasn't used to being addressed without purpose, Brody gave her one.

"You are anything but obsolete, Madame Emily, but it's a different thing to be essential." He stood quietly, waiting to be spoken to again or dismissed. Emily turned slowly to look at him. "You *are* like your mother," he said, quietly. "She never wanted to be the linchpin in the family. But after she died it was clear she had been just that, with the expected results when it was pulled." Emily stared out the window toward the mews wondering what the house must have felt like with her mother so suddenly gone. It was an experience she didn't want any of them to encounter now. Brody bowed slightly and left the room before Emily even sensed he'd gone.

Too much confusion swirled around emotions about her father, sons, and husband. Even Brody added to the sense that the rhythm was off in the Alden house now that they were all in it together. It was as if his commitment and relationship to them all had the essence of a deep friendship, more personally familial than professionally loyal. She wondered why her father had never stressed that fact to her, ensuring she understood what their responsibility to Brody had been and should be going forward. Nothing seemed clear anymore and being in the house at Grosvenor Square had only fractured her understanding of the past instead of pulling it together as she'd expected and hoped.

When her life was muddied so much she couldn't see it anymore, she always turned to her friends for clarity. She knew John Mackay would be just the man to filter her uncertainty through. She went to find Brody to tell him she'd need the carriage after all. It appeared she'd been an unwitting balance for her family's equilibrium over the years, just as her mother had been for hers. "But I haven't been pulled," she whispered to herself. "I'm still here and I can make a difference."

7

THE HOTEL

JOHN MACKAY stared at the electric lights installed just inside the entrance of the Langham Hotel, hanging down as the lovely old chandelier lanterns from an earlier time had. He was more interested in what was hidden inside than what they looked like. Head back and chin tilted up for the best view of the ceiling, he didn't notice the young porter had come up behind him. "There's one on a post in the courtyard, too," the porter said, his pride in full view as he gazed up at the light with the hotel's illustrious guest.

"When did they go in?" John asked. "I was here six years ago, and there were none then. I remember the hydraulic lifts, water closets, and bathrooms, but no electric lights."

"That's about right, sir," the porter replied. "I think we got them in '79. Do you have a special interest in electricity, sir?"

"I suppose," John replied. "I own the Commercial Cable Company, and communications require electricity. But I'm fascinated by new machineries of all kinds. It's one of the reasons I've given in to my wife's desire to stay here in the past, even though it's hideously expensive. She wants to see the people, and I the latest mechanicals." He smiled warmly at the young man, happy to share his fondness for inventions. "It's amazing how science has brought society forward, isn't it?" He looked back up at the electric light in the ceiling. "Creations like the camera allow us to record the present for posterity, and the speed of steam power makes the future reachable in the present. It's all quite wonderful, though some would prefer to rely more on the power of rumor than the power of electricity."

"We have room coolers now too, sir," the boy announced, very seriously. "They've made such a difference in the kitchens. First hotel to have them in Europe!" The young porter had somehow misunderstood the guest's comment about rumors. He was too focused on touting the hotel's specialties, but suddenly froze in place, staring at two men being escorted from a private dining room across the lobby.

"There's the Prince of Wales," John said, following the porter's gaze. An overweight man in a beautifully tailored dark wool three-piece suit waited for a companion to pass through the door behind him. With a neatly trimmed beard, he had the look of someone pleased with life in general, and with himself, in particular. "One can certainly understand why his penchant for fashion is so often touted by the press," John added. Watching the prince moving slowly as he gathered crowds around him like flotsam in a river of humanity, John shook his head slightly. "Can you imagine what it would be like to live with no privacy at all, as if your life was everyone else's business? Not for me. But I think he enjoys it."

"Have you met him?" the porter asked, his eyes growing round in amazement.

"I have," John replied. "It was some charity event my wife worked on with the Princess Alexandra. Now there's a lovely and fascinating woman," he added, thoughtfully. "Her skill with a camera is extraordinary. I wish my wife would take an interest in some of the wonderful new discoveries of our time . . ." his voice drifted off, apparently viewing the attributes of the princess in his mind.

But he was in fact allowing his thoughts to stray to Emily, whom he'd be meeting alone soon at the hotel. She'd broken through much of the resistance to women jeopardizing their reputations and social status by stepping into worlds others would have them barred from. He'd seen her play her violin on stage in London over twenty years ago and fallen in love with her then. Following her career in the press and personally when possible, he'd eventually come to appreciate the courage it took to risk public censure to live as she wanted. They shared that conviction, although it had been then, and still remained, markedly easier for him, he admitted. Those were the handicaps in a society biased toward men.

"And the gentleman with him, who is he?" John asked, as if his mind hadn't just taken the detour from the prince's interests to his own. "I've seen him somewhere but can't place him." The porter moved sideways for a better view, as the two men of interest stood at the far end of the hall surrounded by a small crowd of hotel staff and public hangers-on.

"That's Lord William Alden," the porter said. "He's a diplomat—a good friend of the royals. He's here a lot when he's in London. And do you know him too, sir?"

John shook his head, slowly. "Not really. We've never met," he said. "But I know some of his family in America. I've seen pictures of him in the newspapers—handsome man." His usual lack of interest in celebrity seemed to have transformed into fascination, but what he actually found intriguing was the coincidence of seeing Lord Alden on the very day and in the same hotel where his daughter would be meeting him. "I wonder if she knows he's here," John murmured. The desire for privacy suddenly overcame him as he watched the lobby crowds expanding with the prince's arrival. A few minutes to be alone to collect himself was appealing. He would have time to unpack and read in his room before Emily arrived, and as comfortable as he was in the hotel surroundings, he wondered if she would be as at ease now. *It's a smaller world than we know,* he thought. And with that, John nodded goodbye to the porter and moved into the main lobby, crossing to the front desk to get his key.

"Your Royal Highness, what a pleasure to see you." Charles Stanford stepped from the crowd in the hotel lobby and bowed his head, smiling at the Prince of Wales as their eyes met. "And Lord Alden, also a delight," he exclaimed, clearly surprised to recognize the prince's companion. "Twice in one month, Lord Alden. How fortunate. It seems champions of the Royal College of Music are springing up everywhere like tulips in spring!"

"Mr. Villiers Stanford," the prince exclaimed, lighting up at the sight of the attractive young composer. "If I want to connect with someone, all I need do is lunch at the Langham! What brings you here today? I've been hearing from Lord Alden of your favorable meeting at the Royal College. I'm so glad you two hit it off, though I'm not in the least surprised." For all the criticism the prince received from the press and the public about his multiple ongoing affairs and seeming disregard for his beautiful, talented wife, his charm was legendary and in full view when he performed on the stage of public attention.

"I'm just finishing my meal with one of our former teachers at the college," Professor Stanford said, nodding in the direction of a far-off table at the end of the dining room. "He prefers the Langham for lunch, as he's lived here in the past. He says it feels more like home."

"Mr. Liszt," Lord Alden said, following the professor's line of sight. No one had trouble identifying the elderly gentleman with long white hair and strongly chiseled features. "He's aged a great deal," he added, unable to hide his dismay at the decline in the world-famous pianist.

"Indeed. Ever since that fall he had in a German hotel a few years ago," Professor Stanford sighed. "He's always traveled for his philan-thropies, thousands of miles in a year, if you can fathom it, but I think life in hotels, even those as luxurious as this one, has taken its toll." He glanced at the Langham's manager lingering on the outskirts of the cortège around the prince.

Lord Alden gave the professor a small bow to lean in closer. "Might I have a word once Mr. Liszt has left you, Mr. Stanford?"

"Of course, Lord Alden. Your Royal Highness," Professor Stanford said, offering a bow to both men before leaving to return to his table across the room.

Emily's father watched him go. "It's quite amazing," he said to the prince, "how he wears his confidence so easily." The prince nodded. "One never knows whom one might run into, but he seems as comfortable with royalty as he is with his own colleagues. These extraordinary people should no longer be confined to the serving class," Lord Alden added. The prince nodded distractedly, clearly unconcerned with the professor's comfort with high society as the prince was always at its epicenter anyway.

⊱━━✦ ⚔ ✦━━⊰

The Prince of Wales and Lord Alden walked away from the dining room after their lunch together. The prince moved slowly, carrying one of his favorite cigars that had been lit to accompany a glass of exceptionally fine port reluctantly abandoned back at the table. "May I give you a ride, William?" he offered. "I don't see your man Brody anywhere, and I'm going to visit a lady friend." The prince smiled, no doubt with the delight of both the lady and perhaps more port topping off his afternoon. "I'll be passing right by Grosvenor Square," he added. "I'd be happy to give you a lift." He looked the vision of congeniality as he motioned to one of the porters for his carriage. Four additional porters tore across the lobby in a continuous riptide of competition to reach the conveyances just outside the main entrance well before His Royal Highness could.

There was nothing peaceful about being with the prince. Lord Alden found that he himself no longer sought the vortex and was very comfortable with a quieter existence, as would be the case in his retirement. Was he already adjusting to a different world order as he left his former one behind? Perhaps, if his family would join him.

"That would be most appreciated, Your Highness," Lord Alden answered. "I sent my carriage back in case anyone in the household needed it. I don't keep a full stable anymore, with the overseas travel I do for the Crown, and I'll soon need even less when I retire."

The prince nodded and moved toward the entrance. "Oh, that's odd," he muttered. "Isn't that your man Brody now?"

Lord Alden looked up absently, knowing whoever the prince had seen certainly wasn't his coachman, only to exclaim in shock, "Why, yes it is, Your Highness. I have no idea what he's doing here." He stared out the door at his carriage coming to a halt in front of the hotel.

"There must have been a misunderstanding. He probably thought you needed him back after lunch," the prince suggested, taking a puff on his cigar. But Lord Alden knew there'd been no mistake, since Brody never made them, and so stood transfixed as he saw the carriage door open and Brody reach inside to help a passenger climb down. In a matter of seconds, Lord Alden's daughter stood in the entrance.

"I think it's Emily," Lord Alden breathed, obviously unable to believe his eyes. The prince looked up more pointedly, trying to decipher the events seemingly beyond his friend's control or understanding. And just at that moment, another man strode through the lobby and stopped in front of Lord Alden's daughter. Lord Alden could only see his back but watched the man taking both of Emily's hands in his and bending to kiss her on the cheek. "Good heavens," he exclaimed. "More and more curious. Who do you suppose that is, and how does he know my Emily?"

"Intriguing." The prince puffed on his cigar more intently. "Shall we find out, William?" He started toward the door without waiting for affirmation. He was used to moving on his own initiative, responding instantly to the impetus of his curiosity, and used to people following him. Lord Alden stayed still at first, but finally he took a few steps in the direction of the lobby's entrance. The Prince of Wales was already talking with the people at the carriage when he reached them.

"Brody! I knew it was you," he heard the prince exclaim. "And you're William's daughter, the famous violinist. How lovely . . . lovely. Your father and I just enjoyed one of the Langham's fabulous lunches together." The prince was clearly enjoying both his own good humor after a fine meal and Emily's beauty as she lowered her head and curtseyed. "The family resemblance is striking!" the prince announced, still holding Emily's small hand in his fat fingers.

He beamed at her, no doubt pleased about complimenting a woman on her obvious connection to a man of her father's significance. He himself had never questioned his own relevance owed entirely to his mother's lineage, and couldn't have known how Emily disliked her acceptance resulting from her inheritance rather than her accomplishments.

"Your Highness," she said, eyes appropriately lowered to hide her distress rather than out of decorum. "What a . . . a . . . surprise," she stammered, looking sideways at Lord Alden. "And this is a friend from America, Your Highness. Allow me to introduce . . ."

"Oh, we've met." The prince smiled directly at John. "You're the *Irishman* turned American Silver King. The 'Comstock King,' am I correct?" No one listening could have missed the intended slight from the prince, as John was judged unable to transcend his lowly Irish Catholic beginnings by the future king of England, just as he had been by New York's high society. Apparently his huge American wealth was of little interest, either. "We were introduced when our wives worked on some cause or other together. Am I right, sir?"

"Indeed you are," John responded, calmly and without any discomfort, also bowing his head slightly. "Right about everything, naturally." The prince seemed to miss or simply ignore the implied irony in his acquaintance's voice.

"Father ... this is John Mackay," Emily stuttered, an unaccustomed nervousness taking away her usual easy charm. "John is a good friend of the de Koningh family. He's been visiting his wife in Europe before sailing back to America to advance more business dealings, I assume. John, apparently you and the Prince of Wales know each other, but let me introduce you to my father, Lord William Alden." She was collecting her wits at last, thanks in part to the Silver King's comfort and relaxed demeanor. John inclined his head to Lord Alden and held out his hand.

The two noblemen, one of industry and the other aristocracy, eyed each other directly, neither with any reservations about meeting the other's gaze. One born to wealth and the other poverty, both had spent a lifetime making the most of what they had for the good of themselves and others.

"Your wife is with you?" Lord Alden asked, glancing at the prince and then around the room inquisitively. Apparently he thought the prince had seen and recognized the infamous Mrs. Mackay. There were few who'd ever read a newspaper who'd missed the tales of Louise Mackay's attempts to buy herself the social status her husband had little interest in. But there were just as few who truly knew anything about the woman behind the stories, and so a curiosity lingered with those who might otherwise have paid her no attention. Promoting herself socially might have gained her acceptance to some circles but lost her true appreciation in others.

"Not this trip," John replied. "We have a house in Paris, and she only comes to the Langham when she can't avoid a visit to England for some reason. Her preference is France."

"Surely not over New York," Lord Alden tendered, disingenuously.

"Oh, indeed," John said quickly. "She refuses to return to America for any reason."

"So you live alone," Lord Alden persisted. The experienced diplomat knew how to press for facts to assess any situation.

The prince, unaccustomed to being less than the center of attention, laughed loudly. "What a lucky man," he exclaimed, and John smiled politely, neither confirming nor denying the insinuation that all men would prefer to live without their wives if given the opportunity.

"I would think it an unnecessarily lonely life for a married man," Lord Alden commented, eyeing first John and then finally his daughter for the first time.

"Oh, I'm sure a man as successful as Mr. Mackay can find companionship when necessary," the prince said, as if they were old friends of like minds. Emily dropped her head and eyes, again a useful way of hiding her discomfort. Suddenly she recognized that her feelings of irritation came more from the fact that she had not joined the conversation on her own terms. She raised her head and looked at the prince directly.

"I know his work schedule is backbreaking," she offered evenly. "So I doubt he has any time to be lonely."

"Maybe not," the prince muttered, finally conceding to the discomfort in the group. "But with lovely friends such as you and your family, Madame de Koningh, I'm sure he can weather the workload as well as the loneliness." Emily squared her shoulders and lifted her chin in defiance, but her father feared she might be remarkably close to tears. Not wanting to push her to that level of distress, Lord Alden tried to change the direction of the discussion entirely.

Turning to face the prince, he said, "Good heavens, this hotel is a veritable meeting place of all the society one knows at once. I wonder if you might object, though, to the lack of a little peace and privacy."

The prince shook his head vigorously. "Never! That's why they say the Langham is like home and its staff like family," he said. "Travel has become very comfortable, and although I believe my parents' generation endured its discomforts to gain knowledge of the world outside their circle, I think our generation and your daughter's will do it to enjoy themselves, relax, and feel familiar with sights unknown." Emily was relieved that he'd missed her father's point entirely.

Just then Charles Stanford, passing by on his way out of the hotel, stopped to offer Lord Alden the chance to talk as he'd requested. Stanford proposed that they ride to the college together so that they could speak on their way, since he had a student waiting. He glanced at Emily, and Lord Alden introduced her, making the most of the unexpected opportunity to connect them. "Would there be room in the carriage for my daughter?" he asked Professor Stanford. "We could accomplish two tasks at once." He beamed at them both, pretending to forget his daughter had just walked in the door of the hotel to meet another man.

Emily shook her head. "I came to see Mr. Mackay today, and John and I have not had any time together on this trip of his to London." She looked somewhat defiant, but John shook his head at her slightly.

"We visited in Vienna quite recently," John said, "and I don't want to impose on your family plans in any way." He moved slightly backward as if to begin his withdrawal, but Emily reached out for his arm.

"We planned this day together, John, and you'll be leaving for New York soon. I don't think we should rearrange our schedules." Lord Alden's expression began to darken.

"We'll find time before I leave," John said, gently but firmly with a smile in Emily's direction. "A pleasure to meet you all," he added with a bow to the group as Emily's hand dropped back to her side. "Goodbye, Your Majesty." He backed up farther and turned to walk to the front desk.

The prince nodded in the Silver King's direction, grinning with pleasure as he watched the confusion unfold before him. His years of social engagement with his future subjects before he'd be responsible for ruling the British Empire had not earned him the moniker of "Playboy Prince" for nothing. He knew a romantic complication when he saw one, and he couldn't resist stirring the crock of potential explosives simply to discover what might happen.

"And so, my dear, let me present Professor Charles Villiers Stanford, composer and conductor for the new Royal College of Music, of which I am now one of the main supporters," he announced, gleefully. "Your father and Professor Stanford have some business together at the school, and I believe they need a musician of your experience and renown to join them today." The prince nodded as if there could be no further discussion on that matter, and Emily first looked at him stunned, then at her father, and finally toward the disappearing John Mackay.

"Well," she finally breathed, "this is amazing. Now all that's needed to complete the family brew would be my children." At that precise moment, her younger son bounded through the front door behind a beautiful older woman dressed in a stylish velvet coat and high silk hat wrapped with a transparent gauze veil. "Connie," Emily and her father exclaimed together. Emily shook her head in disbelief. "Just say the word and in comes my son."

The Prince of Wales called out almost simultaneously, "Madame . . . Lady Sandhurst!" He laughed with delight. "The baroness has a predatory streak I rather admire," he said to Emily out of the side of his mouth. "But she gobbles up young men like your cherubic son there. You might want to warn him, Madame de Koningh." The look of shock on Lord Alden's face could not be mistaken for anything but horror, while Emily glanced from one to the other. For the moment, they'd all forgotten the professor as they labored to deal with a cascade of mistaken assumptions of varying degrees.

"Oh, no," Emily cried, "you're quite incorrect. Connie could not be involved with the baroness, or at least not that way . . . I mean she must be a client. He's been pursuing the ones his artist friend Mr.

Klimt introduced him to for fashion design. That must be it." She looked pleadingly from her father to the prince, as if to gain their agreement before she could consider taking another breath. Both men looked at each other.

"My dear," the prince sighed, "why is a mother always the last to know?"

"Don't be naïve, Emily," Lord Alden said. "We must believe what we see. That is my grandson in apparent hot pursuit of Lady Sandhurst. And now it's time to send Brody home, since none of us will be needing him for a while, until we return from the college." Suddenly aware of Professor Stanford's quiet, patient presence, he turned to him to apologize for the mayhem the unexpected arrival of his family members had produced. "What a way to meet my daughter through all the confusion, sir."

Emily and the professor looked at each other, apparently both at a loss for words. Finally Emily found her voice. John was clearly no longer a present danger, and she began to feel it was time to work for balance at last. "I doubt the poor professor wants to meet me at this point," Emily said, eager to steer the focus toward anyone other than her son. But reassured that the professor was still delighted to give both her father and her a ride to the college, she bowed her head in retreat to the Prince of Wales, who had already moved off with his driver. She still nursed a feeling of empty betrayal as her afternoon alone with John had disappeared in a haze of unplanned alternatives. Unsure how her father had outmaneuvered her so completely, she turned to join the professor.

"I'll be right with you," Lord Alden assured them when they stopped to wait for him. "I must inform Brody of our plans." Lord Alden stepped over quickly to his coachman. He came up so close to him without warning that their heads almost touched. "What were you thinking by bringing my daughter alone to meet a man twice her age in a public hotel?" he snarled angrily in the coachman's ear.

Brody stared at him, trying to translate the wrath as well as the words flung in his face.

"I could not stop her," he said quietly. "She's much like her mother."

Lord Alden's face froze, and his expression narrowed with the impenetrability of stone. "Don't you dare say that to me," he muttered with his jaw clenched. "If I ever hear you remark such a thing again you'll be looking for a new employer." His eyes flashed a warning that could not be missed before he spun around abruptly to move off toward Professor Stanford's carriage.

Brody watched Lord Alden's back receding and finally disappearing, as the driver from the Royal College assisted him into the school's coach. He could see his master's struggle to assure himself of the strength of his daughter's connection to him when his wife's had been so fragile. "The closer we get to the truth, the harder it is to unwrap," Brody said aloud, shaking his head almost imperceptibly. "And when the heart of the matter is finally revealed there may be nothing to be done about it, yet surely nothing can be done if it is not exposed and faced."

8

THE PROFESSOR

"DO YOU KNOW where you are?" the professor asked. Emily shook her head. "We've just passed Speakers' Corner back there, and now we're almost up to Reformers' Tree," the professor said, looking out as the carriage rounded the northwest point of Hyde Park. "I've always enjoyed the fact that freedom of speech and the right to protest are protected so visibly here in the park." He glanced at Emily sporadically, but she didn't notice. Lord Alden seemed distant and didn't respond to any of the professor's comments, either. Why he'd requested that they speak alone before his daughter appeared unexpectedly had not been made clear. But it was probably best to let her father come to his own point in his own time.

Reaching into his vest pocket, the professor slid his gold watch out on its chain and glanced quickly at it without comment. It slipped back out of sight so smoothly he thought Emily hadn't noticed; but she had. "We've made you late, haven't we?" she asked, looking out the window. "I'm embarrassed by the chaos my family caused at the hotel when you were in a hurry to leave." Why had her father not pressed her to say more about her appointment with John Mackay? Surely the shock of seeing her there while he dined with the Prince of Wales could not have been pleasant. And why had there been no more comment about Connie's liaison with Lady Sandhurst? If so many questions swirled around in his mind right now, why did he not say so or simply cancel the trip to the college? It was as if a matter of greater importance had displaced all the other family tribulations.

"No need to worry," the professor said. "We have less than three miles to go from the hotel to the college. It's just around the other end of the park, and we'll be there in about twenty minutes if we avoid traffic." Emily looked in from the window, a pained expression on her face. "I mean it; no need for discomfort on your part," he assured her. "My pupil will wait for me and practice piano exercises while he does. He probably missed most of his practice this week anyway and will be delighted for less time in the lesson with me."

She chuckled, two dimples deepening for a moment and then disappearing again as she looked back out the window. "When does that magic moment come to them, when they suddenly want to practice for themselves instead of for their teacher?" she asked, looking back at the professor and meeting his eyes directly for the first time. "I don't know because I always had it. But I sense most students don't feel it when they're young and just perfecting their motor skills. I suppose that's something a teacher must understand before engaging a student successfully." She looked out the window again, hoping the young professor would judge her question to show genuine interest in his profession, which she didn't truly have at that moment.

Layered on top of her sense of disorientation and disappointment at her failed rendezvous with John, she recognized a profound discomfort with who she was. The awkward chance meeting with her father, the delay of the handsome young professor by the confusion swirling around them all after Connie appeared with the apparently carnivorous baroness, and her own foolishly unguarded explanation of the nature of his relationship to Lady Sandhurst made her feel naïve and thoughtless.

She was usually comfortable inside the shell of Emily. She'd always been proud of herself, what she'd accomplished on stage and off with her music. And lately, she'd also taken pride in the family she'd formed in spite of the unconventional way she'd been brought up and lived. Most certainly, mentors in her childhood had done their best to help her, Klaas de Koningh and Robert Haussmann specifically, but no one could take the place of her mother. She wondered if the cracks in her family had their origins in that early loss. Bringing up two young boys without an example of how to be a mother might have originated the pains they were suffering now.

"Teaching is much like parenting: neither one has a guaranteed outcome." The seemingly clairvoyant professor smiled at her gently. "And you're right. A lot of it employs an inexplicable form of magic." She looked at him more closely. "But much of it is intuitive—teaching and parenting I mean—don't you think? My father had a penchant for hearing himself talk more than listening." His eyes slid sideways to glance briefly at Lord Alden and then move back again to Emily's face. "I'm sure I became a teacher in reaction to his treatment of me," he said, thoughtfully. "But teaching soon became my calling for vastly different reasons."

"You find teaching as satisfying as performing?" Without waiting for his answer, Emily turned slightly to face him fully on the carriage seat across from her. "You did your adult training in Leipzig, did you not, Professor Stanford?"

"I started in Leipzig with Carl Reinecke," the professor said. "But I finished in Berlin with Friedrich Kiel. The two teaching styles gave me every example of how to motivate students, as well as how *not* to." His grin had a childish devilment about it. "I learned more from Kiel in three months than from all the others in three years."

"And do you know why that is?"

"Expressiveness, Madame de Koningh. My upbringing in Ireland in the '60s benefited from an intense brilliance of imagination. I think artists who grew up after the Famine developed a sense of fearlessness and adventure not known before in our history. Those of us drawn to the arts need to express that spirit in our music. Life's tragedies create a great heat in the artistic spirit just aching to get out. A teacher who doesn't know how to give a student his head is going to crush him or her. Kiel taught me that." His eyes seemed to increase their intensity. "From a distance, your son seems to show that sense of expressiveness so necessary in an artist. He wouldn't feel safe to do that if he didn't have people who'd appreciated him."

Emily nodded slowly, but whether it was in response to the professor's description of the impact of tragedy on the artistic soul or his belief in giving his students room to express themselves couldn't be determined, and she didn't ask. Possibly because she was suddenly wondering at her father's silence, whether he was simply riding with them to make her comfortable in answering the professor's questions. She felt well beyond the need for a chaperone, but her father's penchant for organizing her life was too familiar not to be suspect.

"And you, Madame de Koningh. How did your musical training affect you?" There was no way for her to include her father now, so she narrowed her large dark eyes to bring the professor into sharper focus. Finally she looked out the window again and said, "Profoundly, Professor Stanford. My training affected my life completely, just as yours did. But mine was more about confidence and a belief in oneself, something almost impossible to get from a world that would stop you from doing what you're born to do because of your gender. It is not something you could understand, and you should thank heaven that's so. I, on the other hand, thank the same heaven that I had a teacher who believed in me despite society's estimate of my limitations."

He smiled at her and nodded. "And that is why you, in turn, could be a great teacher as well. It's why your son is the way he is. How lucky for him," the professor said, turning to glance out the window again. "And there is the Crystal Palace now, the former site of Prince Albert's Great Exhibition. We'll be back at the Royal College in no time." He turned to look from Emily to her father, seemingly deciding to bring him back into the conversation they were having. "Lord Alden, might I prevail upon you to show your daughter around the building when we arrive? I'll be less than an hour with my student, and then I can join you. I'll have some food brought for Madame de Koningh in the meantime, as I noted she missed her meal . . . at the hotel. She must be ready to faint by now," he added, looking a little concerned.

Emily was suddenly aware that she indeed felt like fainting, but not from hunger. Why had the professor focused so closely on Connie? Was he trying to draw her out? Perhaps her confusion in the lobby made him suspect she knew little about her son's intimate life. What if the professor had heard rumors? Now she was being ridiculous . . . A sudden movement by her father jarred her out of her thoughts, bringing her back to the purpose of their visit to the college. The professor was the link, and her father had been the one to discover him first.

"Why did you get so involved with this project at such an early point in your own career, Professor Stanford?" she asked. "Your reputation for expertise in composition and conducting is already so strong I can't imagine why you'd need to resort to teaching. Could that not have been saved until old age removed you from the stage?"

The professor smiled patiently. She had the impression it was a question he'd answered before. "I didn't resort to it. I leaped to it," he said without a pause. "It's time for the United Kingdom to take its place next to the great countries' cultures, if not be in the lead." His head nodded thoughtfully with the movement of the coach. "The spark has already been lit. I can feel it, and I think fate sent Prince Albert to us just when we needed him most. The college was his dream. Britain is at the edge of a new dawn for music education. I find it most exciting that the greatest musicians will come from the next generation that I will teach on our soil; more exciting than making music myself, even though I do intend to continue doing that, as well. We'll create a pathway to the future instead of a dead end."

It seemed to Emily as if Charles Stanford had looked inside her and recognized her discontent. The "dead end" he spoke of had already taunted her, and she'd mentioned it to those she trusted most, hoping for relief. Her friend Pauline von Metternich had suggested finding a new direction for inspiration when they'd talked in Vienna. Perhaps this young man was pointing the way. She looked at her father for the first time since they'd entered the carriage, raising a questioning eyebrow. He nodded slightly and smiled.

"I'll gladly show my daughter around the college while you're busy, Professor," he announced with a renewed vigor that surprised them both.

"And I'll join you as soon as my young student can be dispatched, Lord Alden. I do apologize for the interruption to Madame de Koningh's plans but admit the opportunity to speak with you both is timely, and I'll make her meal up to her someday in the future. I promise."

"I agree," Lord Alden said, and Emily surprised herself by agreeing with him as well. There was something about the young professor that made her more comfortable than she had been in a long time. Somehow he made her feel understood again.

"How interesting to believe your legacy is to live in the students you leave behind rather than the music you compose," she said, almost as if speaking to herself. She watched him gathering up his hat and gloves in preparation to leave the carriage. How odd that she'd paid no real attention to him until now. She noticed the long, fine fingers, even more impressive than other musicians' hands she'd studied carefully. She couldn't miss the beautifully made clothing that spoke of wealth and good taste. It was simple and elegant with a quality of workmanship she could recognize after years of discussing her own handmade costumes with her seamstress. He was not at all what she'd expected.

Admittedly the professor's most intriguing aspects were his youth and confidence housed in a person so wise and sophisticated that a lifetime for most would be too short a time to acquire them. She was struck by his point about the hell his countrymen in Ireland had lived through, and how those trials had formed artists of uniquely different character. She watched fascinated as he descended with easy grace from the carriage to talk with its driver, wishing that she could drop the last decade and be the professor's age again. But perhaps leaping from the carriage was not something she still needed to do. She knew her father saw her watching.

"I wish we had more time to spend here this afternoon," Lord Alden said, "but I'm glad we came." She would have said the same thing had he not beaten her to it.

"Ah, you'd best be careful what you wish for," the professor answered, reaching to help Emily out of the carriage.

"I know that all too well," Lord Alden agreed, bowing slightly as the coachman assisted him to climb from the carriage after his daughter.

But wishing was the technique Emily used most often to get what she wanted or where she wanted to go, so she felt no need to take care. She recognized the emotional lift her new acquaintance had given her, obscuring the worry about her children, her father, and her career. Even her disappointment in John's disappearance was gone. "I'm delighted to have this chance to get to know the college, and you, better," she said, smiling up at Professor Stanford. The clouds were breaking up and cracks of blue sky allowed shards of sunlight to fall on the shiny dark hair tied at her neck.

"As am I," he said, glancing at her father to be sure he was properly cared for and following close behind.

9

THE PRINCESS

JOHNNY DUNNE arrived from New York in 1871 to write for *Le Figaro*, the oldest national daily newspaper in France. There had always been journalists who competed for news flashes, and telegraphic services to provide world access, but "war specialists" like Johnny helped keep loyal readers with a focus on the serious political issues of the day. And there were always plenty of conflicts in the world to keep him employed. That was Johnny's specialty—making sense of the senseless. He didn't need to be in the middle of the fray like a war correspondent. In fact, his ability to rise above the conflict to assess the situations igniting and perpetuating disagreement was strengthened by his distanced point of view. He'd made a reputation at the *New-York Times* during the Civil War running a weekly insert, and presumably his fame had grown from there.

Le Figaro almost disappeared after a shaky start in 1826, but war in Europe had expanded its offices and now it boasted the highest circulation in France. By 1871 the Franco-Prussian War had just ended, and dailies were booming. It was a perfect time for a newspaper man like Johnny to be in Paris. Newspapers were finally affordable for the masses, powerful, unrestricted, and representative of every facet of life. Everybody read them, even just to keep up with the latest gossip and fashions. Johnny was not above reporting on those, either.

The paper took its name from *Le Mariage de Figaro*, Pierre Beaumarchais's play parodying privilege. Its motto, from Figaro's monologue in the play's final act, was *without the freedom to criticize, there is no true praise.* Johnny had become more comfortable with the paper's increasingly centrist outlook than he would have been twenty years earlier. Even *Le Figaro's* occasional royalist tilt to the right (very slight, he always emphasized to his younger friends) could easily be ignored amid the high quality of its reporting and writing. And besides, there were plenty of opposing viewpoints to balance it out. France offered a feast of reading choices, and Johnny knew his paper was at the top of that menu.

Standing at his desk in the newsroom in front of a nameplate reading J. R. DUNNE, Johnny looked down at the banner for *Le Figaro.* The familiar profile of a courtier kneeling on one knee, plumed hat on his head and hand outstretched in supplication, presented the paper's title, subtitle, and list of sections within. *Le Figaro, Journal Littéraire,* was superimposed over the list of subjects making the paper the most sought after in Paris: theater, arts and sciences, finance, literature, critiques, and the less than specific overflow identified as ETC., ETC. But along with those was a heading for scandal, as well as "morals." Who would have the audacity to feign an expertise in scandal or morals? Certainly not Johnny. And yet that proficiency was exactly what he needed now rather than his own ability to explain and summarize the many facets of war. What he really needed was a consummate gossip. Not the kind that made up false news, but someone like an Honoré de Balzac or Émile Zola, documenting society in a realistic and reliable way. He tried to fashion himself in their design.

Emptying his pockets of extraneous coins, Johnny put an extra handkerchief in their place and adjusted the sleeves of his shirt. He pulled them down to show just a half inch below his suitcoat cuffs. No more the sandy-haired reporter who used his hands to tame his full head of hair. His light brown hairline was thinning at the temples, streaked with gray, and always smooth and ordered. He'd become more aware of how he presented himself now that his youth was behind him, and knowing the young staff reporters watched his every move, carefully patterning themselves and their careers after their mentor.

"I don't know why you bother with these chic restaurants," his assistant Louis muttered. "There are plenty of good cafés in the neighborhood." Louis shook his head, as if his American boss needed help navigating the Parisian landscape even after more than twenty years of working and living in France.

"Not for the likes of the lady I'm meeting," Johnny chuckled.

"One might think you'd been moved to the society column." Louis knew he could get away with poking fun at his supervisor because they enjoyed each other's company. "How many great restaurants are there in Paris now, chief, five hundred or more? And no doubt you've been to all of them, but the cafés are where the talk gets interesting, not where the fancy people are too stiff to say anything worth hearing." Johnny glowered at his young assistant, but the small smile he couldn't fully hide gave away his affection for his acolyte.

"Not this lady," he said again, checking to be sure he had his pocket watch and wallet. "Because, strange as it may seem, I like to eat good food, well prepared and impeccably served. I also like to entertain, therefore dining out is a must for a bachelor with a maisonette the size of mine. Today I have a princess on my hands, so the Café Anglais is the only possibility. I've always thought it ironic that the best restaurant in Paris should be named after some of the worst cuisine in Europe!" He put a folder from his desk in one of his drawers, locking it with a key returned to his breast pocket. "Odder still that it should be named for a peace treaty with Britain rather than its food. But war is never far off, I suppose, even at the dining table."

"On your hands, eh . . . really?" Louis laughed.

"Really." Johnny nodded.

"And who is the princess?" Louis asked, standing up from the stray chair he'd borrowed from another desk when he'd stopped to chat. "There's so much displaced royalty floating about Europe these days, it's hard to keep track of them all." He looked Johnny up and down, no doubt noting he was better dressed than usual.

"She's a friend of a friend," Johnny answered, pulling on the lapels of his jacket to make sure it hung straight. "Princess von Metternich if you must know. Her grandfather was the Austrian statesman and diplomat who was at the center of European affairs for three decades. She knows a thing or two about politics, I'll wager. She's a fount of information, and I need an update on . . . certain people." He picked up his hat and gloves from the desk, making it clear Louis had all the information he was going to get. "I'm off," Johnny said, "but if you're good, I'll bring you some of those madeleines you love from the dessert tray. And if you're not good and press me too hard for gossip, I'll eat them myself, right in front of you." He winked at his young assistant and moved down the row of desks placed all the way to the door.

"Are you doing a story on European royalty?" Louis asked, following Johnny to the office stairway. Johnny usually enjoyed bantering in English with the French reporters who could do it, but today it was annoying at a time when he wanted more privacy than camaraderie.

"No. I want to see her because she's so well connected, and I trust her." He turned to face Louis and they almost collided. "I need to find out some things about a friend's family, and the infamous Pauline will be the one who knows. That is, after all, how we work in the information business, right?" He started down the stairs, a little slower than he might have once, but he was still too impatient to wait for the ascenseur to carry him down. Patience had always been elusive for Johnny Dunne, and probably would be for the rest of his life.

"Well, why not one of the restaurants with a more literary crowd?" Louis answered Johnny's query about information gathering with another question. Johnny stopped on the stairs again without turning around.

"You've made your point," he said over his shoulder. "You know your restaurants, Louis, but I know my sources, and I don't want this one attracting undue attention. The princess will be only one of many notables at the Café Anglais, and we have one of the private rooms." He sounded as if his tolerance was running low. "And now, my young friend, you have work to do and so do I, but in a blessedly different direction. Au revoir, mon ami. I'll see you later . . . much later," he added as he disappeared around the corner at the bottom of the stairs.

⊷⊶ 𝒲 ⊷⊶

"*Bonjour, Monsieur Dunne, et bienvenu. La princesse est déjà arrivée.*" A white-aproned waiter announced the princess's prior arrival as Johnny stepped through the entrance. The six-story, triangular white building famously formed the corner where the Boulevard des Italiens and the Rue de Marivaux met. It had an austere façade belying its sumptuous interior, but that was part of its charm. He was led quietly through a sparkling front foyer to an interior staircase and upper hall lined with molded doors suggesting discreet hotel rooms, each in fact a single or double private dining room.

The building's exterior was understated; much like the lady Johnny was coming to meet that day who was dressed uncharacteristically, almost like any other well-to-do woman of Paris. A layered, cream-colored short coat covered a dark crimson skirt. But a small, light fur hat topped her dark curls, a stark contrast to the oversized bonnets of feathers and tulle worn by many fashionable Parisiennes. The stylish little cap tempted Johnny to comment on how many elegant women would be running out to buy hats just like hers after their lunch together. The entire millinery industry of Paris would be scrambling for months to catch up. But he wasn't quite as comfortable as usual and so stifled his remark. Princess von Metternich was barely more than a stranger to him, and he worried that any personal comment on his part might alienate her immediately. Had it not been for Emily's attachment to the princess through the latter's support of classical musicians and women in general, Johnny might not have secured a meeting with her for lunch in the first place. For him, the meeting was purely informational, but he didn't want to jeopardize Emily's personal relationship with her in any way.

The princess smiled and extended her hand to shake Johnny's first, as if she were the hostess. He wasn't surprised, knowing it was her superior rank prompting the advanced greeting. He pressed her small fingers firmly but gently, letting her hand go again as he spoke her abbreviated title. He looked at the princess closely, fascinated by the reality of the woman who had always been more fantasy than fact to him. Her strong features were not beautiful in themselves, but her confidence gave her an intensity that fascinated everyone who met her. She was known by the press as "La Belle Laide," or "the Beautiful Ugly Woman," a title she herself had no doubt fostered. She appeared to be very tall and thin, almost wiry, and though her clothes softened her shape, she was by no means the ideal of womanhood sought by most men of the day—or women either, for that matter. But despite her own chosen nickname of "*le singe à la mode*," or "the fashionable monkey," her clothes were always captivating and unusual, suiting her well, like the small fur cap today. Her fashions also made more of an impression because she moved with dynamism, unlike the women of high society in Paris whom she called "the waxworks."

Princess Pauline had survived the horrors of war as a child. It might just as well have turned her away from danger, but the opposite had happened, suggesting something in her character was responsible for her unusual courage. Perhaps her early exposure to hardship created the desire to protect other female royals, such as her best friend the Empress Eugenie, from the trauma of political conflict. In 1870 she'd stayed close to the empress in Paris during the Franco-Prussian War, eventually helping her escape to Great Britain, and then surreptitiously sending the empress's jewels after her in a diplomatic courier's pouch. Rumor had it that the empress would not have survived without Pauline's help.

"Are you staying in Paris long?" Johnny asked, accepting the seat offered by a waiter. "I'd heard you'd returned to England after many years of travel around the continent." He noticed a gleaming bottle of chilled white Bordeaux already nestled in a bucket of ice standing beside the table. The princess had apparently already been busy preparing for his arrival. Johnny felt more comfortable seated now at her eye level than looming over her as he had when he'd first arrived.

"Oh, yes, too much back and forth," she said. "When one government replaces another it quickly becomes necessary to disappear to a safer, less exposed vantage point. But like most people, Paris will always light my spirit. One can't stay away forever. I can be faithful to my homeland and still appreciate the beauty of Paris." Johnny smiled as he pictured the draw the City of Light had for so many people, including him. He noticed the princess also imagining something she hadn't shared out loud yet, but then she spoke again, fixing her gaze on him more directly.

"Queen Victoria and the Prince of Wales both show sympathies for Prussia, understandable with their ancestral family ties, but they still enjoy the comforts of life in Paris. They profess a love for the French yet also embrace their enemies. One learns about duplicity moving from place to place as I have done. I fear the covert hypocrite far more than the overt assailant."

Johnny nodded, realizing the princess was a woman he could deal with head on. "You lived through some terrible conflicts in Vienna as a child, I know." Johnny watched to see if she could acknowledge a frightening memory or would need to hide. But she seemed resolute rather than sad, and so he let her continue uninterrupted.

"Much bloodshed, of strangers and family, was spilled on our front steps in Vienna. The horror of what human beings will do to each other," she said forcefully, "is a waste and totally incomprehensible." She stared past Johnny now, and he watched her viewing her reminiscences, wondering if it was time to break the cycle of trauma memory with a recognition of the wine waiting to be served.

"You've experienced in reality what I've only experienced vicariously," he said, marveling at her composure. "Yet the irony of it is that I've built my reputation on communicating the ravages of war to society, while you are the one who has actually experienced it." She nodded almost imperceptibly. "I do hope our paper hasn't reported your life in circumstances that might have been less than accurate or embarrassed you in any way." She shook her head, looking past him now to one of the windows along the façade.

"It's one thing to experience horror as a child," she said, quietly. "I'm not exactly sure why, but somehow one takes it in a different stride, as if it's a part of the craziness governing most of the world a child must navigate. But when events upend us in our later years, robbing us of things and people we've come to know and treasure, then we have a difficult time adjusting." Johnny was careful not to show any lack of attention or need to speak himself, noticing how deeply she was concentrating now.

"The empress and I have seen our lives and families turned upside down by war. I and a few other dedicated royalists made sure she escaped the bloody revolution here and had enough money to live initially after arriving in England. Slipping her jewelry out of France for her was a mission I took on and completed without hesitation, as there would have been no life for her without them. No one, including the press, ever knew of her or my whereabouts until we'd completed her escape abroad. I know how to avoid the papers and ignore them when necessary."

Johnny smiled to himself, remembering she'd been the compatriot of choice for the empress when the latter wanted to see what Paris looked like from the top of an omnibus. Everyone had heard that Pauline dressed them both as men and slipped out of the palace, though they were eventually caught by local gendarmes. The press got hold of the incident and reported it with its usual flourish, but Johnny was convinced the adventure was only the tip of Pauline's iceberg. How much else had slipped public scrutiny, he could only imagine.

Three waiters had somehow moved unnoticed into the room and now hovered by the entrance. But they were still well out of earshot, and so Johnny felt no hesitation to announce his reason for inviting the princess to lunch. He realized he hadn't seen her in person for months, not since Vienna, where Emily's friends and family had congregated before their departure to England. "The last time I saw you, Princess, was in Vienna," he said, "at Emily de Koningh's farewell party with her friends and family." The princess nodded slightly, but one cocked eyebrow showed she'd been unprepared for his quick change of direction. "Emily is the woman I need to discuss with you," Johnny said, waving a waiter off from their table and pouring the wine for the princess himself.

"How is my dear Emily?" the princess asked in her fluent English. "Has she made some friends in London now that she's had time to herself and her family without performances getting in the way?" Johnny waved another waiter off and took the menus from the third garçon himself. Knowing them both to be regular diners at the Café Anglais and familiar with the menu, the waiters left them with small bows, closing the door silently behind them.

"I don't know if Emily has made friends in London. I haven't seen her since we parted in Vienna, but I rather doubt it, don't you, Your Highness?" He took another sip from his wine, appreciating the unusual pleasure of having a cool, refreshing white Bordeaux in the middle of the day. Its subtle lift was lessening his anxiety about the topic he wanted to discuss with the princess. "I've always had the impression she has few close female friends, other than you, Princess."

"Perhaps, but she has many male companions, and I assume that will continue while she's in London. Male or female, a friend is a friend," the princess said, smiling warmly, no sign of cynicism on her face as she took a respectful sip of wine. "And truly, she does have some women friends," the princess continued, watching Johnny directly as if she was on firmer ground than he was. "But it's harder for her because of her work. Female musicians are still a rarity at the level of Emily's skill, and a woman who isn't immersed in the culture of music and performance has little to offer her. Yes, there are a few women today in all professional spheres, even yours, I dare say," she added with a smile. Johnny nodded, grudgingly. "But they are rare, and so focused on their own personal struggles they often lack the time and energy to expand their female connections."

"I see your point," Johnny said with a nod. Narrowing his eyes to look off into the distance, he added, "But maybe that's her problem. She's corralled herself entirely in a sphere of music and others have trouble getting in. That makes her unaware of what's happening in the rest of the world, leaving her with an outlook solely her own." Johnny hoped that by drawing the line to his friendship with Emily, perhaps he'd be able to draw a parallel one with the princess as well. Her keen intellect and curiosity made their talk distinct, but also made him more aware of how much more comfortable the princess seemed talking about Emily in her absence than he was.

Pauline shook her head emphatically. "I have never found her to be introverted, nor simple and naïve," she added. "I believe her to be a woman of the world, especially because of her work and travel. When I first met the Empress Eugenie, I was drawn instantly to her sophistication due to the full life she'd already led. Ordinarily no woman born to royalty would have acquired the education or been allowed to experience the outside world the way she had. But she had an unusually permissive childhood, and Emily has much the same demeanor." She smiled broadly, apparently picturing her introduction to the empress many years ago. Then focusing again on Johnny, she continued.

"But I think Emily sees what she must, Mr. Dunne, and chooses not to see what she doesn't need. After a lifetime of challenges to her strength, courage, and resilience, she has a right, as we all do, to deny what she doesn't want to let in. It's how we survive without collapsing." Johnny stared at her, aware that she'd overcome a great deal by seemingly facing her challenges head on, just as he felt Emily had in her own way. Avoidance had never been a trait he'd assign to Emily, but he supposed both women had designed their narratives in ways they could be comfortable hearing them. Either way, theirs were stories with resonance.

"You and she are much alike," Johnny said, letting his admiration for the princess show clearly in his smile. He rearranged himself on his chair. "My apologies," he added, "I should have asked you sooner if you'd like to order. If you're ready to dine, I'll call the waiters over." He didn't even have to signal them to move into the room, suggesting, however, that they were not as far out of earshot as Johnny had thought. "Garçon, could you bring us the potage Germiny now, followed by the sole Dugléré in about twenty minutes?" he called out to the waiter moving toward the table. The princess put her hand on his forearm resting on the tablecloth for a second.

"I'd prefer the soufflé à la reine today, if you don't mind." She raised her voice just enough for the waiter to hear when he'd arrived next to them.

"Of course, you shall have what you want. Forgive me," Johnny said, nodding to the waiter, who was as surprised as he to find that this lady chose to order for herself. "And then," he added, "I will plumb the depths of your knowledge about something especially important to Emily and her family, as soon as the potage is served, and our helpful friend has disappeared for a while." He picked up his glass, refilling it after glancing at the princess's, which was still half full. He took a large sip from his, reducing the volume by at least a third. The fact that he'd not written Emily to ask her permission to speak with the princess about Connie was suddenly staring him uncomfortably in the face.

"This is so difficult?" The princess winked at him, eyeing his swiftly draining flute.

"It is," Johnny replied. "I need information from you, but you might be upset by the request." He eyed her directly. Her reputation for controlling the kind of gossip that made or broke people's reputations also made her as feared by her friends as by her enemies.

Pauline's eyes narrowed to study Johnny more carefully. "You need me to confirm whether your information is accurate or not, yes? You require my expertise as a . . . *gossip*," she said. "If it concerns Emily de Koningh, I don't think I like the implication."

Johnny shook his head. "You misunderstand me, but rightly so. I haven't explained myself well." He worked hard to resist the desire to look away. It wasn't easy. Her height made her seem taller than he, though she'd been seated when he'd arrived, as straight as her royal posture could support. She seemed to be looking down at him. He was unaccustomed to being intimidated by anyone, especially a woman.

"I'm a man who makes his living using the written language," Johnny said, feeling he needed to reintroduce himself. "So I've always had an affinity for word derivations. Do you know the origins of the noun 'gossip'?" He picked the wine out of its bucket of ice water, and seeing the bottle was almost empty, offered it to the princess first. She shook her head. He poured himself a full glass, putting the empty bottle back in the bucket upside down and draping a napkin over it.

"Such a short life," the princess said, shaking her head sadly at the Bordeaux's demise.

"Ah yes, but so delicious while it lasted," Johnny added. No sooner had he finished his comment than the waiter returned with another bottle, perfectly chilled, and instantly opened it. The empty disappeared as if by magic, and the full bottle took its place in a fresh bucket of ice.

"One can't even get a thought completed, much less a request," Johnny chuckled.

The princess nodded and smiled. "The service in these luxury cafés consists of the very finest of those who served the French aristocracy, and sometimes even finer!" she added, with a laugh. "The emperor's Summer Palace was no better than a second-rate hotel. Still, it was impossible for most of the highly skilled chefs and servants to find employment in private homes after the revolution. These elegant restaurants have provided them with new opportunities." Johnny knew France had been positioned to implement its emperor's grand vision for Paris as an imperial capital. Change and modernization had revived the French economy, making Paris into the centerpiece of Europe. Parisian demand for luxuries had risen beyond anything seen even before the revolution. He could appreciate that he and the Princess von Metternich were both being cared for at this moment as only she would have been at an earlier time in a different place. He thanked the waiter and paused, his silver soup spoon held expectantly above the potage Germiny as he watched the waiter retreat and close the door again. He knew his need for privacy hadn't escaped the princess but felt that could only serve his purpose. She was paying attention.

"Now back to my lesson in Old English," Johnny said, unwilling to start from a different place. "The origin of the noun 'gossip' comes from the two nouns 'gods' and 'sip.' The 'sip' refers to a sibling, or someone as close as family. Therefore it came to mean a woman who could serve as family to a friend." He enjoyed the look of amusement on the princess's face. "And so you can probably intuit what comes next . . ." He paused, assuming she probably couldn't, and relishing the suspense that guaranteed her interest. "It's barely a step to gossip actually meaning 'godparent.'" He smiled at her, feeling her growing pleasure in the irony behind the slur. "Please, don't let me keep you from your lunch," he said, nodding gently in the direction of her delicate porcelain soup dish.

"Not you, Mr. Dunne, but your narrative," the princess said, looking just past his shoulder to someplace else. "You see, I find it so interesting how close our languages are. The derivation of 'gossip' in French is much the same, did you know?" She looked directly at him now, that same amusement playing at the corners of her mouth. Johnny became aware that she'd probably been prepared to better him from the start of his English lesson.

"Ah well, then I shall tell you," she went on, cheerfully. "As a man of words, you'll appreciate the knowledge. It comes from the French word for godmother, which is 'commère.' It came to also denote a female friend or familiar acquaintance but is now used only in a derogatory sense." She picked up her spoon, allowing it to hover above the dish and finally lowering it into the soup, commenting on the perfection of the taste and temperature as she enjoyed her first mouthful of the café's famous wild sorrel soup. Johnny wondered how the rest of his planned conversation would unwind. He glanced at the dining room door to be sure the waiter had not returned to his sentinel post. Satisfied that they were still alone, he continued.

"I can't speak as a godmother, but I've known Emily's sons since they were born, and I've even served as a godfather of sorts to them all this time. Primarily because of their mother, but also because of my affection for them, I find I am tied to the de Koningh boys' happiness in unexpected ways for a bachelor. And so, it's in that capacity I need to ask you if Emily has confided any . . . worries to you about her youngest son, Cornelius."

The princess raised an eyebrow, leading Johnny to wonder if she was ignorant of a truth he knew or simply curious about it.

"Worries?" she asked. "Of what nature?"

"I shall tell you of it," he said, glancing again at the dining room door. "So long as we're entirely alone." The princess remained still and silent. Johnny drew a breath. "I gather you've not heard the rumor circulating about the young de Koningh and his proclivities toward . . . sodomy." Johnny watched the princess's face and body language, but as there seemed no change in either, he continued quickly. "It's not the usual stuff of *gossip* in its current meaning, easily discarded and ignored. The criminal nature of the lifestyle is possibly overblown but is still, nonetheless, illegal."

He wanted her to see his disdain for the overbearing sodomy laws in Europe and America, but still needed to ward off any attempt to minimize the importance of Connie's offense. He knew enough about direct communication to know her face would give away much of her own feelings about morality and punishment, but the princess said nothing and sustained her level, uncompromising gaze, as if an interruption on her part would be unthinkable. So, Johnny was forced to continue without a chance to recover his composure. He took two more attentive portions of his sorrel soup, finally putting the spoon down and pressing his napkin to his lips as if to seal them against what might come next.

"Perhaps it's my work in the newspaper business, but I've always been peculiarly sensitive to the difference between news and gossip," he said, keeping his face as stoic as he could. "The ramifications of the news and of a rumor can seem similar, but they most assuredly are not in this case." He looked to see if she was ready to jump in with a response, but she was not, so he had no choice but to continue again.

"I've always felt the facts behind the information being communicated differ broadly from news to gossip, and often the consequences are far more punitive. Sodomy accusations and trials are front-page news, not merely titillating mutters over glasses of port. The consequences to the accused's reputation can topple whole families as well as the respondent. In other words, not only would Connie de Koningh lose his young life and career, but Emily could lose everything she's worked so hard for, as would Connie's father and brother, and his grandfather with his fine old family name and a lifetime of service to the Crown. And let's not forget the boys' American grandfather and his family's reputation, although the Atlantic Ocean does help to soften that blow." Finally, Johnny found a way to stop, knowing there was little left to be destroyed by his damning tale. "I hope I haven't distressed you too much," he added.

The princess took a deep breath, which seemed to raise her another inch in her seat. "Mr. Dunne, I hardly know how you could consider a meal after such a story." She quickly smiled to show her fondness for teasing, while she continued to move her own spoon in and out of the cream soup, raising it to her lips in a slow, steady rhythm as if nothing could deter her. The room was silent. Finally she said, "I appreciate that a reporter's perspective might be a little grimmer than that of a mere citizen. But when you've lived through as much torture and bloodshed as I have, it takes more than a whiff of rumor to upset me."

She smiled at him reassuringly, apparently unscathed by his horrible news of Connie's ruination. "I do know how seriously the sodomy laws are upheld," she said. "However, I also believe that the recent Labouchère Amendment has reduced the punishment for 'gross indecency' to two years' incarceration instead of life imprisonment. Although his intentions were not entirely humanitarian, the result is at least merciful."

"Yes . . . ," Johnny said, eyeing her carefully to figure out what might come next from the unusual woman. It hadn't occurred to him she might know anything at all about the laws controlling sodomy, especially as they were softer in the French society she knew best.

"I met Henry Labouchère in his days as a diplomat." She raised her chin. "I found him eager to move with the popular will, but he himself was clearly on the side of increased punishment, even though it would appear that indictment and conviction for this so-called *unnatural crime of gross indecency* is rare. So he removed the need for proof, the burden of that being impossibly weighty."

"I see," Johnny said, slowly. "But what is more common today seems to be the connection to fraud and extortion even if incarceration is avoided, which would certainly shake Connie's family to the core!"

"No doubt, and that is the danger, but I can assure you that Emily knows of the rumors already and is trying to address them herself. She asked me if I'd heard of them, knowing my reputation for curiosity and the ability to put myself squarely in the middle of controversy."

Johnny pulled himself up. "Good heavens," he muttered, "why didn't she come to me, then?"

"I think she felt your position would require that you get more involved than she wanted you to be," Pauline said lightly, but none-theless suggesting that Emily hadn't trusted Johnny's discretion as a friend first and reporter second. "A mother will often trust the judgment of another mother before that of anyone else," she added. "The worry one feels for a child under siege of any kind is over-whelming, and hard to describe to one who isn't a parent, let alone to a man," she added, looking him directly in the eye to emphasize the factual nature of her comment. Johnny seemed doubtful, as if Emily's choice of confidants was highly suspect.

"Oh, you think I don't know?" the princess declared. "My parenting credentials are impeccable." She straightened up in her chair. "My children are roughly the same age as Emily's. I have three daughters, instead of two sons, but the care and worry over them is

never as balanced as any other concerns in my life. The eldest is
unmarried, but uncaring about it. I find that unnatural, which makes
me worry. The middle girl is married, too young, to an insane,
alcoholic Czech prince who abuses and beats her. There is not a day
or hour I don't fear for her, even though the law says she is his
property now and basically has no rights. I know that, and knew it
when she married of course, but I cannot let it go. And my youngest
daughter who is only fifteen was mauled by one of our dogs when she
was a child. Her face is so scarred she has declared a life of celibacy.
And even though she is the healthiest of any of my daughters emotionally, I weep every day for how her life has been decided for her
with one brief accident. So you see, Mr. Dunne, I understand the
depth of commitment to one's children coupled with the frustration
of our utter lack of control. If I can help Emily with hers, I most
certainly will." The princess's shoulders seemed to relax imperceptibly, and she finished her soup and replaced the spoon gracefully
beside her dish. She finally also reached for her wineglass, as if the
narrative of her own daughters had released her somehow.

"What did she tell you about how she heard of it?" Johnny asked.
"It's important to know the facts of how this got started. Whoever
delivered the first blows meant to do specific harm to the boy and his
family." Johnny worried that he was pushing too hard, a failing of the
impatient.

"I'm sure she's fully aware of that, too." The princess nodded at
the waiters and raised her hand for a moment. They approached the
table to remove the appetizers and deliver the entrées. She was
clearly less concerned than Johnny about being overheard. "But I
assume you have suspicions of how this got started, Mr. Dunne. I
could probably help Emily better if you took me into your confidence." Johnny shook his head slightly.

She adjusted herself on her seat, replacing the napkin in her lap
and moving closer to the table. "So why don't we drop the subject,
then, and enjoy what's left of this delicious meal." She smiled at

Johnny with the assurance wrought of power and confidence, clearly saying the discussion could go no further without his contribution.

He stared at her, knowing well what she wanted of him but not whether he could meet her requirement. "Your Highness, how precisely did she broach the subject with you? I'm sure she was guarded, even if she was upset enough to expose her feelings." Again, he was being too aggressive. The waiter removed soup with spoons and placed a soufflé dish in front of the princess, rearranging the silverware at her place to make the proper implements for eating her entrée more accessible. She nodded her thanks and waited for Johnny's meal to be served as well and the waiters to move toward the dining room door again.

"I see you're genuinely worried for Emily's emotional well-being," she said, quietly. "I can tell you she mentioned only that she'd heard the rumor and asked me about the reputations of Connie's artist friends. When she told me he'd been adopted, so to speak, by Gustav Klimt and his compatriots, I told her she need fear nothing from them. Her son is in the best company personally, socially, and professionally with those men if fashion art is his chosen calling, and truly I know quite a good deal about that, as it's somewhat of a calling of my own." And as if they had slipped smoothly away from news of the most horrifying corruption, the princess closed her eyes in appreciation of her golden soufflé with creamed chicken.

She opened her eyes again to lift her fork and start her meal. "I did question Emily about her son's qualifications for the level of couture career he wanted, knowing the reputation of his Austrian artist friends couldn't be higher. She described to me a beginning in Connie's youth much like that of my old friend Charles Worth. You know of him, Mr. Dunne?" Her eyebrow shot up again, punctuating her query without interrupting her delicate maneuvers to open the center of her soufflé to release its heat. When Johnny nodded briefly, she continued, "The House of Worth is a world-famous couture establishment today, but Charles began with a simple training in fabrics, and a skill like Connie's with artistic drawing. And none of these particular men of fashion engage in the 'unnatural crimes' of which Connie has been accused. They're all devoted to their families and mistresses, not necessarily in that order." Waiting for the steam to escape the soufflé, she paused in her narration of Emily's visit in Vienna to call Johnny's attention to their primary reason for visiting the Café Anglais for lunch.

"Look at your sole Dugléré," she exclaimed, leaning a bit closer to him to appreciate the imaginative presentation on his plate. The rolled filets of sole gleamed with Monsieur Dugléré's elegant wine sauce and cheese, lightly glazed in the oven to bring it to the table with a soft brown glow. Without straightening up, she looked into Johnny's eyes and asked again, "Who told *you*, Mr. Dunne? As I know it wasn't Emily, I can only assume it's someone with a connection to the informer, if not that very person him- or herself." He shook his head, feeling instinctively that the more people who knew of the accusations and the circumstances surrounding them, the more likely that Connie would go to jail.

"Ah, you fear the disclosure will add weight to the allegations," she said, reading his expression accurately and nodding slightly. "But you said yourself that the only way to protect against the assault is to know who is behind it. I have lived through many conflicts, Mr. Dunne, and the diabolical planning that goes into them can resemble the precise placement of a damning piece of gossip in many ways. The right catalyst will always cause a fire eventually, harder to put out once it's roared into full frenzy."

She picked up her spoon and, looking deeply into the crater she'd created in the middle of her soufflé, apparently decided she had nothing to fear from the heat within and started to eat. She smiled broadly in anticipation. Johnny watched her innocent pleasure knowing she was giving him time to change his mind. He was fully aware that to gain her confidence he had to earn her trust, and that would only happen if he offered her at least some of what she wanted. She was confirming that collaboration was the only way she'd help him help Emily.

"Your Highness," Johnny said very quietly, "you are a woman of royal blood, and you're used to getting what you want both privately and socially. But even more important to me is one of my oldest, and dearest friends, Emily de Koningh. Somehow I must find a way to protect her from the ruin that would crush her son, to save her. You apparently can't or won't help me unless I disclose information that might hurt Emily even more. I can't take that chance."

"That is fine," she said slowly, though he wasn't sure if she referred to his statement or her first taste of the soufflé, until she continued. "I admire and fully support your protection of Emily, but if you change your mind about including me in your plans, I'll then have a suggestion you might find useful." She looked up, shook her head slightly, and then smiled as if she and Johnny were both in complete agreement, making him feel that perhaps they were.

"I truly know very little." He could have added, *Which is why I asked you to lunch*, though that was already clear. He glanced at the door to the dining room again, but it was still closed, and the sentries had deserted their posts. He suddenly realized it must have been Pauline's shake of her head that had kept them away.

"I've signaled they must leave us alone," Pauline assured him as she read his glance. She'd accomplished what Johnny could not. She seemed in complete command of the meal now, so it was time for him to allow her control of the conversation. He dropped his voice, though there were no others present.

"The little I heard came from some of the young reporters who work on my paper," he said. "A couple of them belong to the gentlemen's clubs as well as the literary salons. I heard them discussing young Connie's fortune as well as his talent and suggesting that he'd be an all-around wunderkind if only he hadn't given in to the weakness of these 'high crimes.' Naturally, I tried to question them further, but I had no sense any of them knew anything definitive. Like most gossip, it was all speculation and innuendo, and I had to work particularly hard to appear disinterested." He bowed his head, and dropping his eyes to his dish, spoke with a little more force. "I've been upset by such dangerous talk since I heard it, and—if Connie continues his behavior in England, where the consequences are worse—I feel my hands are tied unless I can get the help of some of Emily's friends who might be concerned for her, too."

Pauline continued to eat her soufflé with steady determination, although it appeared she was nearly finished. Johnny on the other hand had barely touched his fish. "Mr. Dunne, if you do not finish your meal the chef will not allow us to return!" She laughed gently. "If you'll eat, I'll talk," she said. It seemed her care for another unusual woman of substance had given them a reason to befriend each other. He wasn't used to thinking of Emily with such a connection. He smiled back at the princess uncertainly, picking up his fork and fish knife to tackle his sole Dugléré, which was blessedly still warm. She waited for him to finish the first mouthful and start another before she spoke.

"So, my friend, it seems we are of one mind in many ways." The princess smiled easily at him, making him feel that large dark eyes were probably the best communicators of all. "We must protect Emily, which obviously means we must protect her son, from scandal. I care not what life he chooses. That's his own business, and if I could guarantee his happiness for both his and his family's sake, I certainly would. But I know nothing of what would assure that, and I challenge any human being to have that power."

Johnny wondered why he'd waited so long to make the princess's acquaintance. "So then, how can we do that—ensure Emily's happiness?" he asked, realizing immediately that he asked the impossible.

"Well, I don't have all the particulars fully thought out yet," Pauline said, quietly, "but there is only one person who owes me such a debt and knows it."

"And can you tell me who that is?" Johnny asked, wishing he hadn't finished the second bottle of wine, as he was beginning to feel less in control and assumed it must be because of the delicious white Bordeaux.

"Certainly," the princess answered, hands folded in her lap and a firm smile on her face that seemed to grow by the second. "It is particularly convenient that he happens to be the master of haute couture in the world today." Her dark eyes gave a snap of delight, just as Johnny found his voice.

"Charles Frederick Worth," he muttered, almost without thinking.

"Definitely," she answered, her smile now becoming a beam of delight.

"But how can he help us if he knows nothing?" Johnny asked.

"By finding out some facts," she said. "Who started these rumors and who is perpetuating them. Isn't that what you want to know?" She fixed her uncompromising gaze on him, holding his eyes with hers. "And the benefit to us will be his absolute commitment to silence and secrecy. He is the only person in the world I can say that about with confidence."

"I suppose the benefit is also that he's the very top of the profession Connie de Koningh wants to enter himself." A plate of fresh-baked madeleines had appeared magically on the table with a tray of deeply pungent coffee, and Johnny wrapped two of the delicious little sponge cakes in his extra handkerchief. ". . . for my assistant at the office," he explained with a sheepish grin.

"I understand," the princess responded. "You see the human connections very clearly, Mr. Dunne." He placed the delicacies gently in his coat pocket.

"But even if Mr. Worth promises not to utter a word of his discoveries to anyone, how can you be sure he'll keep his promise?"

"Because he owes me his life," the princess said with a smile.

10

THE POST

"THE POST," Brody announced. He'd have left Emily's letters on the hall table next to the mail chute if her door hadn't been standing partially open. He knew she'd been preparing to practice her violin, but he could see that she hadn't started yet. He held up two envelopes and nodded, suggesting they were both for her.

"Thank you, Brody, but you didn't need to . . . I'd have found them eventually. I'm not used to the regularity of the post here in London." She smiled her thanks as he started into the room to place the letters on the embossed green leather of her desktop.

"Not if the dog ate them on the floor right out of the letterbox," he grinned, shrugging a little as he knew full well Lord Alden had never owned a dog in the city. "You're not used to letterboxes in every front door, either." Lifting his elbow slightly to expose a brown package held against his side, he beamed at her like a child on his birthday. "I've been waiting for this," he said, with an unmistakable twinkle. When he was running the house on his own without her father's supervision, Brody had a lift to his voice, step, and expression, making him look younger than his sixty years.

"Has Christmas come early?" Emily asked. "If so, I hope you got what you wanted."

He nodded. "New reins for the carriage," he said, crinkling the package between his fingers and palms. "I can feel them! Straight from Italy, which is why they took so long." He looked as if there could be no more wonderful present in the world.

"Why from Italy?" she asked, trying to focus on her father's groomsman rather than the envelopes he'd just put in front of her. Both were of fine white paper, but one had unadorned male handwriting and a stamp for the Royal College of Music on the left side. The other was larger in every way, the envelope, the handwriting, and the decorative flourishes all standing out. Both letters were sealed with gum, but the larger one was also fixed with a red sealing wax stamp of the Metternich coat of arms, the plumes, helmets, and trappings of war predominant. Emily wanted to discover what was in the letters more than she wanted to know why reins must come from Italy.

"Because the leather is so fine there, and the more delicate the reins the better the communication, though the sooner they break, as well." Brody looked as if he wanted to open his package just as much as she wanted to read her letters.

"Really, Brody? I thought reins were only for slowing the horses down. Isn't calling it communication putting rather too fine a point on it?" She reached for the letters so she could feel them, as if the touch alone might reveal something of their contents as Brody's package had.

"No, no, Lady Emily. Communication isn't about one having the power to force the other to do what you want. There is a give and take making it a shared operation. Do you play your violin just to force people to sit down and look at the stage?"

"Of course not. But I think playing the world's most beautiful music on an ancient instrument is more communicative than holding a pair of reins in your hands." Brody looked at his wrinkled brown package for a few seconds. Then he looked back at Emily very seriously.

"The reins transfer information from the sender, the driver, to the animal, or receiver, to affect the behavior of the receiver. That is the purpose of all animal communication."

Emily stared at him. "Oh Brody," she sighed. "Will the influence of the stable never leave you?"

"I hope not, my lady," he chuckled. "Any more than the pull of the stage will ever leave you. But, let me point out that Britain's development of the post advanced our lives greatly. As we now have a prepaid postage stamp and regulated postal system, we know a thing or two about communication."

He looked so serious she almost laughed. She was not going to upset his equilibrium by pointing out that France and America were already moving down the same path as England, even if in a slightly different manner. "You send a letter to someone," he nodded in the direction of the envelopes in her lap, "to give them information that will affect them in some way, isn't that so?" She looked somewhat doubtful. "And it all starts with the animals," he added, bowing slightly, spinning on his heel, and disappearing out the door as fast as he'd appeared.

Getting up to close her sitting room door so she could be alone with her letters, Emily relished the thought of private time with her correspondents. A somewhat disquieting thought stirred as she realized she seldom had the kind of talks with others in person that she had in her letters anymore. Her early life as a child with Corey had been the last time she'd truly engaged another human being that fully in person. She wondered if it had had something to do with their shared passion for music. She'd sensed that possibly her new acquaintance with the young professor at the Royal College might have the same connection, in which case it would be the music again opening that same door.

She took the envelopes to the bureau next to her window seat. Natural light made reading easier, a benefit she'd discovered when setting her practice music up to play her violin. The house welcomed fresh air and sunshine with its big windows and high ceilings, and Emily always found ways to use the window seats to get closer to the outside. They reminded her of the dormers she'd read in as an adolescent in her father's rented house in New York.

She propped the envelopes side by side against the perfume bottles and studied them. Both followed the correspondence proto-col of the day, using the requisite pure white paper (never cream) and black ink (never blue). But there the envelopes diverged, already communicating separate messages. The smaller was addressed to her in a neat hand, the letters neither too small nor too large, and without any flourishes or ornamentation. She knew from the return address of the Royal College of Music this was probably from Professor Stanford, to whom she'd sent an apology only yesterday. The multi-ple mail deliveries a day in London sped up connections. None of the other capital cities of the world had anything like that kind of efficiency. Was it because of Queen Victoria's promotion of the Uniform Penny Post with her picture on the Penny Black stamp; or had that been Prince Albert's idea? Either way, Brody was right that it had encouraged the growth of the British society. She could feel an acceleration of life everywhere in England that hadn't been notice-able when she was a child.

The larger of the envelopes was, in fact, a little too big to be considered entirely tasteful. The beautiful handwriting was too bold to be as ladylike as it should be from a woman of prominence. The scrolls and flourishes had given away the writer's gender even before Emily noticed the Metternich coat of arms stamped into the sealing wax. That, too, was an unnecessary embellishment as the envelopes were both gummed at the flaps in back. But the wax was red in a nod to convention while stepping just outside the bounds of propriety. There could be no doubt the envelope was addressed by Pauline Clémentine Marie Walburga, Princess of Metternich-Winneburg zu Beilstein. Emily smiled at the divergence of styles, clearly demon-strative of the discrepancy of lives as well. She'd leave Pauline's for last, knowing it would throb with her friend's intellect and passion and she'd need time to absorb it.

Professor Stanford's note would no doubt simply acknowledge her apology for her father's waste of the professor's precious time. She'd affirmed no interest in teaching violin on a regular basis and admitted she had no idea where her father had gotten the idea. She privately worried at his obvious manipulation of the professor's attention but wrote she hoped a sizable donation to the new college would make up for the inconvenience. She'd added her own willingness to help on an occasional basis, depending on the professor's need.

She picked up the delicate silver letter opener that had been her mother's and slit the flap on the professor's envelope cleanly and quickly. She was surprised to see there were two sheets of paper, creased together with a tight fold, and the second one had a small, hand-drawn sketch of a violin and piano together next to the signature. How had he found time between his teaching, composing, conducting, and attending to his own personal life to answer her letter mailed only a few hours ago? His response seemed instantaneous. She held the letter open with both hands and started to read.

My Dear Madame de Koningh,

Thank you for your thoughtful note just received. I assure you time spent in the company of both you and your father has been nothing but a pleasure. In fact, I look greatly forward to more time together enjoying our shared love of music . . .

How could that be? Had her father suggested a greater involvement to the professor than to her?

. . . It was such a pleasure to meet you in person, and I would love to hear more about your experiences performing in Europe and America and share anecdotes of the musicians we have both been blessed to know.

How had he ever gotten the idea that they should discuss other musicians? Did he think she wanted to meet him socially?

I was certainly sorry to learn of your disinterest in teaching, but I understand. It is not for everyone.

It had never crossed her mind before . . .

I suppose I am motivated by the creation of a musical legacy, a dynasty for this country, more than anything specifically for myself. When I am with the students, faculty, orchestras, and choruses at the college I feel I am home with my family. It is the best place I can be.

There was family or there was work—what did he mean that work is family?

I hope you will find an afternoon to share lunch with me at one of our better restaurants, such as the one at the Langham Hotel we passed through recently like ships in the night. I feel sure we have a collaboration in our future and hope we can pursue it together.

All my best wishes to you for now, and the morrow,
Professor C. Villiers Stanford, at the Royal College of Music

Emily stared at the letter in her hands. It was perfectly contained and the tone polite, but instead of the Royal College closing its door, it seemed to have opened wider than before. Professor Stanford seemed not to have entirely accepted her refusal of his offer to teach, but she wasn't quite sure if she'd imagined that. Perhaps she was inventing reasons to accept his invitation to lunch. The time left her to react and reply had also been shortened by the unaccustomed speed of the post, so Emily felt lunch with the professor at the Langham Hotel looming imminently and irrevocably. The charming sketch of a piano and violin next to the professor's signature did little to ease her discomfort at not understanding her own motivation. She folded the letter, slipping it back in its envelope and putting that aside on the lace dressing tablecloth, facedown.

Still propped up on her bureau and waiting to be acknowledged was the unusual envelope from Princess Pauline. With the contents of the professor's letter so gently coercive, Emily felt herself bracing for something overwhelming inside the other. Maybe she should wait to open it, giving herself time to think freely about the first. No one would know, after all. Just because the envelope had arrived in the post box she didn't have to read it. Actually, she did. The reliability of the post made a letter impossible to ignore. Everyone knew when they stuck the stamp of Queen Victoria in the right-hand corner that it would arrive safely at its destination, and, perhaps within hours. Professor Stanford would expect a response, which is what kept his door propped open, and Pauline would wonder what was wrong with Emily if she didn't hear from her soon and might start concocting theories. Her letter clearly and loudly demanded attention.

Rejecting the precision of her mother's letter opener, Emily broke the wax seal on the back of the envelope, sliding her thumb under the flap and prying it up with a jagged tear she thought her mother would have forgiven. The four-page letter slid out easily, however, a testament to the quality of its beautiful, smooth white paper. She could see the oversized handwriting undoubtedly accounted for the extra space needed before the signature affixed to the last page. A large and decorative "Your true friend, Pauline," hailed her as she carefully collected the pages together and moved to the window seat, dropping down with a small sigh.

Always there seemed to be an interruption when she wanted to practice her violin. It had been that way ever since she could remember. She spent less time practicing now than she had when she was young, but she reasoned that was because all the hours between the years added up to enough preparation to satisfy any performance requirement that could ever be made of her. She'd had to spend a little extra effort getting used to her new instrument when she'd first come to France, but that had happened within the first year, and then she and it were as good as old friends—as close as Professor Haussmann's Guarneri she'd grown up with in America.

So the interruption of Pauline's letter was probably not responsible for her tension and anxiety. It was as if both Professor Stanford and Princess Pauline were sitting beside her. The pressure of social interaction bothered her most of the time. Now that she'd raised her children and promoted her musical career, she'd come to realize she preferred her own company and that of her instrument and music to others. Yet she truly was part of this world, and she knew the loneliness of abandonment only too well, with a mother who'd died when she was thirteen and a father who'd left her on a friend's doorstep in order to travel more freely. If Professor Stanford was right about one's collaborators being family—and she thought he might be— then the family she'd always wanted could be positioned around her if she reached out to the musical community directly. She launched into Pauline's letter with a sigh.

It began, "My dearest friend, Emily." She knew Pauline tended toward hyperbole, yet also that she felt everything at the deepest level, and so it didn't seem outrageous to be identified as one of her "dearest" friends. There were so many wonderful composers and musicians of the day the princess had discovered and adopted; Emily could only take the suggestion of intimacy as a compliment. And truthfully, she felt an odd connection to Pauline, bordering on the kind of friendships she usually had only with men. The princess's intellect and interests, to say nothing of her energy and approach to life, were unapologetically similar to those of the males of European society. Americans were a little different, but not much. Pauline most resembled that careless freedom Emily had claimed for herself when she was young, only to find out she couldn't ride it easily into adulthood. Pauline's tone and the events she chose to focus on and relate made Emily feel as if the two of them had been galloping off together, playing, dancing, and laughing through the princess's myriad costumed parties, private theatricals and salons all leaping to life on the pages of her letter . . . until she reached the unexpected account of the princess's lunch at the Café Anglais with Johnny Dunne.

Emily put the letter down in her lap and looked out the window toward the stables. What a powerful and daunting twosome the princess and the editor made, the vision in her mind taking on a sense of unreality as she imagined them running the world together from a private dining room at the famous café. She laughed silently and shook her head. She'd been the one to introduce them at her family's farewell party in Vienna and it hadn't seemed as if the princess even noticed Johnny more than to register him on a list of "once met" acquaintances.

How had the impression of each on the other been made so strongly? They were both such influential people, but one was paid to exert his beliefs through information gathered openly in pursuit of his work, and the other surreptitiously in support of her social life. Yet the results were much the same, and both were trusted by those they led as experts with knowledge not available to everyone else. Their social relationships were their greatest assets, and just as Pauline recognized the artistic connections with men and occasionally women she promoted to their and her advantage, she'd apparently recognized that Johnny also had that wealth of shared contacts. The difference was that he'd obtained his one way and she acquired hers another.

The ramifications of the lunch at the Café Anglais ran around in Emily's head like the warning rumble of thunder in the distance. There was still another page to finish the letter, plenty of room for trouble Emily didn't want to face. She knew them both too well. Stiffening her back and sitting up straighter on the window seat, she read on. Before she knew it, she'd arrived at Pauline's signature with no earth-shaking discoveries of talk shared between two friends. A suggestion from Pauline to write to Johnny so he wouldn't worry about her certainly made sense. But she couldn't ignore the fact that her friends were more engaged in her trouble with her sons than she was. She'd said nothing further to Connie about his arrival with Lady Sandhurst at the Langham, and had ignored William's often sullen presence in the house, as always. And in addition, there was an announcement of a pending trip for Pauline to London to have some dresses made by Charles Worth, who'd traveled to his place of birth for family matters. It was just like the princess to be unable to wait for his return to Paris for a fitting. She trusted no one but him to take the measurements. And perhaps she could introduce Emily's younger son to the master of haute couture while she was there. That made Emily's heart jump with pleasure, as it could do nothing but good for Connie's career to have Monsieur Worth critique some of his fashion sketches. What a wonderful opportunity! And an easy way for her to put difficult thoughts behind her and focus on a happy outcome for her younger son.

Emily smiled, thinking of the pleasure it would give her to connect with Pauline again, but this time in her own birthplace—London.

"I'm here at last!" A cry rang out, ricocheting down the entry hall of the Alden town house on Grosvenor Square. Emily's head shot up as her mouth formed the words "Aunt Clara"—unexpected, unwanted, and undeniably her father's busybody spinster sister they'd found ways to avoid for the last thirty years. It was not by chance that Lord Alden had removed his daughter from the home that would have been dominated by Aunt Clara after his young wife died. "Clara is not the solution," she'd heard him say to Klaas de Koningh. "She is the problem."

And so Emily had been able to avoid her aunt with her father's help, other than a few visits in New York and chance meetings during performances in Europe. Yet here she was, without warning or preparation, invading Emily's family life and privacy as if they were nothing. She jumped to her feet, Pauline's letter slipping to the floor unnoticed, and glanced quickly around the room as if for a place to hide just as the door flew open and Clara sailed in. "Oh Emily, dear," she crowed, sweeping across the floor in a full black skirt with many crinolines beneath, looking for all the world like a relic from a portrait of some bygone era. "How lovely to find you in repose and uninvolved." She shoved her face up to Emily's, presenting her cheek for a welcome kiss that she didn't get. Instead, Emily stared at her aunt incredulously.

"I had no idea you were expected," she said, firmly. "And I rather doubt my father did, either." She did her best to hold on to her patience and stay as calm and polite as possible. But she would not be intimidated by the likes of Aunt Clara when she'd spent most of her life dealing with concert managers who wanted to push her around and cut her pay any chance they got.

"Oh dearest," Aunt Clara warbled, "there wasn't time. I knew I'd be welcome whenever I got here and I didn't want to miss your visit, although I know your father feels you'll be staying indefinitely!" Emily's look of polite disbelief began to sour, and she pulled back enough to stare at her assailant, eyeing her from her head to her feet.

"Have you ever heard of the post, Aunt Clara?" she asked. "There was most certainly plenty of time to reassure yourself of a welcome in a house that is full to the brim with people now, all going in different directions with different needs and scheduling demands." She had started to feel surer of herself, knowing her father would have been even less accommodating to his sister than she was. "And in fact, this is not a good time at all. I don't know that we can accommodate you even overnight."

"I saw Brody outside and he said the boys can stay together so the guest room will be available for me. He's always so willing." She smiled innocently, taking a couple of large hat pins from the top of her bonnet wrapped in a dark lace veil, and removing the hat while she lifted her puff of gray hair where the hat had smashed it down. "The post is not for families," she said, looking at her image in the bureau's mirror. "It's just for industry—for making money and other vulgarities. Not for nice people." She turned to face Emily again. "Will you let your father know I've arrived?" Emily wondered if she'd lost some of her legendary determination. She wasn't communicating well, but was that her fault or because her aunt refused to hear her?

"It seems to me you could have done that yourself, Aunt Clara. You've had no trouble communicating your wishes in the past, but the post would really have been the thoughtful way to do it this time. What if Father had been away on one of his trips for the Crown?"

"Oh, I knew you'd be here, and you're the one I came to see. Brody," she called out, somehow intuiting he was coming in the front door at that moment. "Brody, will you take my bags up to the guest room please, and let Lord Alden know I've arrived. Lady Emily is not in a mood to be helpful." She swooped out of the room, leaving with a sardonic glance in Emily's direction.

"Oh, Lord in heaven," Emily groaned, leaning down to pick up the princess's letter she'd just noticed at her feet. "I don't know if I can live through this."

Then, feeling the weight of the letter in her hand, she put it on the bureau with the professor's, a slow smile spreading across her face. She would need to be away from the house in Grosvenor Square as much as possible while Aunt Clara was in it, and the letters offered opportunities to make that happen. She took them over to her desk and pulled out her white stationery, black ink, and pen. She could rely on the professor getting her answer fairly quickly and so would count on him first as her means of escape. He might even be able to provide some engagement with his musical "family" for her, keeping her away from her own home and family. Pauline would take up the slack in the schedule when she arrived, and Connie would keep them all busy with his new possibilities at the House of Worth. There would be no time to get tangled up in one of Aunt Clara's webs with so many other social connections to be made immediately. *Thank heaven for the post.*

When she'd finished answering Professor Stanford's letter with a grateful acceptance of his suggestion of lunch, she'd go out to one of the pillar boxes to send it so there would be no questions about it, or opportunities to slow it down in the house. Pauline's would take a little longer to write and leaving that response on the hall table for posting later might solicit the kind of curiosity from Aunt Clara that Emily could welcome. Her aunt would know that the Princess von Metternich was well out of her league where social relationships were concerned. The possibility of meeting her might even frighten her enough to encourage an early departure! *Yes, indeed, thank heaven for the post.*

And yet, Emily couldn't push the burning fear for Connie's reputation down far enough behind these distractions to avoid its pain. Pauline's letter made it clear there were rumors around Connie's social connections spreading fast enough to include the news media in France. Johnny's worry about her emotional health suggested those who knew her expected her to be in serious trouble. Pretending to herself that none of this was true would never hold her family together with the threat of the discovery of sodomy swirling around in ways she should have dealt with much sooner. Denying the trial of what they were all going to go through now and in the future wasn't going to stop its advance on her family. If some solution to the metastasizing accusations around Connie wasn't found, she knew they, and particularly she herself, would not survive.

11

SURPRISE!

HE'D SUGGESTED several different restaurants when she'd shown obvious discomfort returning to the Langham Hotel where'd they'd first met. Billingsgate Diner (for fish), Crosby Hall (nice place for proper ladies), the Saloon Dining-room at the Crystal Palace—there was really no shortage of respectable places to eat with a married woman in London. When she'd finally decided the Langham was just as good as any other, he pointed out that the Langham might be too busy for a quiet, uninterrupted discussion. When he'd suggested Crosby's to remove them from the hubbub of London, she'd said she was fine with whatever he thought best. How just like a woman it was, he thought, even though the change of direction had truly been his. And yet he knew this woman was not like any other. She played a violin on the concert stage, for one thing, and raised a family in a sophisticated European household at the same time, for another. He'd expected to meet someone inappropriately outside the bounds of conservative society when her father suggested the connection, but had been pleasantly surprised by the lovely, intelligent, balanced woman who'd presented herself.

It was interesting, and even a little exciting, that she wasn't what he'd expected. Perhaps he'd surprised her, as well. He knew his students and even his colleagues thought of him as deeply and fervently conservative in music and politics. Yet he knew there were many areas where the traditionalists would break ranks with him, his passionate belief that women belonged in the profession of music among them. It was enough to make anyone with a sense of irony chuckle to think of how eagerly he'd rebelled against his early music teacher's desiccated ideals. Carl Reinecke had forced him to find his own way with the romanticism of Brahms and Schumann, both of whom Reinecke loathed and sneered at. Yet perhaps his own love of that classic idiom had in turn forced his own students to rebel in ways he couldn't yet appreciate. They might surprise him yet.

He looked out the door with more purpose, focusing on the few arrivals of carriages but seeing no one he recognized. He'd realized how much more inconvenient Crosby's was to get to, offering to pick her up in his carriage, but she'd demurred, saying she could get there on her own. Of course she could. Her father had a coach and driver. So now, Charles Stanford awaited Emily as he watched with some impatience unfamiliar Londoners coming and going. There was much he wanted to discuss with her. It had been so long since he'd visited France or Austria, and he wondered how she felt the audiences there were changing with the modern influences of Wagner and Liszt, and the waning interest in Brahms, Schumann, and Mendelssohn. He also wanted to share with her the discovery of Schubert's incidental music to *Rosamunde* in his nephew's home by his composer friends Arthur Sullivan and George Grove. He knew she'd be thrilled about that in a way few today would understand.

Feeling a change in the anticipatory energy around Crosby's front door, he cleared his vision again to see what might have caused it. Suddenly Emily stood before him, her dark eyes shining and cheeks as pink as if she'd spent a scandalous afternoon hatless on a sunny beach. Her black hair was tied tightly under a small-brimmed straw bonnet with a beige ribbon circling the crown. A double-breasted dark brown jacket with fitted sleeves exposed a white blouse filling in the chest, and her neck was protected with a silk ascot. A light woolen skirt appeared to be no more than three-quarters of the way down her calves, which in turn were covered with high brown kid boots.

"Where did you come from?" he gasped, realizing he'd been staring at her in surprise as if at an apparition that had magically materialized from a vapor. "I never saw the carriage." He bowed slightly, an apology for his lack of alertness. Beaming as if thrilled by the amount of dislocation she'd caused, Emily wiped her forehead with her gloved right hand, pushing a recalcitrant strand of black hair back under the brim of her hat. He worried that her face was glistening with the exertion that must have come from descending from her carriage without his help.

"I didn't come by carriage," she said. "I'm sorry to upset you so, Professor, but I rode my bicycle here. Father's carriage was gone early, and I had no intention of waiting, or keeping you waiting, for that matter." His pince-nez spectacles dropped and hung uselessly by their ribbon from his vest as his eyes opened wide. Her delightful laugh when she saw the surprise on his face sounded like bells ringing in his head.

"You didn't!" He stared at her with the confusion of a far-sighted man.

"I certainly did, and the half hour or so it took me was the most fun I've had since I came to London! Do you ride, Professor? Well, you should if you don't. I sense it's just what a sedentary musician needs to stay healthy and fend off the ravages of middle age—although on second thought you don't have to worry about that quite yet."

"Madame de Koningh, how did you learn to ride such a contraption? Probably in France." He fumbled for his glasses and replaced them on the bridge of his nose, looking at her closer once they were settled.

"Not at all. I learned indoors in one of the London riding schools. There are so many of those gymnasiums here." Her breathing seemed to be slowing down and she started to remove her gloves.

"I had nothing like that in Paris or Vienna, but England leads the way in the art of cycling, and my younger son and I decided to make the most of it. I saw an advertisement for a gymnasium in Sloane Square that rented English cycles, and so off we went. We both did rather well at it, though it took a few lessons!"

"I can't fathom why you were ever interested in it," the professor said, staring at her as if he had trouble believing her.

"I found the whole idea intriguing when I read about them years ago. The idea that a woman can be entirely emancipated from the need to rely on others for transportation enticed me, and when you add the health benefits and sheer exhilaration of the speed and contact with nature, one's interest in it is anything but surprising. In fact, I think the bicycle could be the most influential, revolutionary change in society we'll see in our lifetimes."

"Revolutionary—"

"Absolutely! It's even been suggested the composition of society in England will change with the increased mobility. There will be new opportunities for people to connect to others they'd never have met without it. Mr. Darwin's theory of natural selection may have a whole new pool to draw from."

"M-Madame de Koningh," the professor stuttered.

"Emily, please, Professor. And would it be possible for me to call you Charles? I do hope so, as I believe we may become friends." Professor Stanford nodded his head. "And to promote that, could we start into the dining room? I've found that riding a bicycle for any length of time greatly increases the appetite!" Turning toward the inner dining room, in full view from the doorway, Emily started to lead the way as if the invitation to lunch had been hers rather than his. "And I do apologize for my somewhat disheveled appearance, Professor. I know the accepted preference for women who ride is for a calm, ladylike demeanor with no change in feminine fashion to rational clothing and no heightened complexion. I can handle the call for decorum now that I've conquered my balance on the two wheels, but the exercise makes one's complexion glow, much as a half-hour performance on stage might. There's no way to avoid that, and frankly, I wouldn't want to. I think cycling every day has given me more stamina for the violin."

Charles finally stopped staring at his guest, moving after her to the dining room and noticing that much to his amazement, her skirt was divided in back. The pantaloons were not visible from the front where a flat panel of matching fabric covered them as a front fold of a kilt might.

"Clever," he said, laughing a little.

"What was that, Charles?"

"Your . . . partial skirt," he said. "It must make the riding a lot easier, and it's only half of a commitment to rational clothing."

"Why Charles," Emily smiled, two dimples showing on either side of her mouth. "I'm surprised you approve. Maybe you're not as conservative as I thought," she added, accepting the seat he pulled out for her with a small, gracious nod of her head. He seated himself opposite her, but as the tables were barely big enough for two, they were still quite close. He pushed his chair back slightly, ostensibly to make room for his slightly longer than average legs. She laughed quietly, almost to herself, and then remembered to include him.

"I was just remembering the first time I wore 'rational clothing' decades ago on a mountain-climbing expedition in Switzerland," she said. "It was my first trip to Europe, ostensibly my 'grand tour' with my teacher to experience the violin's pinnacle of performance with the world's best musicians. I discovered many things on that trip at the age of twenty, and one was the 'new' rational clothing, which I purchased to shock my teacher more than to free myself, I fear." She chuckled again. "Oh, if he could only see me now on my new bicycle!"

"I was just thinking before you arrived that I'm viewed as especially conservative by many, but in many ways, I'm not. I suspect that's true for all of us. We just need to take the time to discover our shared values." Emily looked up at him as if she hadn't seen him clearly before. "For example," he said with a twinkle in his blue eyes, "I quite like the idea of riding a bicycle to work at the Royal College. I might have to get the name of that cycling school you mentioned. I sense my students would think I'd become eccentric early in life, but they might also appreciate me as a vibrant contemporary instead of a dried-up old fossil. Shall we order?" he asked. Emily's smile spread across her face, and she nodded slowly.

Having eaten her meal with a gusto undoubtedly resulting from her ride across London that morning, Emily now settled down to enjoy a large cup of purposely lukewarm tea, the perfect rejuvenating beverage before her return ride to Grosvenor Square. As the professor had little time to eat during his narratives about teaching the future great musicians of Britain, and the discoveries of musical treasures by his colleagues and friends, Emily drew his attention to the food still awaiting his commitment. She made conjectures about the part of London they were dining in, and the old Crosby Hall itself, to give him time to finish his meal at last.

She reminded the professor that she hadn't spent much time in London as a child, and almost none once she'd started touring with her violin as a young adult. She knew they were now in a portion of town dating back to the Roman era and that Bishopsgate was part of the original defense system of that pre-Norman world, but that was where her trivial knowledge ended. She'd found it surprising that there was so much history infusing everything in this city she'd considered vaguely inferior to the other capitals of Europe. Whether that was just because she had a natural disregard for the place she'd been born and a reverence for all things other, she didn't know. But Charles tried to ignite her interest without overburdening her.

"Shakespeare was a resident of this area for a while," he told her. "And Richard the Third and Thomas Moore both lived here." He had to work to finish his roast beef and Yorkshire pudding.

"In this very building?" Emily asked, incredulous with the

possibilities. She would take a better look at the architecture outside, remembering out loud that when she'd spotted it first on her cycling trip, the four-story structure had looked surprisingly like an ornamented house in a country village.

"And also the first printing of the *Communist Manifesto* happened right around here, if I recall correctly," he offered, pausing over his fork. She smiled at him, raising an eyebrow in disbelief. He nodded back, ruefully.

"There are many complex layers to the culture of this country going back so far," Charles said, as he glanced around at the old beams and floorboards of the inn. "It's time our musical culture receives some of the reverence shown the more antique cultures of Europe. I've always felt Prince Albert was trying to help us take our rightful place in so many ways. I'm working to make that happen in the Royal College, and especially where both musical composition and conducting are concerned." He pushed his cup away with a small sigh of contentment.

"Composition . . . and conducting?" Emily asked, staring at the professor with curiosity. "Orchestral works, choral pieces, operas, songs . . . ?"

He nodded, tapping the table in time to her musical queries. "Of course. They're my main commitment, although there are too many to mention. Why do you look so shocked? Do you think one has to be Austrian or French, or maybe Russian, to compose with any level of success? Nonsense. Of course Britain can join those ranks, and I predict the next generation we train will do just that!" He slipped the lovely old gold watch from his vest pocket, and looking satisfied with whatever it revealed, signaled a waiter to refill his cup. "We have time for another if you'd like one as well," he added as an afterthought. "I seem to be forgetting my manners. It must be your emancipation."

"I would join you, then," Emily answered, nodding when the waiter came to the table. "Your involvement in a whole different area of music education fascinates me. I'd like to hear more," she said, obviously genuine in her attention. Even the slip of the burly waiter, missing her cup and adding some tea to the saucer, didn't distract her. "Correct me if I'm wrong, Charles, but you personally teach piano and composition, as well as chorus and performance. You've also mentioned teaching new conductors and using the college's orchestra to give both them and the composers a platform. Have I left anything out?" He smiled, nodding slightly.

"Many things," he said. "But they're all adjuncts to those you mentioned. Do you not see yourself somewhere in that panorama of musical offerings?"

She smiled back at him and shook her head. "No, Charles, I'm not a teacher like you or my first great mentor, Professor Haussmann. I don't share your calling."

"Yet there are so many other needs. A professional to stimulate and guide the string quartets in chamber music is essential, and as we have no Brahms or Haydn to do that for us, I was hoping perhaps you would see that position of musical leadership as more to your liking."

"I suppose," Emily said almost under her breath, "maybe . . . I remember in France I worked with some young men on the Schumann String Quartet in A Major. They were professional adult musicians, but we accomplished quite a lot, I think." She chuckled a little at the memory. "I was first violin, but the second and cello got so tangled in poor Mr. Schumann's crazy tensions I thought they'd fly off their chairs. It was a blessing that the violist understood, so we were both able to bring those two hot air balloons down to the ground safely, with Mr. Schumann's anxieties a bit more subtle and contained. It worked well, in the end." She smiled with obvious pleasure at the memory, and the professor nodded with delight.

"You see?" he said. "I knew it. You'd be a wonderful tutor for our chamber music groups. I hope you'll at least consider it if you won't run the entire violin department." He excused himself, finding the waiter and paying him thoughtfully out of his female companion's sight. When he returned to the table, Emily was already standing with that sense of earnest eagerness he'd come to appreciate during their lunch together.

"Charles, could we put my bicycle up in the luggage compartment of the carriage so I could ride with you back to the college?" she asked. "There are many more things I want to discuss, and I don't want to waste any time with you in the carriage while I'm on my bicycle."

"Don't they have bicycles for two?" he said, smiling at her so fully she thought she'd not known him at all before today.

"They do," she nodded with her dimples in full evidence again, "but from what I've seen of them a thoughtful discussion would be impossible. I can't imagine anything but a courtship being a success while trying to balance together. I also think one or the other must be in charge of the directional control, and it seems to me that defeats the purpose of emancipation." She grinned at him again, clearly enjoying the shared foolishness of the challenges of such a contrivance. "You're a composer, Charles. Could you compose a song about the trials of riding such a contraption with another?" she asked, perhaps more coquettishly than she'd intended.

"Certainly. The lyrical narrative line is all it takes. I'm a romantic of heart and head, and that must always rule the song," he said, looking down at her.

"How interesting. Is that my first lesson in composition? I'd like a few more."

He nodded. "Well then, we shall certainly stow your cycle on the carriage, although I'm surprised you'd put up with the loss of freedom. But if it offers me a chance of you coming to work with me at the college, I'll gladly support the cause." He led the way out to the carriage, instructing his driver to collect Emily's unusual cargo.

While they waited for the cycle to appear, he smiled at Emily and said, "This is a good opportunity for us both. I had hoped for our conversation." She looked back up at him, then turned to watch as the driver and restaurant manager lifted her cycle up to the luggage compartment and tied it down carefully for her approval. She nodded, but to whom, Charles couldn't be sure.

"Oh, it's not me you need, Charles," she said, leveling her unwavering gaze back at him. "It's indubitably my husband!"

12

STABLE FAMILY

DARLING BOYS. It was Aunt Clara's favorite identification for William and Connie. Everyone was suspicious she couldn't tell them apart or remember their names—a strange anomaly if true as they looked so dissimilar, but Emily had always given her the benefit of the doubt by reminding the family Aunt Clara saw them only occasionally. William was annoyed by the label, but Connie found it amusing. Hearing the unwelcome greeting ring out through the entrance hall in a clarion call from the library, Emily knew the family had come together for tea, an exceedingly rare occurrence.

She smiled ruefully at the irony of her aunt's visit. She longed for the family to congregate more often, afternoon tea being the perfect time, yet the one day they did, an annoying, gossipy maiden aunt greeted them unannounced. That would probably make them turn and run from gatherings in the Alden house in the future to avoid unwelcome surprises. Emily hesitated in the hall, picturing her boys dealing with Aunt Clara in the timeworn ways. William would be rolling his eyes and sighing. Connie would be laughing and hugging her, which seemed to upset her more than eye-rolling.

In addition to her aunt and her sons, Corey and Lord Alden were in the library as well, truly a full family congregation. How the two senior men of the clan were dealing with the inconvenience of Aunt Clara, Emily couldn't imagine. She started toward the front hall with a wish to disappear before she entered the library. "Clarissa," she heard her father say forcefully, "we are anything but a typical British family, but we won't be changing our ways to oblige you. Like it or not, we will all continue as we are, and that includes your niece, who was teaching this afternoon at the Royal College of Music. Her conference was set up prior to your arrival. She has nothing to apologize for— Ah, here she comes now." He'd spotted Emily poised in the doorway and gave her a look filled with meaning. A greeting, a warning, a plea for help, and complaint of outrage all seemed wrapped up in that one glance. Lord Alden was clearly unhappy with his sister's spontaneous arrival and her comments before Emily entered the room. The mistress of the house was tempted to turn around and run off to the stable, grabbing her bicycle and spinning off someplace with no predictable tension or demands.

"Good afternoon, everyone," Emily said, trying to stay calm as she looked around the room. "I apologize for missing tea, but when you get involved with students, scheduling can be a very fluid thing. I had no idea I'd been at the college so long." She smiled at her father standing with Aunt Clara in the middle of the library. Emily knew how invested he'd become in her participation at the music school, though not exactly why. Yet she was not above using his questionable motivation to her own advantage now. "I know Father represents me well, although I am the lady of the house and thus in charge of the family's social responsibilities." She smiled at Aunt Clara pointedly, making sure she understood where her niece was positioned in the hierarchy. "Though it's hard to fulfill those duties if people arrive without warning."

One last look at her father who tried to smother a smirk, obviously proud of her improvised performance, and she knew they were at least momentarily in complete agreement. It was an oddly satisfying instant. Scanning the room again, she saw that Corey sat in the reading chair next to the windows, a book resting on his knee as if he'd forgotten it with the surprise of their guest's interruption. William and Connie both perched on velvet ottomans near the fireplace, seemingly prepared to take flight at any moment. And Aunt Clara could not have been there long as she still hovered in the middle of the room.

"And I, too, must apologize for missing your entrance, or arrival if you will," Corey said, winking at his sons as he stood, putting down his book and moving past them, and then turning to take Aunt Clara's hand and kissing it with all the chivalric courtesy he could muster. "You look very chic in a Victorian kind of way," Corey told her. Turning to his younger son who so resembled him in a shorter package, he said, "Connie, stand please to greet your great-aunt. Now, what can you tell her about ladies' current fashions in Europe that might contribute to the wardrobe I'm sure she's here to purchase?" Corey gestured to offer his wife's aunt his now vacant chair, but Aunt Clara shook her head.

"I can't tell her much," Connie said, unable to choke back the laugh he and his father were sharing, "as I'm newly in London myself. But I can see from her choice of color and material she's copied the queen's widow's weeds to perfection. I could only suggest fewer crinolines beneath the skirt to give it a more updated look. But you might also consider a short skirt, Aunt Clara, all the rage now; though then the hoops must definitely be abandoned, or you'll resemble a tea tray about to take off in a wind. Still, you look lovely as always, Aunt Clara . . . and youthful beyond your years," he added, blue eyes dancing under his waves of blond hair, and two remarkably familiar dimples inherited from his mother deepening as he tried hard not to smile too broadly. Everyone else snuck furtive peeks around the room under lowered lashes, trying to hide the merriment Connie's evaluation of Aunt Clara's personal fashion statement had brought to the surface.

"Please excuse me as well as the other latecomers," William said, rising and bowing slightly to his great-aunt. "I can add nothing to this cultural exchange, but I must dress for drinks at Grandfather's club. I'll be out for dinner, too," he added with a glance in Emily's direction.

"Darling, darling boy, why would you want to dine away from the family in one of those clubs? You have such a lovely home right here!" Aunt Clara accepted the two requisite kisses from William, one on each cheek, but she strengthened her grip on his sleeve like an osprey in possession of a catch. It made his imminent escape all but impossible. "Which club is it?" she asked, still clinging to William's arm with her remarkably strong grasp while she looked over at her brother, Lord Alden. "Is your grandpapa assisting in this domestic defection?"

Lord Alden moved over to the tea tray to pour another cup for himself. "It's White's or Boodle's, I suppose, depending on whether he wants to gamble or not." Raising an eyebrow at Emily, her father caught her nod and started to fill the last unclaimed cup for her. "No, he hasn't been accepted for membership yet, but yes, I have put his name in for both clubs at his request."

"My, you are a jack-of-all-trades, aren't you, Your Lordship," Aunt Clara said, noting her brother's adaptation to serving the tea for his daughter, and finally letting go of William because it was clear he could no longer escape without knocking down his grandfather at the tea tray if he moved forward. "Have a little port or something with us now," Aunt Clara said to William. "We can offer you anything you can get at that club, whichever one it is. My, haven't you become the handsome man!" she gushed, looking William up and down as he paused in flight.

"Yes, do stay a while," Emily chimed in. "I haven't seen much of you over the last few weeks, and it would be lovely to talk with everyone together, the way it should be in a family. Tell me, William," she said, thanking her father for her tea silently with a smile and a nod, "why do men feel they need those places? Women don't, which I suppose is a good thing since they won't let them join anyway. But men's clubs have really gained in popularity, I think, and I honestly don't know why. Do you not miss the company of women when you have free time to socialize?" She looked pointedly at William after glancing around the room again.

Then, turning to Lord Alden, she said, "Father, since this is one of your clubs William is frequenting, can you explain to the rest of us what you men see in them?" She took a deep sip of her tea, then went to one of the small side chairs with her cup to show she was intending to settle in with them. Connie had already moved over to hold her chair for her, and then sat down next to her to share a small table between them. His face still shone with pleasure, but he clearly had no intention of adding anything to the discussion. He was a member of the audience enjoying the family show.

Corey, obviously used to his wife's familial role as chief provocateur, stayed seated by the bay window in the wing chair he'd been enjoying before his reading was interrupted by the arrival of the tea tray and Emily's aunt. As a child, he'd shared that role of instigator with her, no adventure too daring, no prank too outrageous. But that had changed after their marriage, and even his commitment to writing music had all but disappeared, even though he and his wife still performed together because he was such a good intuitive accompanist. There was an unspoken connection between him and his younger son as well, both adopting safe positions as cheerful observers rather than continuous participants. Aunt Clara still stood close to William, keeping an eye on her quarry in case he tried to wriggle away.

"You're not mistaken," Lord Alden said to Emily. "London has hundreds of clubs now, which shows they must fill a need." He glanced at William and the two most class-conscious Alden family members exchanged a knowing smile. "Of course there's an exclusivity that appeals to some people, a way to climb the social ladder." Emily's focus was already drifting, and Aunt Clara seemed exasperated by her brother's interruption.

"But surely that has no appeal to you, Darling Boy," William's great-aunt gushed, almost swooning in appreciation of her great-nephew's fairy-tale good looks. "Your grandfather is already on the top rung of that ladder, so you must be after something else. Why would you forgo a lovely evening here at home with—" she looked around the room, waving her hand as if at a loss for words, "—with us, or with some beautiful lady of your choice?" she finished triumphantly.

"I agree completely with Aunt Clara," Emily said, "surprising though that may seem," she added under her breath. "It's very hard to keep a family together emotionally if they're always apart physically. Life with you all is like herding cats!" she exclaimed in exasperation.

William stepped purposefully around his great-aunt with one large stride sideways, and having opened up a path of escape to the door, he now felt free to turn and face the audience. "A gentleman's club is meant to be the antithesis of his family world," William said, looking at his mother, and then to his grandfather for support. "It's a means of confirming his . . . masculinity," he added, finally in possession of the exact word he'd been searching for. "It provides a safe place away from women, where a man can practice the roles required of his gender . . . be in charge of everything he's meant to be."

"It also provides a place for gossiping freely," Connie added lightly, looking as if William's definition of the gentleman's club was reaching a high level of foolishness.

"Yes, indeed it does," William said, very seriously. "Gossip is a weapon to attack or defend oneself from the outside world. Clubs offer the privacy and secrecy for a gentleman to employ those weapons without censure from those who have no right to intervene in a gentleman's business."

"Good God," Emily said under her breath. "Well, if that's so, I can tell you that men are no match for an accomplished female gossip, my friend the Princess von Metternich being the perfect example. But Father, do you approve of all this? Do you belong to these places to launch salvos against the society . . . of women, and others?"

"And you as well, Corey," Aunt Clara piped up unexpectedly. It seemed that she and Emily were playing a rare but well-matched duet. "I gather you almost never come to lunch or dinner here, and can't be found in the house at other times, either, because I've tried. I suppose you are also living in one of these clubs and plotting revenge against the rest of us as you gamble and gossip with your men friends."

Corey burst out laughing. He had to put his cup and saucer down on the window seat to avoid spilling what little was left in it. "Hardly, Aunt Clara," he chuckled. "I know many men prefer the all-male environment because they weren't brought up with ladies—attended schools for boys only and had only male teachers and friends. But I, on the other hand, grew up with only women—a mother I had to be concerned for, Emily as my full-time playmate, and maids who cared for me in my father's house. I'd go crazy spending my spare time with only men. Those clubs aren't quite as common in America, and my father certainly never belonged to one, so it never occurred to me. I think Lord Alden was enrolled from birth by his father. It's a vastly different system." He turned deliberately away from Aunt Clara to speak directly to his sons.

"And Connie, you seem to be spending your time with some of the most notorious ladies in London these days rather than wasting it in men's clubs. Did you enjoy Lady Sandhurst's company the other day? Your mother tells me you made quite an entrance with her at the Langham Hotel!" Connie smiled, cocking his head in his mother's direction in mild protest against her obvious sharing of gossip with his father who hadn't been present. Corey unwound his long frame from his reading chair to stand and put his cup down on the tea tray, adjusting his waistcoat as if preparing to leave. "I'm sure my wife would prefer to lock her men away from the females of the species," he added with a wink at Emily, "but those clubs are not for me. And in fact, where were you all afternoon, dear wife? Applying for a new position at the Royal College of Music with the handsome young professor who runs it?"

"No," she said, eyes flashing with a lift of her chin. "I was in fact looking into the college for you, dear husband."

"Me!" Corey stared at her.

"Him?" Lord Alden cried out, glaring at Emily as if she'd lost her mind.

"Yes. I had a nice lunch with Professor Stanford and I went back to the college to talk with him further. It's quickly become obvious to me that his most pressing need right now is for someone who can teach composition with him, assist in conducting, and also head the choral department. Who do we all know fitting that description?" She turned, slowly flattening her hand out, palm up as if offering a gift, and pointing it directly at Corey. "Yes, you, Corey de Koningh." Everyone in the room stared at her in silence, realizing even if they didn't understand the true nature of her disclosure that she had somehow completely redirected attention away from herself to the elusive and self-deprecating Corey. Lord Alden was the first to recover from the surprise.

"Oh, but Emily, my dear," her father said in the soothing voice he probably saved for disobedient horses and the queen when she lost her temper. "Compared to the world-class staff he's already acquired, and musicians of your caliber, how can the college compete on the choral front, or in composition for that matter? There's nothing there for Corey. But you, however—"

"Enough!" Emily cried out, dark eyes snapping with a warning none in the room could miss. But only her younger son seemed to fully intuit the danger signs, leaping to his feet, and suggesting he ring for Brody to collect the tea service. Yet there was no way to act quickly enough to ward off the impending eruption.

"I will have you know," Emily breathed angrily, looking from her father to her husband as if bearding lions in their den, "that the 'handsome, young Professor Stanford' is fast becoming a key performer on the British musical scene, or so Professor Haussmann tells me. I couldn't take your assessment of him on face value, Father, as you don't have the grasp of international performers that Robert has. I wrote him to get a sense of how Professor Stanford is viewed by his European colleagues and learned he has few rivals. That's why I broke down my resistance to meeting him for lunch and returning to the college." Lord Alden beamed and nodded emphatically, ignoring the slight to his critiquing powers where classical pedagogy was concerned. Corey's face took on a quizzical look.

"Truly?" Corey said. "Robert Haussmann has heard of him?"

"Not simply heard of him," Emily said, her voice gaining the strength of self-assurance, "he wrote when he heard we were going to London that Stanford is known for his compositions—songs, operas, symphonies, and church music—as well as his directing for both orchestra and chorus. He said he'd just heard the professor has been made conductor of the Bach Choir here in London, succeeding Robert's old friend Otto Goldschmidt, and Hans von Bülow is discussing conducting German premieres of some of his symphonies." She was almost breathless, throwing her head back triumphantly with the growing list of accomplishments she could rattle off from her former mentor's letter. "It's hard to believe he'd have time to teach and run the college as well. It's a good thing he's so young, and also that his wife doesn't seek his company very often." She smiled at her own humor. "But I believe he does have happy young children, so I assume that neither they nor his home life have suffered from his crushing schedule."

"Children!" Aunt Clara snorted in disgust. "In my day children were kept where they belonged, out of the way and thoroughly obedient. This new fascination with childhood just confuses them, makes them believe they can do as they please, be as creative as they want, get away with anything. That's why they end up like . . . that!" She finally stopped, out of breath, as she gestured toward the de Koningh brothers. "It's all the queen's fault!" she spluttered. "Nine children is a maternal excess appropriate only for rabbits." It was all Emily could do not to laugh out loud. She knew that there was much outrage over the changing status of children in these modern times, but she could easily see how someone who'd never had any of her own would feel even more alienated.

"That's ridiculous, Aunt Clara," she muttered, eyes flashing with the very cataclysm Connie had hoped to avoid. "Why, Pauline von Metternich has told me that her grandfather, the chancellor, would prefer to be with her young children than with all the royalty of Europe. And he's certainly no example of Victorian parental largess!" But in truth, Emily couldn't justify the way her boys treated her or the family, either, wishing for some of the old-fashioned deference that might have kept them home together tonight.

Corey started to move toward the library door, but Emily hadn't decided to let him go yet. "Robert was extremely impressed with the professor's accomplishments and encouraged connecting with the Royal College in any way we can," she said to him. "He advised you to write him yourself, Corey, and you should if you want to discuss the opportunity further. Robert is well, by the way, and sends his best wishes," she finished, as if to remind Corey of the closeness of their family ties with the man who had trained them both in their chosen musical passions so many years ago. In many ways, he'd been their musical uncle as well as a teacher, affecting them both more deeply than either one of their own fathers at a very young age.

Corey bowed slightly to Aunt Clara, as he thanked Emily for looking out for his interests. "The college does sound noteworthy, and Stanford as well," he said. "I shall look into it and write Robert the next chance I get. And now, I'm off for a walk and will be back," he glanced in Aunt Clara's direction, "who knows when?" He smiled at his sons, turning toward the door and leaving quickly. Emily couldn't get over the thought that he was avoiding Aunt Clara's grasp, having seen what it did to William. As soon as Corey disappeared, Lord Alden stood up, glancing out the window and commenting that he was waiting for the carriage. Convinced of an intentional abandonment, Emily objected to the fact that he, too, would presumably be out for dinner.

Her father put both hands on her shoulders and placed a light kiss on her dark head, so like his own before the years had brushed it with white. "No one turns down a dinner invitation from the future king of England," he chuckled, "even to dine with his own family. You must remember that my friends think of me as entirely on my own, as I was for many years before you brought your boys back from America." He smiled at her, squeezing her shoulders for reassurance. "If you'd like to be included in these evenings with the Prince of Wales, I'm sure I can work that out, but I rather doubt you'd enjoy them, knowing you as I do."

"Grandfather, I think Brody has the carriage here." William signaled to the doorway where he must have caught sight of the groomsman hovering so as not to interrupt. "Could you drop me at the club on your way?" Lord Alden nodded, wishing everyone a pleasant evening and leaving the library with William close behind.

"And I, too, must be off," Connie said. "I'm trying to catch up here with some of Gustav Klimt's artist friends to make some inroads to the fashion scene in London."

Emily sprang to her feet, rushing to Connie and folding him in a hug. "Oh, Connie dear, I meant to tell you I may have a connection for you through the Princess von Metternich. Why don't you stay home tonight, and we'll discuss it?"

"You can tell me all about it tomorrow, Mother," he said, smiling warmly and giving her a return hug before moving her gently away. "I made dinner plans with these men, so we'll have to put off the princess's contacts until later. Goodnight, darling Aunt Clara," he said, bowing slightly and turning to leave. Emily stood silently watching the empty doorway as if she couldn't believe it had swallowed up her entire family so quickly and completely.

"I told you," Aunt Clara muttered. "If you'd put them in their places as children, they'd be here now."

"We're all a catastrophe," Emily sighed. "Even the family that isn't family."

"Now what do you mean by that?" Aunt Clara said, staring at Emily through narrowed eyes, as if to see her more clearly.

"Oh, nothing," she said, moving around to collect the extra cups and saucers to put them on the tray, though she thumped them down with an alarming force. "It's just that Brody had the nerve to chastise me for riding my new bicycle recently." She brushed imagined crumbs from the tea cake off her skirt, apparently forgetting she hadn't had any as she angrily emphasized every few words: "It's none of his *business* what I do, and you'd think he'd be pleased anyway about the *pleasure* it gave me. If he's really *like family*, as he says, he'd be more *supportive* instead of warning me of impending *doom*."

"Oh, don't let him bother you," Aunt Clara said. "I can't understand why your father kept him on anyway, after that trouble with your mother." She looked like a clever parrot who'd learned more than anyone else knew. Dark eyes darting and slightly hooked nose guarding the secrets behind her sealed lips, Aunt Clara was throwing Emily a challenge. There could be no doubt that her father's sister had acquired the skill of appearing to have information no one else had, much the same power the men in their exclusive clubs sought to wield over those who didn't belong. Emily wanted to turn and leave the room but couldn't resist the pull.

"What trouble?" she asked, instantly wishing she hadn't as she saw Aunt Clara's expression of deep satisfaction. She looked so content Emily could imagine her actually preening her feathers.

"You know, dear—that inappropriate relationship your mother

and Brody had. I thought he'd be out on his ear the minute your father discovered them, but for some reason he was still here, even years later after your mother died. I never understood it," she said. "Did you?"

Emily couldn't hear anything but the ringing in her ears. "No," she said, staring out the window across the yard to the stables. "I never did because I knew nothing of it." She walked slowly backward toward the library doorway. "I told you the whole family is a catastrophe and apparently always was," she said, finally turning herself around with the help of the door frame, to be swallowed up in the darkness of the front hall as she stumbled toward the stairs and the ultimate safety of her own room. It seemed no one in the family had thought to light the lamps.

13

CHISLEHURST

SUDDENLY EMILY'S DAYS were filling up with luncheon dates to meet new colleagues from the college and old acquaintances visiting London from other European capitals. It was an obvious benefit of a career that had moved her around Europe in a continuous flow of performances since her early twenties. Soon after her meeting with Charles at Crosby's, Emily learned of Pauline's pending visit to see the Empress Eugenie's home in England. She'd thought her friend referred to a "who" rather than a "where." *It sounds like one of Mr. Dickens's characters—Chislehurst!* Pauline was surprised Emily had never heard of it, but Emily had to remind her she was more American than British. Chislehurst might be only ten miles from the center of London, but it could have been a hundred miles, for all Emily knew of the geography of Great Britain.

Apparently, a sympathetic partisan British gentleman had rented his huge home there to the Empress Eugenie at the start of her exile from France, but appearances are often deceiving. It turned out that an English mistress of the emperor, whose father owned Camden Place, had invited Louis Napoleon there often in his youth, and so he'd come to love the mansion as much as the mistress. Emily had been confused as to the connection of the French imperial family to England, so Pauline had explained to her that "your Queen Victoria" was related to all the royal houses of Europe. And so another English beauty later in the emperor's life had her father buy Camden Place and put it in trust for her, as she'd also borne one of the emperor's illegitimate sons. The house was totally renovated in the style of a French chateau, and it seemed the trustee had been paid by the emperor to maintain the house for him "in case of emergency."

Emily found it hard to understand why he and his family were suddenly the receivers of this trust that had been set up for his mistress, but she found Pauline so comfortable basking in the imperial family's radiance that it wasn't worth asking. The Princess von Metternich explained that both the French emperor and his son and heir who died fighting as a British officer in South Africa were buried at the Catholic church in Chislehurst in the 1870s. Thus the empress had initially stayed on at the house in exile to be near the deceased imperial family interred in England but had recently left for good to return to her roots in France. Emily was surprised her friend had any interest in it now that the empress was no longer in residence, but assumed the nostalgia of remembrance was strong enough to draw her back there on the way to visit Emily.

Of Camden Place, Pauline had written, "it is a big country house, richly furnished and situated in the midst of a fine park full of splendid old trees. There were plenty of flower-beds close to the house, and yet there was something depressing about the place . . ." She'd admitted to Emily it probably had everything to do with the sad talks she'd shared with the empress about the calamities of France and the imperial family. Emily felt an odd sense of hope that the empress might regain some of her own life without the family that had torn her apart for so long, even though she had no real notion of whether the poor woman felt that way herself. But Chislehurst would probably be off Pauline's travel agenda for the future.

The princess preferred to return to England this time with a base at Flemings Hotel, a small, private, luxury lodge where she wouldn't be exposed to public scrutiny. Emily was entranced by the stained-glass window in the entrance celebrating Prince Albert's Great

Exhibition of 1851, the same year of the hotel's founding. And she applauded Pauline's choice to avoid the exposure guaranteed (as Emily had learned) by a place like the Langham Hotel, though it surprised her, knowing Pauline as she did, and she told her friend so. They were used to being completely honest with each other.

The princess explained she felt there were times when life should be lived in full view, and others where discretion was the better choice. She'd said she always adopted the latter strategy in England, probably because the imperial family had been exiled there, and although that shouldn't put her own family under scrutiny, she felt the need to be on her best behavior in case it reflected on Their Majesties in any way. Emily sensed this protocol was founded on an opinion that was less than flattering of the British psyche and sensibilities but didn't feel the need to clarify that suspicion as it wasn't personal to her, being more of an American in her own eyes.

Seated in the front parlor of her suite at Flemings Hotel, Pauline greeted Emily as she would an old friend she hadn't seen in years instead of just a few months. Springing to her feet, she reminded Emily of the strength and power the princess had in her lithe, healthy body. The tales of her doing handstands and dancing the cancan on tables in the royal apartments in Paris all seemed possible and even probable when one watched Pauline move across a room. Dressed in one of her matched skirt and jacket outfits, trimmed with black silk braid and elegant hand stitching, the princess was a soothing sight, and Emily told her so. "Everything from your fashion to your figure fills one with pleasure and harmony, Pauline," she said, holding the princess in a longer than usual embrace. "I've missed our talks," she added, not wanting to presume on the princess's affection without explanation.

"Oh Emily, my dear little American, surely you've found plenty of admirers to reach out to now that you're living with your father in London again." Pauline held Emily at arm's length, looking her over as if to make note of any hardships showing on her face or in her manner. But satisfied that nothing she saw warranted comment, Pauline smiled and turned toward the settee she'd just left where her book still lay open on the seat. "Come and sit here with me," she said. "At last we can return to our wonderful conversations so recently interrupted when you left France. The trip to Vienna was a nice interlude, but you were under the stress of travel and your concerns about your son there. We didn't get a chance to just . . . talk. Will you join me in a small lunch?" She rose to ring the bell for room service without waiting for affirmation from Emily. "I can attest to the privacy here, which is excellent, but the food is not. I find the British cuisine so tasteless and insipid I can hardly touch it, and yet one must be nourished. Perhaps you're more used to it." She shuddered a little, as if recalling the quality of the food upset her stability.

"I eat at home with Father much of the time," Emily said. "There's room enough for twenty in that dining room, but usually we're the only ones at home together. But the food is good, I think. You must join us while you're here. My family would enjoy it and I always love your company." She smiled warmly, and Pauline seemed to relax visibly and smile broadly back at her. They grasped each other's hand and moved toward the settee.

"By the way, have you heard from your friend Mr. Dunne lately?" Pauline asked, casually. "He's such an attractive man, and devoted to you and your children, I think. Is the son here who you were so concerned about? Cornelius, or Connie, is it?"

"No, I've heard nothing from Johnny recently, but I'm sure I will when he has some time he can spend thinking of things other than the upheavals in Europe. And yes, my son Connie is here with the family in London. But I'm not as concerned about him as I was. I'm thinking the rumors about his inclinations were unfounded, and nothing new has surfaced since we arrived here." She smiled reassuringly at Pauline, feeling all the while that the clairvoyant princess could look right through her. But Pauline smiled back warmly, giving no hint of skepticism.

"Wonderful," she said without hesitation. "I'm on a mission to have Connie present some of his drawings to Monsieur Worth while I'm here. I think that might help start him on his fashion career, just as Monsieur Worth's future was assured when he showed me his drawings and made me my first dress."

"Charles Worth? Is he here in London? I thought La Maison Worth was in Paris?"

Pauline burst out laughing. "Oh, it is, my dear, of course it is. But Charles is English, if you can believe it, and he comes here to visit that family every year. Naturally, his own family couldn't be more French, starting with Madame Worth and then to their two sons, Jean-Philippe and Gaston-Lucien."

"Pauline, why do you differentiate between family just by where they're born geographically? Aren't they all just the same, his family?"

"Good heavens, I don't believe so," the princess said, looking profoundly serious and drawing her dark eyebrows together in one long line below her forehead. "I think he sees his French family as vastly superior, but his English relatives as a responsibility he must bear. No family is ever the same," she said, shaking her head emphatically and pulling harder than necessary on the room service cord. "But why do you dwell on that point?" she asked.

Emily had settled into the seat left vacant next to Pauline's and was watching her friend intently. She took a breath, as if preparing a difficult response. "I've been challenged uncomfortably recently on the subject of family," Emily said, a grim expression on her face that seemed to have come from nowhere. You know, Pauline, how important my family is to me, partly because I felt as if I started my life without one. I guess we always value what we don't have, sometimes maybe even more than it's worth," she added, still watching her friend intently.

Pauline's expression never changed, and she simply said, "Go on."

Emily took another breath, and this time jumped up, restlessly moving around the room and touching the furniture distractedly as she went past it. "Oh, lately the family seems to be breaking apart, and no one but me cares or will make any effort to bring it back together again." She could tell there were hot tears welling up in her eyes but didn't want to waste the energy to quell them. "And the precious family that existed before, namely my mother, I can't seem to find even in the house we lived in together once. Everything I built my whole life on as I grew up came from my memories of my mother, but they might have been fabrications." She let the hot, salty tears run silently down her cheeks, grateful for the chance to let them go on their own without trying to stop them. She hadn't even been able to cry alone in her own room.

"Emily, what is the cause of this distress?" Pauline asked, watching her carefully. "Your father has revealed something new about the past that has upset you so?"

"No," Emily said, pulling one of her handkerchiefs from her pocket. It was ordinarily used to place under the violin on her shoulder, but this was the rare occasion when it would serve the purpose it had originally been made for. "Not my father," she said. She wiped her face before folding the handkerchief carefully and shoving it back deep in her pocket. She'd need it for practice soon again and didn't want to find it wadded up and unusable in her skirt. She looked away from Pauline's intense stare, knowing it was she herself who'd started this unwinding and only she who must continue it. She took another deep breath.

"I sense the groomsman who was here when my mother was alive knows something more of her, but he won't tell me. I asked my father about her but instead of clarifying her for me, he still refuses to speak of her." Emily sank back down in the indented cushion she'd left beside the princess. Somehow relaying the facts of her discovery seemed to have calmed her, so she could continue without tears.

"I sense something that makes me think my mother was neither the angel I envisioned, nor my father the devil who abandoned me as a child, Pauline. I feel as if my whole past life has been nothing but a lie and a mystery, and that's why my own family has no solid foundation to build on. No wonder the household is all breaking apart now." Emily looked across the room, gazing at a grandfather clock standing against the wall. She'd always found a grandfather clock the heartbeat of a home, keeping everyone safe and together, and prized their unifying influence no matter where she'd lived. She looked away from it and shook her head; making the most of her friend's attentiveness, she decided to let her doubts and misgivings pour out unrestrained.

"I should have known a long time ago, in the beginning of my marriage when my new husband was unfaithful, and repeatedly so. That, in turn, set me on a search for friends to share my life with. Most of them being men probably because of my work, one thing led to another and now maybe I'm no different from my own mother." She could feel herself start to sink farther into the sofa cushion, wanting to disappear before her friend started to comment on her confession. Finally, she sat up a little, braving to look directly at her. "Pauline, how did your empress survive the grief of her own life with a husband who was continuously and publicly unfaithful and a family broken apart by war and calamity? My God, I wish I could learn her secret for handling the pain of it." The princess continued to look at her penetratingly, but finally shaking her head, she put her hand on Emily's hands tangled together in a knot in her lap.

"You Americans do see the world differently," she said. "And it's often to your own detriment. I think your history is too short for you to benefit from your sorrows." Her face softened and she held Emily's small hands in hers. "In Europe," she went on firmly but with a smile, "the lines between relations are blurred over time, and I think that's a good thing. Do you understand what I mean?" She looked at Emily as if to be sure her message had not already been misunderstood.

"Ah, well, let's use my own situation as a prime example," the princess said, sitting up straighter as if beginning a new and important lesson for her pupil. "I assume you know that my husband, Prince Richard von Metternich, is also my uncle. That of course meant that my darling grandfather Prince Klemens von Metternich was also my father-in-law. You can see that the simplicity of most family structures doesn't exist in mine, yet we are a happy, solid unit nonetheless." She smiled at Emily, whose attention was riveted on the princess.

"My own husband has had frequent affairs with actresses and operatic prima donnas," she went on. "Why those particular career women, I'm not quite sure. But even so, we've lived happily together in full admiration of each other's intellectual abilities and clearly comfortable with our private conjugal homelife, as our three children attest to." She smiled warmly and easily at Emily. "You are luckier than most women, my friend," she said, serious now. She caught Emily's gaze with her own and held it. "You have a life and direction of your own, and devoted male friends, and family who love you in many ways, as well as a husband who shares your passion for music and performance. Your children are far more stable than mine, though I know you worry about yours greatly." Emily started to look pained again, and Pauline sensed the mood change immediately. Moving quickly to the most important part of their talk, the princess stood up to face Emily down on the settee.

"Do you know who you remind me of?" she asked. She stopped there, clearly waiting for a response before going on. Emily finally shook her head and raised her shoulders in complete resignation. She held her breath, waiting.

"You remind me of Herr Wagner!" Pauline almost exploded with glee at delivering a surprise so unusual as to finally capture her friend's full mind. She saw Emily's expression slip into something less than pleased. "Oh, I know what you think of him and his music," Pauline went on, almost gleefully. "You've told me often enough, and

I acknowledge that even I am not enthralled with the man personally, though I do appreciate his music. But this is not about that." She lowered herself quietly to sit beside Emily again, and then started to tell her story.

"When I had a party in Vienna for a small group of friends, I invited Franz Liszt and Herr Wagner because they are good friends, and I knew they would add much to the festivities. One of my less-than-worldly guests asked Liszt what instrument he played. When she was told it was the piano, she begged him to play for us, which he did, astounding her with his skill and the beauty of his playing. Still fainting from the joy of his performance, she turned to ask Herr Wagner what instrument he played, and he paused for a second." Pauline grinned and laughed under her breath, clearly enjoying the memory of that party and the moment. She looked back at Emily, her eyes growing bigger with the pleasure of what was to come.

"I wondered what he'd say, because Herr Wagner did not play the piano terribly well, and I knew he wouldn't want to be shown up by his friend who'd performed so brilliantly. But finally he turned to the woman and said, 'I play the orchestra, Madame.'" Emily's eyes started to shine for the first time that day, her dimples deepening along with her smile. "But you, dear Emily, do not play the orchestra. You have your specialty—the violin—which takes precedent over everything else. Most of us cannot play the orchestra. And so it is essential that we concentrate on that which we do best and have the deepest devotion to. Your music has always taken and should continue to take precedence over everything else, because you cannot lead your family as if it was an orchestra, either."

The two friends talked into the early afternoon over a lunch of cold meats and vegetables that they both declared to be filling but less than inspiring. As the lunch progressed and the accompanying wine diminished, the princess regaled Emily with stories of her daring escapades with the empress in their early days together in

France. Possibly encouraged to join the narrative with tales of her own, Emily told of climbing on the roof of the de Koningh mansion to smoke cigars with Corey in her youth. She then moved on to recent exploits with her son learning to ride her bicycle, finally suggesting that she and the princess go rent bicycles at the cycle school. Still desirous of some level of anonymity, the princess secured a vow of secrecy from Emily as to their adventures at Cycledom Ltd. Single lessons were only two shillings, and the school would be open until nine that evening, so there was plenty of time to become an expert for a woman with Pauline von Metternich's athletic abilities.

Later that night, when asked about her day with the princess, Emily found her spirits so high she almost made the mistake of telling the family about Pauline learning to ride the bicycle. But having promised that she wouldn't, she told them she'd spent the day with her unusual friend, learning about Chislehurst and discussing the art of conducting. It had been another wonderful adventure, helping to distract and remind her of the way the lives of others move back and forth in much the same crazy tempo as her own. It was impossible for her to ignore the fact that she enjoyed life outside of her home more than she did within it. As was so often the case, she felt like a stranger who didn't belong entirely to the house at Grosvenor Square or the people therein. But the vicarious "visit" to Chislehurst with Pauline and the empress suggested that acceptance was an important skill to practice, perhaps even more vital than the art of conducting.

14

THE HOUSE OF WORTH

IT WASN'T UNUSUAL for Johnny Dunne to receive telegrams at
Le Figaro. He depended on the service but wasn't fond of Western
Union, the company. In their 1883 contract, the corporation made
the workers pledge not to be part of any labor union and remain loyal
to the company. It infuriated him every time he saw one of their
messages, knowing how costly they were for the sender and how
little of that went to the workers who made the profits possible. Yet
for a newspaper responsible for communicating world events, and
many people awaiting word of lost relatives or other monumental
occurrences affecting their lives, the service was a godsend, no
matter how lamentable the cost. He knew John Mackay was working
to bypass Western Union with his new Commercial Cable Company.
Until Mackay had formed his enterprise, financier Jay Gould controlled all submarine cable traffic between the United States and
Europe. A rate war would now surely follow, and perhaps a better
deal for the company employees at last.

This mustard-colored envelope looked both familiar yet mysterious. He'd leave it unopened on his desk until he'd finished with the
notes he'd been working on for the funeral of Victor Hugo. The
elderly statesman, poet, playwright, and author had been more
important to the French people and the citizens of the world than
royalty. He also needed to report on the continuing agony of the

bugs ruining the vineyards, and therefore what was left of the meager French economy, as well as the ongoing scramble and disagreement with England over territory in Africa. That alone could keep him busy for a lifetime. And yet none of it would be resolved by any news outlet immediately, so he might as well see what the telegraph message added to the barrage of information he'd need to sort through.

Opening it with one quick slip of his thumb, he slid the yellow sheet of paper out of its envelope as if his experience with those messages was so huge he barely needed to touch them to know what they would say. But this time, his brows knitted together as he read the unexpected note from Pauline von Metternich, handwritten as they sometimes were by one of the unseen telegraphers . . . *procured desired information . . . fear its effect on our mutual friend . . . your presence required in London . . . as soon as possible.* Johnny sat down on his wooden desk chair harder than he'd intended to.

There was no possibility he could leave his work now or anytime soon. The military conflict between Serbia and Bulgaria was calling him to cover international diplomatic efforts when Austria-Hungary threatened to enter the war in Serbia's defense. And immediately after that trip he needed to get back to reporting on the telegraph rate war between Gould's Western Union and Mackay's new upstart company. The American in him relished the news of that particular skirmish beyond any European-inspired battle. Still holding the princess's message, he looked across the row of staff writers in front of him. Every desk was filled, and every head bent in determination. The stunning truth making itself felt was that he would not go to Emily's aid for the first time in their long relationship, and that perhaps it would be the most important call for help ever made on her behalf, including the Great Chicago Fire.

His mind already racing, Johnny looked back down at the telegram. Perhaps there was another way. Mackay had been in Paris at his wife's mansion and might still be there. He would go see him immediately to convince him to leave for London before going to New York. He knew Emily would have shared her fears with Mackay and had no doubt he'd be as worried about her as he and the princess were. He composed a brief message of his own to the princess, explaining his plan and promising a follow-up communication soon.

He raced off to the Huitième Arrondissement to see Mackay, but found only the wealthy Louise Mackay, a skilled interlocutor well used to reporters clamoring for information about her husband's latest financial escapades. She informed Johnny that her husband was by now in New York to complete work on the Commercial Cable Company. Disappointed to have missed him, Johnny was nonetheless pleased to learn the fight to best Gould and the Western Union Telegraph Company was ongoing. That would force down the toll rate for transatlantic messages. Pleased with his new discovery, he almost forgot why he'd gone to see Mrs. Mackay in the first place.

⊱⭒𝍦⭒⊰

"Where were you off to so fast?" Johnny's secretary asked when he swept back into the office. "You forgot the address for the message you wanted me to send to London." She waved the blank envelope in front of him as proof of its lack of an appropriate destination.

"I'll take that," Johnny declared, snatching it from her. "I need to rewrite it, and also to meet with a few of the reporters in the conference room. I have a critical story to pursue." He stood tapping the envelope against his other hand. "These will be so cheap soon we'll be able to fling them around the world like rice at a wedding." He chuckled, bending over without sitting at his desk, his hat and coat still on as he wrote another message for Pauline von Metternich.

John Mackay unavailable . . . upset that I cannot go myself due to pressing issues at work . . . he realized it was not the message Pauline wanted to receive, but this was a time Emily must deal with her own problems without her friends . . . *a shame her own family unable to help in such an extreme time of need.* She was a strong woman and he had little doubt she would prevail. Yet somewhere deep down he realized only a short time ago he'd had nothing but doubts that this possibility for scandal and extortion could be handled without a tragic outcome for Emily and her family. Someone was planning and executing a nasty campaign to ruin them all. But his past experience with Emily's unusual strengths helped him push the misgivings back down where he could ignore them for the present, bringing full attention to the story he wanted to work on about the telegraph rate war between Gould's Western Union and Mackay's entrepreneurial experiment. He was rooting of course for someone to give Western Union its comeuppance for cheating its workers out of an honest wage while overcharging the people it served.

It wasn't that he lacked empathy for Emily's plight, but it had no value to the public, and in fact needed to be kept from open view, and therefore it was outside of his area of expertise. It was really more appropriate for the princess's innate talent for gossip. He wondered why Pauline hadn't just handled the difficult news with Emily herself but wouldn't get a chance to ask her now. He moved toward the meeting room purposefully, gathering reporters along the hallway like a parent picking up dropped clothing. They all had a mission to assiduously oil the world's economic rumor mill with his findings. They would try to beat the news itself by getting the next edition of *Le Figaro* out before anyone knew anything specific about the American communications giants' latest battle.

Pauline von Metternich stood next to the window in the sitting room of Flemings Hotel, her jaw outlined against the light in grim determination. She was clearly not happy with the telegram from Paris. She had worked well in advance to prepare Emily's friend, the writer at *Le Figaro*, for his role in saving Emily. The princess knew Johnny thought he'd been the one to call on her, but that's what she'd wanted him to think. It made men feel strong and indispensable to be a woman's chevalier. Pauline wasn't sure about his relationship to Emily over the years, but it actually didn't matter. What did matter was his belief that he was Emily's *knight*.

But where was he now? Pursuing his role as professional gossiper with the most influential public voice in Paris, chasing after rich Americans and their newfangled toys. And the Silver King, John Mackay, where was he? Pulling another million dollars out of the ground to feed those gluttonous telegraph cables. Pauline shook her head, appalled at Emily's abandonment by her businessmen friends when she needed them most. The discovery made by "Le bon Monsieur Worth" had been a shock Pauline felt should be mitigated by a man, conveying the news in what might seem a more direct way. It might be easier for Emily to assimilate, used to a blunt approach from her upbringing with men and being surrounded by them in her work.

The princess felt certain that Emily trusted her not to speak about her fears for her son to anyone else. They both prized that kind of trust. But Pauline knew that in British society the sodomite would be marginalized without recourse. The issue had become how to protect Emily's reputation, both personal and professional, from the lies that grew and magnified in the dark of secrecy like poisonous mushrooms. What Pauline suddenly realized she needed was an artist, not a businessman, to communicate differently with her friend, and she knew just who she could convince to do this most difficult job for her: Le bon Monsieur Worth himself.

Moving to a small desk between two windows in the sitting room, Pauline reached for some of the hotel's stationery. She was relieved to realize anything she wrote to Monsieur Worth would arrive that same afternoon. She felt time was of the essence. Emily needed to learn who had targeted her son with accusations of this illegal behavior. Monsieur Worth had made the discovery at Pauline's behest, and he should be the one to convey it to Emily. Pauline raised the pen, dipped it in the inkwell and set to writing, occasionally glancing out the window without seeing anything as she paused to allow her hand to catch up to her head.

Monsieur Worth would fully appreciate someone of Emily's background who had conquered the realm of classical music and the art of performance, preferring her work to socializing and spending money all day as women of her class often did. Pauline nodded to herself and put the pen to paper again to suggest the venerable designer create a couple of performance costumes for Emily, exposing the troubling truth he'd discovered as if it had simply come to light during his fittings with the wives of men he conversed with often in his shop. The princess closed and fastened the envelope with the Metternich seal and coat of arms. She brought the ring with her for special communications and knew Monsieur Worth would want her to observe the formality so that his workers would know whom they were dealing with. He had a great zeal for distinction and *le grand air*.

Monsieur Worth's gratitude and loyalty to the princess helped her overlook the little airs he gave himself, as well as his self-aggrandizement in creating a unique dress for an important lady on a special occasion. He was undeniably brilliant and had admirable common sense in addition. His judgment about the world was extraordinarily sound, and she knew he would have been a success in life no matter what his direction. Conversing with him was a real pleasure, and she knew Emily would find it so as much as she did. Most important, he would recognize Emily for the very real lady she was, beyond the importance her birthright and marriage had given her and the worldwide acclaim for her musical gifts.

"You will need to go upstairs for your fitting, Princess," Monsieur Worth said, with a slight bow over Emily's hand. "Madame de Koningh will stay here with me so I can take her measures properly without interruption." He looked up at Pauline over Emily's hand without rising fully. Their plan was close to the finish, but they were both practiced at social intrigue and gave nothing away.

Pauline laughed to lighten the mood. "Oh, my, you are special, Emily. Le bon Monsieur Worth doesn't often take measures himself." She smiled knowingly, moving off to climb the curved staircase to the small upper floor at the House of Worth's London office. She was more used to the world-famous Maison Worth at No. 7 Rue de la Paix in Paris, which had a grander feel and luxurious opulence in its furniture. But she had a sense that this store would appeal to Emily more. And she was right. Her friend had taken on a pleased, calm sense of happiness at being out on this excursion with her dear comrade, a mood that would serve Monsieur Worth well when he delivered his shocking message.

"I'm honored, Monsieur," Emily said, with one of her small smiles exposing her dimples. "And I'm most impressed with how involved you are in your business when you are the most famous couturier in the world. Even now when you could turn everything over to others to do for you. Caring about the quality of what one puts one's name to is the first sign of a true artist."

Pauline could tell her friend was entirely sincere, as she could see the designer did, too. That showed in the glow on his round face, which sagged a bit under his chin to match his drooping mustache and aging eyelids. The advancing years had not improved the gentleman's overly dramatic appearance, set off always with a velvet beret and cape trimmed with fur, no matter the temperature inside or out. One might have assumed he was dressing for a costume ball, except that this had become his daily attire. And yet there was a sweetness about the brilliantly successful designer. The affection and regard he had for the Princess von Metternich was obvious, making his slight blush as sincere as Emily's appreciation for his art. The shine spread almost up to his receding hairline, as he bowed again and motioned Emily over to the mirror in his sitting room on the main floor.

"I have admired your work on the concert stage, Madame de Koningh, and was most thrilled when the princess informed me that you would accompany her today. As you may know, I have dressed many artists of our day, and I would enjoy nothing more than creating something dazzling for you." He danced around Emily as if envisioning her in many different poses, which she was not, so he changed his own posture up and down, left and right to accommodate his imagination. "I've been thinking as I watched you move across the room when you entered that small silver paillettes catching the light against a white satin background would be most effective on you. Shall we get started?" He looked as if he could see the dress perfectly before him now. Emily nodded, seeming a little lost about where she should stand and what she should do.

"Oh my heavens, that sounds divine," she said, smiling at Pauline, who disappeared up the stairs. "But I have only a few weeks until my next performance in Dublin. It will be the first concert to raise funds for the new Royal College of Music, and I'll be rehearsing the students so steadily I fear I shan't be able to come for fittings."

She followed the designer across the room, already apologetic for what she assumed would be a terrible slight to his talents. "Madame," he said, stopping short and spinning around to look her in the eye. "There will never be more than one fitting after the dress is cut. I do it right the first time."

He motioned to the mirror, clearly indicating she should stand on the pedestal there as he brought his measuring tapes and record book over to the table nearby. He also motioned to a gentleman he called his "first-hand man," Carlsson, asking him to bring a few bolts of different fabrics. He then instructed the young female assistants hovering about to disappear upstairs and Carlsson to accompany them to be sure they attended to the princess's needs there properly. "Keep everyone upstairs," he instructed Carlsson, "until I call for them." Emily was surprised to be getting so much attention from the world-famous designer but knew from Pauline that he was eccentric and unpredictable, as well as highly intelligent and curious, and so assumed she was being treated with the interest reserved for new clients.

As he turned and measured her, Monsieur Worth spoke only of her work, performances of hers he'd seen or read about, or performances of other violinists including a couple of women, comparing opinions of some of the composers Pauline had championed herself. If Emily brought up musicians he'd missed he queried her thoughtfully about her opinion of them and what made them successful or not so.

"It's a surprise to me how many wonderful American women, such as yourself, have excelled in performance of the violin," he said. "I wonder why. It cannot be the training, but perhaps there is a different expectation for women in America," he finished, looking past her to the mirror. "Arma Senkrah certainly comes to mind, as well as Maud Powell, both of whom I've heard and enjoyed greatly. I was going to say I admired Camilla Urso most of all, yet hearing Miss Senkrah and Franz Liszt performing together was enough to send anyone to a blissful heaven, so I shall take that thought back." He smiled at her mirrored reflection impishly.

"You've certainly contributed greatly to the advancement of female violinists with your open appreciation and support, Monsieur Worth," Emily said. "I've also heard and loved all of those ladies, but ironically only when I was in France, not America, since they've all spent time at the Conservatoire de Paris, and also had European careers."

She turned to look at him directly instead of in the mirror. "I wonder if you're not right to say the original seeds might have been sown in that rebellious soil in America, yet it would seem it took the fertilization of a European education and audience to bring them to full growth." She narrowed her vision, as if to watch the progress of many imagined young girls working with their instruments. "Think, sir, of how vital that training was and how they all sought it. That's why the new Royal College of Music will be so important, to bring that same brilliance to fruition right here in England." Feeling completely at ease with this intelligent, kindred spirit, Emily then happily jumped into the fray by asking the designer about his own career and early opportunities, his creations, and eventually his theories about people and life.

By the time she'd started to learn about how he and Pauline had met, Emily felt she'd known him forever. When he described how his first drawings had been presented to Pauline by one of her maids, who was a friend of the designer's future wife, Emily listened in rapt silence. Pauline had been impressed in particular by one drawing of a layered empire dress showing an embroidered skirt underneath a transparent silk gauze fabric, and she instantly ordered the artist and his portfolio of designs be brought to her directly. The princess ordered three new gowns, immediately referred Worth to the Empress Eugenie, and the rest was history and well known to everyone. But Emily stood straighter, eyes shining, and told the designer that her own youngest son had drawn just such a layered gown when he was very young and was even now presenting his drawings with the help of the Klimt brothers, whom he befriended in Paris and Vienna.

"Madame!" Monsieur Worth exclaimed. "You have a son who designs fashions. How marvelous! But ah, wait one moment, my memory is not what it might be anymore. Is he the one named Cornelius?" He slipped his fur-trimmed cape to the back of the chair, apparently feeling the warmth of being inside and his growing excitement in uncomfortable ways. Emily nodded happily, pleased that her friend had already tried to promote Connie's artistic talents as she'd promised.

"Indeed, Monsieur, but everyone calls him Connie. Cornelius pays tribute to a long, drawn-out family name from the Dutch side of his lineage, but it never suited a cheerful, spirited little boy who loved to draw. Now that he's grown and doing extraordinarily beautiful work, we should probably revert back to the more mature version, but we're all so comfortable with Connie's simplified name we can't seem to imagine him as a *Cornelius*. Monsieur Worth, would you be willing to meet with Connie sometime? Some advice from you would be like an answer to a dream for him." She held herself very straight, her dark eyes glowing and chin raised as if to start out on a new adventure. Monsieur Worth couldn't resist leaning forward and taking her hand. Covering it with his other hand as if protecting a delicate bird, he smiled at her. There was a pause as he looked into her eyes. Emily feared she might have taken one step too many toward familiarity in championing Connie's cause.

"Madame," he finally said after what felt like a very long time, "I would not only be delighted to meet your son Connie, but I will also look forward to evaluating his drawings for him. I am so pleasantly surprised to hear of his chosen profession." He patted her hand and let it go gently. "But tell me, my dear, what is the name of your other son? I have heard of him as well." He suddenly looked very serious.

Emily took a breath as if to clear away the air of concern that had suddenly descended over them both. "My older son's name is William, Monsieur, after his grandfather Lord William Alden. But I don't know how you could have heard of him."

The little round designer lifted his head as if trying to see a memory he'd forgotten was there. "Ah, yes, William." He leveled his gaze back at Emily, his dark brows knitting together again in a solid line over his eyes. He rubbed his hand across his forehead. "I remember now. Madame, may I share something with you of a serious nature regarding your son William?" Emily stayed erect as if preparing for flight. But she didn't move or let her eyes drop, and the set of her jaw indicated she had sensed the designer's discomfort and was bracing herself for whatever he had to share. She nodded once.

"Good," he said, though from his increasingly grim expression she doubted there was anything good about what he had to say, and she was right.

Later that afternoon, after Emily and the princess had left the House of Worth, the designer's first-hand man, Carlsson, asked what he should do with Madame de Koningh's measurements, and whether Monsieur Worth had decided to take on the princess's friend as a new client. He'd noted the look of a wild animal caught without escape in her eyes as she left, and assumed it meant the designer had put her down in his inimitable way. They'd certainly spent much more time than necessary together, and Carlsson assumed the woman's simple clothes and modest jewelry had eventually exposed her lack of social standing with unpleasant certainty.

"Naturally I'll create some new performance gowns for Madame de Koningh," the great designer answered, seemingly annoyed by the foolishness of the question. "Let me tell you, Carlsson, that this was a real lady in our house today. You can tell it by the way she carries her head and everything else about her grace and manner. Most importantly, her intellect is mature. You can see it in her face: a modesty, and confidence speaking of a comfort in who she is. That is someone I'm interested in having a dialogue with, and to me that is key. Compared to so many of the young parvenus who think themselves distinguished, she demonstrates the truth that it is what's inside that makes a woman rich and beautiful." He pulled his velvet beret off his head, rubbing his temples with his free hand as if the strain of his work was becoming too much for him. He glanced up the stairs, muttering to himself as he stared at nothing in particular.

"No matter how exquisitely I may dress them, those others have no more brains than a linnet and will never be anything but middle class from top to toe." He gestured dramatically with his free hand, sweeping it first to the ceiling and then to the floor. "The way Madame de Koningh handles the heat of tragic circumstance tells you she is a *grande dame*—if it wasn't already obvious," he added under his breath.

He snatched his cape off the back of the chair and started climbing to the second floor, most likely to take one of his famous impromptu naps in hopes of relieving one of his frequent migraine headaches. Apparently he'd not fared as well as Emily through their talk. "Madame de Koningh will always be welcome in the House of Worth," he exclaimed, flinging the cape dramatically around his shoulders as he disappeared from the second landing. His first-hand man watched him, wondering if he would ever make sense of the designer's discriminating taste.

John Mackay slipped the envelope into his vest pocket. It hadn't been sent as a telegram because his office, and only his office, knew he was still in London. Ironic, he'd noted, that someone in his field of communications should require only the simplest form of connection. It was fast becoming a fact that mostly business and political conflict traveled by expensive telegraph, at least transatlantic, while more personal, social interaction used the always affordable and universally accessible post.

This letter from Emily had a tone of panic that he thought he'd never heard before. Almost frantic with relief to find him unexpectedly still in London, Emily was begging him to meet her somewhere, anywhere, because she was in such dire need of his help. If he hadn't recognized certain affectations of their shared language—"JW" instead of John William, as well as the use of her shorthand "Mack," for his surname—he'd have wondered if the message had actually come from her. But the chaotic jumble of its plea was so unnerving to him he'd sent a return note to her immediately with his carriage driver, insisting she get right into the cab and come back with it to his hotel. He had to take the ship to New York tomorrow, so this would be their only opportunity to be together. He was waiting for her outside the hotel, watching for the maroon top hat his driver liked to wear above the sea of black on the other cabs. He smiled to himself, wondering if he always attracted people around him who liked to be different.

She was there in no time, slipping out of the cab into his arms so fast it appeared quite normal for him to be catching her so she wouldn't fall. He held her a moment longer to help her stabilize and settle down, but she sprang out of his arms into the hotel entrance past the doormen and other guests the second he let go. Hurrying up to the suite with her in the lift, he felt a pressure as heavy as humidity before a hurricane. Just as it was with those storms, he had no choice but to ride this one out with her. He was no stranger to the ways of human suffering and recognized the signs in her now, as if every moment she breathed was a struggle and her emotions were in a racing, foaming boil.

"What room?" she asked hoarsely, and he told her. She ran out of the lift once they'd reached his floor, luckily passing no guests along the way to his door. She'd clearly stopped caring about anyone else, so it was a relief that there was no one in the hall to worry about. Glancing at her a couple of times as he unlocked the door, John resisted talking even though they were completely alone. This was a time for listening, and it was also evident there would be plenty to hear. He thought for a moment of how many of his employees' trials he'd had to share in his business life; many, if not all of them, were founded in some kind of human cataclysm. He'd had a lot of experience dealing with people's troubles, yet they were always unique, as all mortal events were, and so he could guarantee no successful outcome. Especially when one's own emotions got tangled up with those of the person in trouble. He knew she came to him specifically because of his involvement with and commitment to her, and so impartiality had no place with them today. A caring father, a proud mentor, an occasional lover, and always a good friend, he accepted his responsibility to her without restraint, partly because she so seldom called on it.

Turning around to face her after he'd closed the door, he suggested she sit on one of the side chairs nearby. Her dark hair had escaped around her face as if she'd been running against a stiff wind. Her hat offered no help as she held it in her hand, a tight grip crushing the straw brim in her fist. Looking at her now reminded him of the very first time they'd met, over twenty years ago, after a frightening day with her youngest son in New York's Central Park. His chubby little leg had been caught between the bars of a bear's cage at the zoo, and she had just recovered from that fright after Connie's rescue, starting home on foot with both her boys in tow. John had recognized her as the world-class violinist he'd seen at a performance in Paris he'd attended with his wife. That day in the park, he'd noticed and admired her unusual absorption in the care of her children. Most mothers of her social standing would have simply turned them over to a governess and spent the afternoon attending to their own affairs.

She was obviously very unusual as a female musician of deep familial commitments, and her bareheaded frenzy today reminded him greatly of the Emily of half her age, just as crazed and wild in a natural, resolute way. There was a focus even in her desperation, and he sensed that when it was so narrowly directed, it was targeted at her family. It had been a long time since he'd heard any distress about her music, so he braced himself, without realizing it, for the expected personal challenges instead. "Do you wish to sit?" he asked again, gently, without moving from the door. He wanted to give her space, ensuring she had the freedom to unfold her troubles in a way she could be comfortable with.

"No," she said. "I just want to talk with you. I need your help."

"Then I hope you won't mind if I sit," he said, slipping the key back into his pocket and moving to a small settee. He sat down with the grace of an athlete, filling the seat with his muscular body, but still also appearing to be a distinguished, refined gentleman turning his full attention to the problem at hand: Emily. "Please, go on," he said.

It all came out fast. "John, you remember our last talk in Vienna—" He wasn't sure and must have shown it. "—when I told you about my worries over the rumor William repeated to me about Connie!" The anguish had returned to her voice and her straw hat was crushed and rolled even tighter against her skirt. He said nothing, feeling she should get rid of all her demons as quickly as possible. He nodded slowly, remembering that day in his hotel room before she'd left for London. Her obvious distress over her son had translated into a final afternoon of shared intimacy for them both, although he realized now he might have taken advantage of a more serious hurt for her than he'd appreciated at the time.

"Well, I've just learned from someone I trust that it's happening again." She stood entirely still, her eyes wild and desperate. "But this time, the rumors have been spread in public to men in high places throughout the best clubs in town, and from there carried who knows where! Why, you might have heard them yourself if you didn't shun the men's clubs as you do." She swung her arm up as if suggesting the allegations were flying through the atmosphere, permeating even the air above them now. He was afraid to take a breath that she might note and attach to some kind of sign. She was not depleted yet, and he needed her to be totally satisfied that the poisonous report had all been expunged. "Well what do you say, John?" she almost screamed at him. "Is that not a shock to be confronted with just after arriving in London?" He knew she was pushing him to react.

"That isn't all, is it?" he said, staying as quiet as he could in his seat even though every instinct in him said to jump up and hold on to her before she broke apart. She stared at him.

"No," she said, her hands dropping to her sides, the crushed straw hat bearing no resemblance to anything that could be worn or used for sun protection again. "You're right. There's more, and much worse." She looked across the room as if seeing a vision very far away. Her voice dropped down and she now appeared to be in shock. "William has been the person spreading the rumors about Connie. And even though I made it very clear he would be in serious trouble with me if he continued, I've had little effect on him before and certainly not this time. It's horrible on the surface, but much worse inside his motivation." She sank down on the upholstered stool next to John as if her legs could no longer support her. "I've been told the reason he made such a spectacle of Connie was to divert attention from himself, John, from himself! Not because of his innate jealousies, coldness to his brother, or air of superiority as I've always believed, but because . . . he is the sodomite." She stared at John, as if she expected him to collapse or explode with her news, glaring at him when he did neither. "And he not only didn't want to be exposed but wanted his brother to take the blame for what society would see as his own crime." She seemed to rock a little, buffeted by an unseen wind.

He reached out instinctively to steady her but removed his hand when he saw her balance was good enough to keep her centered on the stool. He could hear the tall clock next to the settee ticking in rhythm with his pulse. Knowing she had come to him for more than his sympathetic ear or infinite appreciation of her, he finally took a breath and said, very softly, "That is truly terrible, but I assume it's William's disloyalty to his brother that upsets you the most. Am I right?"

She stared at him as if she couldn't believe his reaction, then answered with a small cry, as if she were being strangled, "Of course! What else? You must know I don't care how either one of them live their personal lives, and both Corey and I believe everyone has the right to live as they please as long as they don't trample on someone else's rights." She sat very straight on the stool, the straw hat having slipped to the floor unseen, and clasped both her hands tightly together to bury them in her skirt. "Oh, I see from your face that you're surprised by that," she went on, every muscle in her body seeming to tense at once. "But you of all people shouldn't be." She sprang up from the stool, staring wide-eyed at Mackay. "Clearly William has demeaned Connie not only emotionally and professionally, but crushed this family as well. And it's all been done *intentionally*! That's the worst of it. John, what in God's name can I do? And why do things like this keep happening to me?" She looked lost, unable to explain how she'd gotten there.

She knew, and had known for a long time ever since she'd moved to France from America, that her relationship with her sons had not retained its closeness from their early childhood and her early marriage. Once, in the de Koningh house in New York, she'd felt completely at ease with her boys and even enjoyed her life with them as they started to learn about the world around them and the people in it. Certainly, Connie had always been easier to relate to with his warmth and love of all things artistic. William had shown his discomfort in his own skin from an early age, manifested as an air of superiority, which was both annoying and seemingly lacking in empathy. But she'd worked on being close with him on his own terms, and Corey had done well with both boys, too, never losing his playfulness and comfort with their disparate personalities. They had been good parents until . . . until everything had fallen apart with Corey and his father's trip down south. What she saw as both of her men's disloyalty had changed the family irrevocably. Corey's affair with a young southern woman and his father's connection with and ultimate marriage to the woman's aunt had forced Emily and her young family out of the de Koningh family home in New York. Their move to France had been an escape—a necessity rather than a choice.

After that she couldn't trust either one of them again, and the move out of the de Koningh mansion and into the new home in France marked the beginning of her changed life toward a full-time performance career, where her music would make up for what she'd lost in her marriage. Her boys had been well cared for, fed, clothed, and educated. But something had been lost between them and their mother while she found herself again. And it was not just their loss. All of them had dropped away from each other because she hadn't been able to accept another abandonment in her life. She'd driven the wedge between them all, angry and sad about what was gone forever instead of being grateful for what they still had. She wondered now in a brief flash if she'd been as wrong about that as she had her father's neglect after her mother died. Things were not always what they seemed, and the changing perspective of time confirmed it.

"Things like this?" John's need for clarification broke through her thoughts. He was clearly unsure he'd understood all of her message, where precisely her sharpest pain lay. She couldn't answer and as the silence between them grew, she saw herself coming apart. John started to reach for the carafe of water on the table to pour her a glass, but quickly thought better of it and waited to see if she wanted to speak again. She stared at him now with her fists clenched by her sides, partly hidden by the folds of her skirt. "I can't stand it anymore, John," she breathed. "I don't understand why so much pain and . . . testing, is sent my way. What is all this for?" Her voice suddenly dropped, as if her oxygen was depleted and her will to gasp for more gone. John knew the fire must be almost out for the moment with no more fuel to reignite it. He rose easily, handing her the glass and suggesting she take a drink before he put it back on the table.

"Now sit with me here, on the settee," he said, moving her gently with both hands guiding her, one on each arm. She'd become unresponsive in her depletion. She sat down without a will of her own, and he sat again in his own seat, but sideways so he could look her in the eye. "How can I help?" he asked, looking at her directly as if to say he had no intention of either shirking his duty to her or forcing an opinion on her.

"I . . . don't know what to do next," she said.

He nodded slightly. "I think . . . you must speak with the others in your family," he said very quietly, but firmly. "They are all affected by what's happened and what might unfold in the future. I think a predisposition towards secrecy will be the surest way to bring you and all of them down." He continued to look at her directly, even though he could tell she was beginning to disintegrate as she heard him now and started to register what he was saying.

"All of them?" she asked. "Talk with all of them about it?"

"Not yet. Not William and Connie. Your sons can wait until you've decided with the others what to do for the sake of the whole family." She sat up a little straighter, still looking at John directly.

"My father and Corey," she asked, "the three of us must decide what to do?"

"I believe so. For you are not the whole family, nor are you responsible for it solely. And the two boys most directly affected by the lies cannot be expected to be impartial."

"I am not the conductor," she whispered. "How ironic." Emily rose slowly from her seat, and John found himself doing the same so he could be at her level, no matter where she might be going. "I must go home to the family now and wait until I can speak with each one of them alone," she said, almost as if she'd started to come out of a hypnotic trance.

He reached out, taking her small, graceful hand in his strong, workworn grasp. What a surprise her small fingers always were to him, so capable and sure on the taut violin strings in spite of their childlike appearance. "You are being tried as silver," he said, without hesitation. "I think that process never ends for a parent, and you're no exception. I know it comes to us all." He felt her grip tighten in his hand not so much for support but more as a sign of her growing resolve. He bent to pick up her crushed straw hat, coaxing it back into a recognizable shape and handing it to her. "Will you focus on the betrayal rather than the act?" he asked. "What will you tell them?"

"The truth," she said, "I'll tell them the truth. What else?"

15

DIPLOMACY

JOHN HELPED HER into his carriage and gave the driver her address at Grosvenor Square. "I have a feeling your true mettle will shine through in ways you can't imagine now," he said, as he leaned toward her, lifting his hat to shield them both as he kissed her cheek. The door to the carriage shut him out and her in as it took off, leaving him on the steps of the hotel. She'd considered trying to walk home very slowly, perhaps using Hyde Park to give herself plenty of time to think. But she knew John had been right. Time was not on her side with this test, and she needed to know what she was made of now.

It was unlikely any of the men in her family would be home when she got there. Her father was often called out to dine with one of the parliamentary participants, or a close friend of the Crown. Corey would be with one of his new musician friends introduced through his connections in Paris, or working late with some of his potential new students at the Royal College. He was meeting with them on a volunteer basis, but the numbers of pupils seemed to be growing as favorable reports of his skill and humor were passed around. And Connie was ever pursuing a young female of the upper class in need of a gorgeous new gown. What William would be up to, she never knew but often wondered. How would she get through the rest of the hardest day of her life? Waiting while the hours got longer and longer, feeling the dread rising ever closer to the surface where she couldn't hide it from herself, let alone anyone else, would be a torture she feared would shut her down. There was only one way she knew of to keep the panic at bay: by practicing her violin so the hours would fade.

Arriving back at Grosvenor Square, she'd considered giving a message for John to his driver, yet held off as she thanked the coachman for bringing her home. She told him she hoped to see him again when Mr. Mackay returned to England, which she hoped he'd do very soon. She requested his driver pass that along. Entering the apparently empty house using her key after ringing at the front door with no success, Emily stood for a moment, collecting herself from the confusion of her time spent with John at the Langham. She felt as if the emotional chaos had spun her off in every direction, yet now the silence overwhelmed her with emptiness at the very moment she craved action. Nothing seemed to be working the way it should, and it might be hours before either her father or Corey came back. How would she make sense when she told them about William's betrayal and secret?

She knew how her mind traveled to another world when she played her music, surprising her with its total immersion even after a lifetime of familiarity with the violin. Luckily there were new pieces to work on for the fundraising concert in Dublin. She seldom played chamber music for a paying audience, and Ireland was a special challenge for the Royal College staff, as it was Professor Stanford's birthplace and thus meant more to them all. His family had been and still was involved in government there, and his reputation had already made him the pride of the country even at his young age. She and Corey would not perform together. He'd conduct the choral works and help with some of the student compositions. Charles would be accompanying many of the student performers on the piano but would not be joining Emily's quintet. He preferred that she lead it on her own, a way of showcasing her talents for the future.

Schubert's sublime final chamber work, the String Quintet in C Major, was Professor Stanford's choice for her group's main offering.

It was possibly the greatest composition in all chamber music. Bypassing the most popular instrument of the day, the piano, it was created for two violins, one viola, and two cellos, a unique group of musicians producing a very different, very deep, mellow sound. She needed to work hard as first violin to know all the parts well enough to lead and support, while also preparing her own occasional moments to solo. Her practice would give her that wonderful sense of losing herself in the resonances, not just the ones under her left ear but those in her mind as well, leading her down different paths, in different directions. Would the imagined sounds match the heard ones, or would that take more work? Her hardest job was always to make the reality meet her expectations. That's when the hours dropped away.

But fearful her father and husband might come in and leave again without her knowing, Emily put the violin down and walked through to the back of the house to see if she could find Brody at the stable in the mews. She could have him inform both men she needed to speak with them as soon as they arrived. Through the window, she saw movement in the back, suggesting that the family groom was most likely working in the tack room, and she suddenly grasped a thought that pushed all sense of time and practice from her head. She should have considered it long ago. It would solve the family mystery, bringing her understanding of her father's life full circle. She needed to talk with Brody before speaking with anyone else. Going out to the mews, she prepared herself for Brody's possible lack of cooperation. But she wanted answers and would permit no diversion.

Brody looked up from the harness he was working on, neither smiling nor frowning, saying quietly, "Can I help you, Lady Emily? Are you looking for something?" She stopped abruptly, balancing on one foot for a moment as if unsure of her own direction.

"Yes," she finally answered. "I need to speak with my father and Corey before dinner. Did they say what time they'd be home?" She planted her other foot down securely to steady herself, creating the impression that she'd come for a long stay instead of a fleeting moment.

"I don't know if they'll be home for dinner tonight," Brody said, still holding the harness in his hands, expecting Emily to move off as quickly as she'd come.

"Would you watch for them, please, and tell them I must speak with them as soon as they do arrive?" He nodded and started back to cleaning the leather. "Brody," Emily said, so sharply he jumped. "I need to ask you something." He looked up at her, slowly putting the harness down with his rag on the workbench. He said nothing but collected his full attention for her benefit even though his work had been interrupted. Emily took a deep breath to steady herself. "I know about your relationship with my mother, and I know my father did as well. For that matter, apparently a lot of people did because I heard of it for the first time from my aunt Clara." She realized her dark eyes had hardened, but she was too drained to regulate her expression for his benefit.

Brody lifted his chin, pushing his thick gray hair off his forehead with the back of his hand, but other than that neither moved nor said anything for a few moments. Finally he asked her, "What do you want to know?"

Emily watched him through a slightly narrowed gaze. "Why didn't my father have you leave immediately once he'd discovered your affair with my mother? And why did he keep you on indefinitely? No wonder Aunt Clara was surprised to find you here to greet her when she arrived recently—unannounced, as she so often does! There's very little about the whole situation that makes sense to me."

"Why does it need to make sense now?" he asked, staring at her as if unafraid to take on her accusations he'd been expecting for a lifetime.

She glared back at him, infuriated. "Because a friend of mine reminded me of how poisonous secrets are, and how they have an insidious way of hurting people they don't even involve. One might think the only way I can start to put my family back together again is by beginning with the truth. And if it doesn't break us apart forever, it may heal us. Brody, why are you still here?"

Brody sighed slightly, resting his hand on the harness for a moment in resignation. Then he looked back up at her. She noted the quiet strength in his face, the firm jaw and high forehead completing an appearance that was uniquely and strikingly Scottish. Emily felt she could almost remember that sandy-haired young groom who'd let her work in the stable with him before she'd left for America.

"Your father always traveled a great deal for the Crown," Brody began, "as I'm sure you remember." She nodded, working hard not to interrupt. "The queen had just given him the assignment to go to America when your mother was found ill and unlikely to recover. He couldn't take her with him and wanted someone to care for her here in her own home; someone he could trust to put her needs first before anything else. So, he left her, and to some extent you, as my responsibility, and his sister Clara in the house for the look of propriety. He knew no one would work harder than I to keep your mother as happy and comfortable as possible, or you any safer than I did." He talked as if he'd told the story many times before in his own head.

"You see, we became a family of a different sort," he went on, smiling gently, as if his memories had a calming effect. "It appeared to be an arrangement of convenience for your father, his work being so important and necessary. There were many diplomats and politicians working for the government at that time who had to live apart from their families. But truly, it was rather a loyalty created of love. After your mother died . . . ," he sighed and glanced out the window at the courtyard dividing the mews from the house, ". . . your father needed someone to take care of the house, and he wanted to keep a connection to your mother's memory, and so he asked me to stay. That is why everything was and is as you find it now."

Emily was shocked. Not so much by what Brody had told her, but she was unnerved by the fact that she understood perfectly how the unusual arrangement had come about. There was and had been a community of caring, connected people, creating a structure around each other and her mother. But where had the young daughter Emily fit into that family? Somehow Brody intuited her thought and leaned slightly on the workbench for support.

"Your father brought you to America when he had to go himself, making it appear as if he'd brought you with him to live with his dearest friend, yet truthfully his lifelong friend took on the responsibility of raising you with his son. In fact, Lady Emily, you've had a large, extended family almost since you were born. As I see it, you've been unusually blessed."

He smiled a little, but she looked at him steadily and said, "That's not how I saw it then." She took a deep breath before speaking again. "Brody, what of all the traits you've mentioned do you find the most important to the strength of a family? You've said that you and my father had it here with my mother, but what was the key to that relationship?" She knew he couldn't possibly understand how important his answer would be to her, and she tried not to let him see how close she was to breaking down.

He didn't look away, but didn't speak immediately, either. Finally, he said, "Loyalty. Not the blind, unquestioning kind given to a cause or creed, but the kind shared with others who care for one another. To know that no one's loyalty need ever be questioned is the power of a family bond. Do you not agree?" he asked, noticing her growing agitation.

"Oh, I do. I most certainly do," she said, tensing her whole body. "And now I have some work to do with my violin before the men come home. Thank you for sharing some difficult memories with me, Brody. Somehow I knew I could count on you for the truth." She turned slowly but deliberately toward the stable door, aware that she'd never asked the groom how his affair had developed with her mother in the first place, because it didn't matter. "And thank you for your loyalty," she said, turning to give him one of her warmest smiles, knowing they'd always meant a great deal to him since she was a small child. But just as she took a step forward, she stopped again, and without turning back to look at him, dropped her voice to a deeper level. "If loyalty is the key to a family, then what should be done about those who betray that trust?" She stood with her back to him.

He misunderstood her question, trying to read her expression when he couldn't see it. "I didn't betray it. We didn't. Your father—"

"That's not what I'm asking," she said, her back rigid.

"Well, your father sent your aunt Clara away this time because he'd told her specifically he wanted you to have your memory of your mother untouched by any gossip. She pointedly violated his wishes, as if your mother had been involved in a scandal. If you want to know what I think should be done about something like that, it's just what he did. She has no place in the family when she treats his feelings and yours with so little concern."

Emily turned partway around to look at him again, nodding slowly. "It's like the packs of animals that ostracize one of their own for behaving in ways that aren't good for the rest of them."

"Yes," Brody said, reaching for the harness and his rag again. "Simply put, the family must protect itself from members like that."

"And there's no second chance?" Emily asked. "No possibility for someone to change?" She was stuck halfway between the door and the groom.

"Not when it comes to family trust," Brody said, unaware that she'd moved on from Aunt Clara. "There are some people who are made differently. They don't share the values of the family, and no amount of time or effort will change them at their core. That's just their nature."

✦✦✧∙᳀∙✧✦✦

"What are you doing here?" Emily stood just inside the hallway of the Grosvenor Square house, staring into the light outside on the front stoop where someone had just rung the bell. A stranger would not have been a surprise, but the unexpectedness of Johnny Dunne's arrival in London, let alone on her doorstep, knocked the breath out of her.

"Not quite the welcome I'd hoped for," he said, standing with his hat in one of his gloved hands and a small dark leather briefcase in the other. "I haven't even been to my hotel yet," he added almost apologetically, lifting his briefcase harboring all his worldly goods with him like a carpetbagger. "Coming to see you took precedence over everything I was doing for myself," he said with a little smile. "Princess Pauline sent me," he added, lowering his voice, "in a way. She told me more than enough about your situation with the boys to convince me you needed support. I'm so sorry the mystery has resolved as it has. Would we be able to talk privately here, or if not, could you suggest someplace better?"

"Johnny!" Emily breathed with a smile growing from dimple to dimple despite her worry and distraction. "You're always there to catch me before I fall. I must talk to Corey and my father about William before they go out for dinner but got tangled up in my thoughts. You've come just in time. But what in the name of the Lord did Pauline tell you that caused you to drop everything and rush to save me, as you so often do?"

"She told me more than enough to convince me I had to be here," Johnny said, returning her smile with the true concern he felt. It was something he'd never been able to regulate in her presence. "I'll catch you in any way I can. Shall we go inside?"

"No," she fairly snapped at him. "They'll all be coming back to change for dinner. We need to talk somewhere else." She pulled the door shut behind her, careful not to let it slam and thus announcing her departure from the house. "Let's walk in the garden if you're not too tired after your trip," she said. But before he could agree or oppose, she'd already leapt off the stoop onto the pavement below, and Johnny stared after her as she started down one of the footpaths leading into the somewhat untamed garden across the street. He had no choice but to follow, having come across the sea to talk her through her predicament and help her start to make sense of it. Clearly, he'd been right to worry she might explode without someone's help.

Almost running to keep up with her, now intent on finding privacy to talk through her plans for the family's salvation, her friend from her earliest adult years found himself looking around with surprise. He didn't know London well and had never been in the garden park at Grosvenor Square. Providing almost six acres of open landscape, the park was the second-largest garden in central London. He knew that from its reputation, but had never given it any thought until now, running behind Emily into what appeared to be a magical sylvan landscape.

"Where did this come from?" he asked, slightly out of breath as he caught up with Emily sitting on a carved bench behind a small cluster of evergreens.

"What, the park or the bench?" she asked, a hint of her old familiar spirit shimmering through the obvious fear gripping her.

"All of it," Johnny said, gesturing at the expanse of park around them. Emily sighed slightly, relieved to have the chance to think and talk about something other than her own troubles.

"Grosvenor Square was originally laid out by a gardener," she said. "Can't you tell? It was supposed to be his 'wilderness work' design, a celebration of the countryside in the city, just like New York's Central Park. But this is just for the owners of the houses around the square, more like Gramercy Park. And it did come first, about 150 years first—in fact, before America was founded. I must say, I don't think it compares favorably with the American version. I miss Central Park," she said, looking away down another path leading around the garden's perimeter. "I hadn't really thought of it until now. I suppose a longing for a better time and happier life is part of that." She still didn't look at Johnny directly, so he reached over with his gloved hand and turned her face toward him.

"Those were not always better times, and most certainly not a happier life," he said, forcing her to look in his eyes directly. She said nothing for a few seconds, nor did she move to get out of his grasp. Then she pulled her head up like a willful animal while putting downward pressure on his hand with hers.

"You're right, of course," she said quietly. "But in those days, I had hope: hope I'd become the world's greatest female violinist, and hope I'd create a solid, loving, and dedicated family of my own to gather around each other and keep the bad things of the world away." She stared back at Johnny believing he'd have had little idea of how straightforward her goals had been. She finally looked slowly past him, searching for something far off in the grove of trees standing so close to one another you couldn't see through to the other side.

"Neither one of those dreams have come true," she finally said, in a dull, flat voice, "even with all my work and commitment." She looked back at him again and found that it was now he who had trouble meeting her gaze. He had looked away down the footpath they'd taken into the garden as if trying to see something that wasn't there.

"And in fact," she went on almost cruelly, as if she would make him experience her pain whether he wanted to or not, "I feel I've created a monster at home that, far from keeping away the demons of the world, has brought them all into the family circle, affecting every one of us with a kind of loathing and pushing us all away from each other." He looked back at her in shock, still unable to say anything to stop her onslaught. "How can anyone create beautiful music in an atmosphere like that?" she asked, clearly not expecting, or needing, an answer she already had. "Where is home when all the dreams have left and only the nightmares remain?"

Johnny knew something about personal accomplishment erasing the stains of a hard childhood, as, for that matter, did John Mackay. It was something they shared. And in many ways, Emily did as well. He thought perhaps that was the strength of the bond holding them all together. He wanted to tell her so.

"Have you decided to tell your father and Corey about William's betrayal and ask them to help with a decision to deal with it? Have you done that yet?" He felt cruel pushing her back to such a difficult place, but it was necessary. She nodded.

"I've decided to speak with them together so they can't say they heard different stories from one to the other," she said quietly, almost sadly.

"Wise," Johnny said, nodding as if he took some pride in her handling of a difficult situation. "But what reactions do you expect?" He was having trouble imagining the scene between the three of them yet didn't want to push her to describe it simply to satisfy his curiosity.

"Well," she sighed, as if growing suddenly too weary to talk, "Corey will laugh, saying we've always felt the boys, who are now almost men, should live their own lives their own way. He often reminds me we used to discuss that they must have the freedom to deal with their problems as well as their victories, and not look to us for remedies to troubles of their own making." She shook her head slowly as if watching a scene in the library all over again. "He not only won't take the sodomy charge seriously, but he'll probably refuse to get involved with the evil that William tried to do to his brother and this family." She stared at the grass in front of the bench they sat on. "He lives in his own world, Johnny, and it's not ours." He took off his gloves, laying them on the bench beside him and putting his hand on hers in her lap, feeling he might warm it as she'd grabbed only a small shawl when she'd run from the house with him.

"And how will Lord Alden react to that—I mean to Corey's noncommittal approach as well as your disclosure before it?" He squeezed her hand a little, perhaps hoping she'd realize she had support to go on, but her voice continued to weaken, and he realized she'd done too much talking in the hours just past.

"Oh, as you know, he's of an even temperament in general, but the danger for all of us will be clear to him, as well as for Connie, who got caught in something he shouldn't have even been near." She pulled herself up straighter on the bench, working for a stronger voice and clearer diction. Finally, she went on. "I know Father heard some of the whispers about Connie himself in his clubs but found ways to silence them. He didn't explain fully, but I know he still commands a certain respect that people defer to. Once he knows the full story, he'll see where those rumors came from and know they must be stopped immediately. I'm sure my father will feel William must be made to understand there is no other recourse, other than being turned in to the authorities by his own family or leaving for good to pursue a life and career someplace else." She slumped down again, as if the last effort had been too much. Johnny put his arm around her, lifting her up against him and hoping the contact would give her the strength she needed now. It seemed to help a little, just enough to keep her going.

"I'm going to discuss moving William to another European capital where he could make his own way and have no contact with any of us," she said against his shoulder. "I think Father could find William a position as an assistant in the Foreign Office, involving him in the pressures of court politics and intrigue, something he has a natural proclivity for. I'm sure Father could find someone through his own connections, or possibly Pauline and her husband; or even you, Johnny. We need to move quickly so William understands that the crime he's committed against his brother must be punished and paid for, and so that he stops his campaign of lies before he makes it worse for himself. I believe Father will speak with him about it directly, thank heaven, because I couldn't do it." She suddenly pushed away a little to look Johnny in the eye.

"Just think what it means not to be able to count on the loyalty of one of your children," she said. "I can't even look at William. It makes me wonder; did I cause that malevolence? Was I not the mother he needed, and most certainly Corey not the father? Did I permit that to happen because I was too selfishly involved with my own life?"

"No more," Johnny ordered. "You know we're all responsible for our own lives. But how do you feel about sending him away, for good?" He stared back at her, returning her direct gaze. "Do you truly feel it's your only alternative? Will you ask what they think about that decision, and are you sure?" Emily nodded before he'd finished, slowly at first and then more emphatically. He continued to watch her carefully.

"Think about it, Johnny. My firstborn son, not even all that much younger than I, barely a generation, so amoral he would sink the family I've cultivated so lovingly. How does any mother get over the pain of that?"

He looked down at her small hands, clenched now in her lap so tightly he was afraid she'd injure her precious fingers. He reached over to cover them again with both of his hands, trying to uncurl and release her terrible grip. Unwinding the fingers one by one, she finally let him place her hands flat and open on top of each other in her lap and left them there. "But every time I see a beggar in the street that no one will help, I'll think, *It might be my William*. And every time I wonder if there's anyone to care for him when he's sick, it will kill me not knowing."

"All right. I understand," he said, patting her hands once to be sure they didn't spring back into the vicious coil they'd been in before. "Now, I have a job to do with your father and the others to find a good . . . situation for William to live and work in. You need to rest and step back from it for a while; let go. It's time for you to stop trying to control everything on your own." He stood slowly, picking her up in one piece from the bench as if he was afraid she'd break if he didn't keep her together, though he'd never seen her do that, no matter the pressure.

"Forget the hotel," she said. "Stay with us while you're here." She held on to his arm as if she needed help to walk. "My aunt Clara is gone, and the guest room is empty again."

"I will," he said. "I need to talk with your father and Corey, and once we have the right position secured, then the boys themselves. Dear Lord, who would ever have imagined such a meeting all those years ago when we used to go Christmas shopping together in New York?" Emily looked stunned by his reference, and realizing he should have kept the thought to himself, Johnny added, "But William was dissatisfied with life even then, and disconnected from his brother as well. I'm afraid it has come to haunt him now. One never thinks of a young child as amoral, but I suppose it can start at that age."

"How will my father explain the decision to him?" Emily asked, trying to give up her front-row seat in the drama she'd been living, and move to the rear of the family theater.

"I don't know," he said, with a small smile, feeling honesty would satisfy her the most. "But do you know the meaning of the word 'diplomacy'?" Emily nodded. "Of course you do, especially with a father who's served the Crown of England his whole life. But there's so much more to it than the political implications. He's very practiced. He'll find the words." He started moving slowly, retracing their steps into the garden from the perimeter where they'd first entered. Emily followed, still clinging to his arm but moving with him. He stopped, worried that she was so exhausted she might not make it out of the park if he didn't give her time to collect herself. But she seemed to be following not only his lead but also his explanation, so he started walking.

"I can't think of a timelier moment for the art of diplomacy in the de Koningh family than right now," Johnny said, grateful that the town house was coming into view across the street. He held her tighter, gently placing a kiss on her forehead. But Emily's legs gave out at last, exhausted in the wake of the storm, and she found herself clinging to him like a life preserver.

⊱✦⊰ 𝒲 ⊱✦⊰

Emily always found herself drawn to the warmth and safety of her practice space. Following the lure of that escape now, she decided to start her day in the library with her violin. Breakfast with Johnny and her father in the dining room had brought back a strange, diffused memory of a morning long ago at breakfast with Lord Alden in the house he'd rented in New York just after the Civil War. Emily had confronted him then about his manipulation of her young life and career, and she could feel the tension and anger of that moment again as if it were happening today. She'd been surprised at how accepting her father had been of her feelings that day long ago. He'd acknowledged his control and misuse of power over her then, and the conflict had ended with a new understanding of each other, albeit a constrained view.

Now here she was again, thousands of miles and two decades away from that first talk, explaining the dissolution of her family to her father at the contrivance of her eldest son. Power, manipulation, and treachery had been a part of this event in a way far worse than that experience when she was twenty years old. And again, surprising as it was, her father had listened, absorbed what he heard, and agreed that immediate action must be taken. He suggested that she step back from the fray to save herself a traumatic scene with

William that she might not ever be able to put out of her mind. Johnny had agreed to join with her father to design a separation plan for William. The men had accepted the assignment to rid the family of its clear and current danger in the form of Emily's eldest son to save her from the trauma of doing it herself. They'd left the dining room with the look and movement of purpose suggesting a potentially explosive situation was about to be disarmed.

But Emily felt no relief, and she needed some. A sensation much like anticipation of an incendiary bomb cascaded through her with the relentlessness of a natural force. It reminded her of all the hells so many artists had endured, convincing her that some time spent with Beethoven or Mozart might offer the strength she needed to face the unimaginable horror of who William had become, and what he'd attempted to do to his brother.

Her father and Johnny had the buffer of their expertise in maneuvering society—diplomacy is what they called it. She, on the other hand, was on the other side of that barrier, a certain lack of subtlety always with her when emotions overtook her discretion. So now she'd turn to those other musicians from the past to find a little of the balm she needed. The library door was partially open, so she pushed it further and headed with singular purpose toward her instrument case lying on the piano just as she'd left it a few days ago. It reminded her how little time she'd had recently to practice. In fact, her concentration was so extreme she walked right through the room without noticing William reading on the window seat.

"Good heavens, Mother. What brings you to the library with such momentum? Is it a guilty conscience stirred up by the dust gathering on your violin?" She jumped, visibly shaken by the shock of his presence, or the leap of her heart; she wasn't sure which. He smiled easily, a calm, handsome vision of assurance that brought the pain of seeing him instantly to the surface, her heart so gripped with the dread of what he'd done she could hardly breathe. Never again would she face this young man with her true feelings about him, nor had she expected to do so now. But the time had come to make her position clear, even though she knew it would mean nothing to him, though it meant everything to her.

"William! You're here . . . What are you doing?" she asked, although it was clear.

"Just what it looks like," he said, lifting the paper slightly to indicate its presence. "Would you like me to leave so you can practice?" But he made no move to change his position to accommodate her need for solitude. She saw the cool, imperious expression and heard the arrogant voice she'd come to know so well, but somehow refused to acknowledge as a harbinger of who he was or might become. She took a deep breath where she stood and straightened her back, as if facing a difficult passage she needed to perform perfectly.

"This reminds me of a time so long ago, when you were very young and insisted on badgering me and your brother in the library of Grandfather Klaas's house in New York. Have I always been searching for a place to play my violin, while you have ever been toying with manipulating others?" She watched his smooth features for some sign of recognition but saw no change. "I felt then as if you were practicing the art of pulling the wings off of human flies, but never understood that it might be an inborn trait." She stood rigid in the middle of the room, staring at William as if seeing him for the first time. He laughed under his breath, folding his paper and putting it down deliberately as if conceding that her interruption would be permanent. He leaned back against one of the cushions lining the side of the window with a small sigh.

"What's all the drama for, Mother? I don't remember having anything to do with the wings of flies in my youth." She was surprised by the antagonism in his voice, as if he had somehow intuited her message and was already beginning his defense with an offense.

"Oh William, you know exactly what I mean," she spat out angrily. "Even as a young boy you worked every angle to make

Connie look a childish fool and include me in your judgment just for good measure. I thought that might all be out of the natural competition between brothers, as well as mother and son. But I've come to realize there's nothing natural about your relationship to this family." Her voice had slowly lowered with increasing intensity, and her eyes flashed a warning she wished William would heed, but knew with growing assurance that he would not. She would be forced to say what she didn't want to hear herself. She stayed standing rigid in the middle of the room, hoping irrationally that a little more silence might help William find his own voice. But he was a consummate chess master when it came to planning his moves ahead, and she feared she'd been outsmarted before she began.

"Mother," he said finally, making it clear with the ennui in his voice that he was only indulging her because she was so obviously vulnerable, "what are you upset about? The day has barely begun, and you're already agitated over something. Why has the sight of me caused you so much aggravation?" Sighing as he pushed his paper aside, he made the mistake of changing his expression to one of exasperation, as if the interruption his mother represented was a burden too great to bear with grace. The shift in his mood served as the spontaneous combustion for Emily's rage.

"You!" she cried out. "You are the one responsible for every negative reaction coming back at you." William frowned slightly, caught off guard by her vehemence. "You lied about your brother and did everything in your power to make him the scapegoat of your own actions. I sense you have no idea why anyone would find that reprehensible, the perfect definition of an amoral character. And I see that you have no remorse and no guilt whatsoever to weigh down your soul. Do I feel guilty at not having played my violin for too long, you ask?" She'd begun to lean forward toward him, trying to hold his big dark eyes so like her own in a viselike grip. "Yes, of course I do, because I have a responsibility to a beautiful instrument and all the people in my life who've helped me learn to play it. And yes, I am so grateful to them all and feel culpable when I let them down. But you!" She fired a look of disgust at him. "You understand what you owe the family and others in your community but have no intention of delivering on your debt—nor did you ever."

William stayed seated but had begun to look fully engaged, as if he understood the importance of what his mother was saying. "What brought all this theater on today, Mother? I feel I've missed some important narrative and gotten the short end of the argument." They glowered at each other, clearly aware of the truth of what was being said on both sides.

"You know perfectly well," Emily said, more calmly at last. "You lied to implicate your brother in your own illegal behavior."

"I'll tell you what I know perfectly well," William said, rising to stand at his full height, a handsome, menacing specter of simmering rage. "My *illegal behavior*, as you choose to put it, is nothing compared to the horrors perpetrated by governments on innocent people who fall unhappily under their rule all over the world. Society legalizes its own crimes and ostracizes those it chooses to condemn."

"I'm not judging your behavior or the way you choose to live," Emily cried out, "and what's more, you know it. I won't get mixed up in your rhetoric, William. I've done it too long to get caught in that trap. I'm accusing you of putting your own desires ahead of the well-being of your brother and your family by lying to condemn us all instead of honestly carrying the burden of your lifestyle yourself."

"What do you know about carrying the burdens of life?" he sneered. "To be different from almost everyone else, an outcast, treated as if you're lacking something essential when you know many people are actually jealous of what you have and can do, is a nightmare you've never had to face." He glared at his mother, an enemy he needed to defeat.

"Don't be ridiculous!" she shouted back at him. "I've never been like everyone else. I've always been treated as if I were different and strange, and I've often experienced the jealousy of the people who are the hardest on me. But that's life, William. You deal with what you're given and in all instances, with the people in your life, truthfully and kindly." She pulled herself back up and finally took another deep breath. She seemed to slow herself down to a controlled place where she could finish her speech with the emphasis it deserved.

"This is the last time I will meet with you or talk to you. Your grandfather and my friends will handle your leaving from this home, and if you don't follow their instructions perfectly, you'll be turned into the law for the crimes you accused Connie of. I advise you to seek your grandfather out immediately before he moves to have you incarcerated without waiting for the right situation to present itself."

Suddenly, Emily stopped talking as abruptly as she'd started. She turned, moving to the piano to grab her violin in its case and running to the open library door. Did it matter if anyone had heard her argument with him? No. It only mattered that she'd finally told him he no longer held a position of good faith in her family and heart. She knew he'd probably always considered their relationship invincible, as it was meant to be between mother and child. But she wanted him to know without any doubt that was not the case under his broken rules of morality. He had lied to hurt others who were entirely unprotected and innocent of his intentions. He would not darken her heart again, and now he knew it.

16

HOME AT LAST

CHARLES STANFORD unfurled the pristine white tablecloth with all the grace his musician's wrists could summon. The soft cotton floated airborne for a few moments before it settled gently over the top of his desk. He smiled in anticipation of what was to come. One by one, he removed the two white napkins wrapped around silverware, the loaf of crusty bread, the cold chicken, the cheese, and the fruit all from the first hamper. From the second hamper, he triumphantly produced a chocolate cake. Emily watched spellbound as each piece took its place on the desktop, finally joined by a bottle of wine and two glasses conjured from the bottom of the second hamper. All was arranged with a care and precision that reminded Emily of preparations for a ceremony. She'd visited Queen Victoria's Japanese-inspired teahouse on the grounds of Frogmore in Windsor, which attested to the importance of marketing British imperialism through the ceremonial consumption of tea. Yet this was only lunch at the professor's desk in lieu of a trip to a restaurant of choice or no lunch at all. Surely it wasn't meant to be anything of major significance.

"Well, I never . . . ," Emily breathed appreciatively, with a small laugh.

"Nor I," the professor said, surveying the feast spread out before them. "My cook has outdone herself. It reminds one of Édouard Manet's *Le Déjeuner sur L'herbe*." He chuckled, adjusting his pince-nez glasses as if to study the picnic better. "In a way . . . except it's not *'sur l'herbe,'*" he added.

Emily worked hard not to laugh out loud. "But I'd prefer if this one could be Claude Monet's, if you don't mind." The professor, first obviously taken aback by her comment, finally burst out laughing when its meaning sank in. He looked like a naughty child caught with a frog behind his back in his mother's parlor.

"I can't imagine what your objection could be to Monsieur Manet's greatest work," he said, "according to Émile Zola. Or can I?"

"I don't particularly like the fully dressed Monet one."

"Boring in every way," the professor agreed, nodding vigorously. "Which is something we are not. Nor is Manet, who seeks only to paint with all the tools made available to him by his skill. There is no subversion of morality in the story the painting presents. That sedition lies only in the naïve purview of the public." He reached for the corkscrew he'd laid out when placing the wine and glasses down, beginning the sometimes-laborious process of removing the seal and cork as easily as if he could do it with his eyes closed. Pausing for a moment of reflection, he looked directly at Emily and said, "This is the first time I've ever had lunch at my desk." She frowned slightly, but a faint flash of her dimples said she was entertained rather than surprised by his disclosure.

"Where do you usually have it?" she asked, without taking her dark eyes from his blue ones.

"I don't," he replied.

"Not at all?"

"No. Not unless I'm dining out at the Langham with potential donors or revered colleagues . . . such as was the case when I first met you in person." He unwrapped one of the knives and started to carve the small roast chicken. "But this is a lot more fun," he said, nudging his glasses back up the bridge of his nose with the back of his hand. "Can I serve you?" he asked. Emily nodded. "Fruit as well as cheese?" he asked again, gesturing to both offerings on the table. She nodded again.

"And why did your cook prepare this feast for you today?" she asked.

"Because I told her I wanted to eat in my office hosting a fellow musician. And I persuaded her by promising to eat more if she made an especially delicious picnic for me." His eyes twinkled with merriment as he looked at Emily over his glasses, and she grinned back.

"Persuaded! It's more of a seduction, don't you think?"

He shrugged and nodded, handing Emily a plate perfectly balanced with just enough of everything and not too much of anything. "Can I pour you some wine?" he asked, as she put her plate down and started to unfold her napkin with silverware. Somehow he'd managed to fill his own plate with the same meal he'd given her without being noticed. She looked at him a little harder, trying to figure out how he was producing such an unusual performance. She was beginning to feel rather like Lewis Carroll's Alice at tea with the Mad Hatter.

She studied the wine bottle and nodded slowly. "I suppose, since I'm neither teaching officially on the college staff yet nor performing today . . ." Her voice trailed off as she watched him pour a chilled glass of Chablis just one-third full, handing it to her with a bright smile.

"No harm done with this," he said. "I'm teaching all afternoon and hoping the wine will get me through it cheerfully! Now, a quick toast." He raised his glass toward her, and she raised hers to meet it. "Welcome, Emily de Koningh, and I hope this new beginning benefits us both and our future students as well." He tapped her glass lightly with his and a pure note rang out, hanging in the air between them for a moment. "Perfect crystal," he said, taking an appreciative sip from his glass and replacing it on the desk next to his plate, "makes perfect pitch."

"And the perfect touch," Emily said, clearly in awe of the young professor's social skills as well as his good taste. "Not just the glasses, but all of this." She motioned with her head as if bowing to both her host and his table at the same time.

"Well, thank you. I'm glad it pleases you. I wish I'd done this a long time ago. It's much pleasanter than dealing with the public crush at a restaurant, although I must say I enjoyed our outing at Crosby's in Bishopsgate. I found my introduction to ladies' cycling most thrilling. Still, if I can convince you to join us full-time here, we could have many more of these lunches to discuss our work and our students." Emily shifted uncomfortably in her seat, a little wary now that an ulterior motive for their picnic might be rising to the surface.

"I don't truly know how my life will be moving along," Emily said, looking out the small window behind the professor's desk to nothing. "My performances, my home, my family . . . I just don't know," she said again, with a deep sigh she was totally unaware of. "I'm at rather a loose end right now, Charles, and not to be counted on."

"That just means you're in transition," he said, cutting himself more chicken. "Oh dear, I forgot the bread," he added, shaking his head. "Let's have just a little so Annie won't berate me when I take the hampers home." Without asking, he placed a piece of dark, crusty bread on each of their plates, nudging a small pot of sweet butter closer to her. "Let us help you tie up those loose ends of yours," he went on, as if he'd never stopped talking or been distracted.

"Oh, you couldn't." Emily let her eyes drop with her voice so her host couldn't see the shadow that had come over her. But Charles had never taken no for an answer, and he wasn't about to now. His intuition was sharp and well trained to serve him.

"Tell me how your family is doing here in London," he said lightly, putting no more emphasis on the matter than he had his query about her preference for cheese or fruit. Professor Stanford was a consummate teacher. He knew when to talk and when to be silent, and how to encourage his students to open their wary souls without ever seeming to coax or entreat. Emily's discomfort now was clearly a result of some trouble she'd brought into the room with her, not a reaction to anything in the discussion they'd already shared. He intuited that he had to be gentler with her than he would be with his young students, or he'd never get anything back.

He watched her expressions go from hidden to an emerging kaleidoscope of uncontrolled emotions, keeping his focus seemingly on the elements of the picnic he oversaw. Reaching for the bread again, he sliced himself another piece, using that as an excuse to look at her directly. "I shouldn't," he said, with a wink. "But I will. I so prefer the Irish peasant bread of my youth to those bland, washed-out white loaves. They're so proud of the Chinese silk sieves making finer, whiter flour today. Everybody feels wealthier with that kind of bread but it's nowhere near as good." He used his seconds of study-ing her to plan his next question.

"So, you say your younger son has had some wonderful luck, thanks to his introduction to Charles Worth through the Princess von Metternich. It sounds as if he's landed squarely in the middle of his artistic dream. Has he always wanted to design clothing?" He smiled warmly at Emily, trying to make her feel that the success of her younger son reflected on them all, as if he was a member of a community of artists who reveled in each other's accomplishments. He watched her face start to relax as they discussed the possibility of Connie working in the House of Worth's London office, at least for the present. She described her own visit to have a dress designed for the upcoming Royal College concert in Dublin, clearly enthralled by the designer's intelligence and artistic sensibilities. "You feel your young son to be in the hands of a trustworthy and inspiring mentor, then," Charles said, in full understanding of the importance of such a relationship when an artistic temperament was at stake. He watched Emily finally settle in to eat her fruit and cheese with some gusto, pouring a little more wine for her without asking. It was time to move on.

"And your other son, is he enjoying London as much?" Emily's breath caught so fast it caused him to look up, and he could feel the silence tighten. But he knew the importance of acting as if he'd noticed nothing. He started to rewrap the chicken to place it back in the hamper, working hard to keep his expression friendly and safe.

"Not really," Emily said, seeing her host shift his expression to watch her, seemingly out of politeness alone.

"I'm sorry to hear that," he said. "Has he not found anything to involve himself in?" He saw from the pain on her face that this was the trouble she'd brought with her and what they must get past before her own needs could be discussed. "Tell me about it, if you can." He purposely avoided asking it as a question.

This was the subject that would plague her, plague them all for the rest of their lives. How was William doing? Where was he? This was as good a time as any to practice her response, as Professor Stanford didn't really know them or him, and was seemingly interested in only one or two things in the world: music and teaching, with his school and his students following closely behind. He clearly held *society* and its mores at arm's length and had no need to involve himself in anything outside of his family of artists. She'd heard him tell the students that musicians at their level made up a very small community, and they'd best not burn any bridges on their way to their careers or they'd find everyone they needed for support abandoning them. This was a world utterly foreign to William, yet entirely familiar to her.

"My older son, William, is at that age of discontent with his lot in life," she said, nodding slightly as if Charles already understood her point. "He's always been interested in politics and the important, powerful people who make countries and governments revolve." She pulled herself up straighter, wanting to appear confident in the speech she was giving. "His grandfather has always been involved with diplomacy for the Crown," she went on, able to look at her host directly when discussing her father. "But involving William in British politics with any of my father's contacts would be too close to home." She thought her voice was suddenly sounding a note of desperation. "I mean, it might take away some of his initiative to perform on his own," she added. She didn't wait for the professor to comment as she might have under more normal circumstances, afraid she might not be able to continue.

"So we've put together a coalition of sorts, comprised of the Princess von Metternich, my father, and a friend of the family who works for *Le Figaro* in Paris. They will come up with the best opportunity for William to start his career in the Foreign Office. Of course that means he'll have to live elsewhere, but it's the best time for a young man to strike out," she rushed to finish, hoping her explanation sounded plausible. She noticed the professor looking politely interested as he listened and slowly put away some of the picnic until the chocolate cake sat richly and conspicuously alone in the middle of the tablecloth.

"It sounds ideal," her host said. "But does he mind the involvement of so many others in his future? I remember thinking the same thing when I heard your father's plan for your future here at the college. And then I realized it's what we do for the people we love. And what a wonderful group to stand behind your William and further his career. I can't imagine more advantageous connections than those of the professional statesmen and ambassadors you have working on his behalf. I'm sure between the Metternichs, *Le Figaro*, and Lord Alden, a wonderful situation will be found for him somewhere." Emily's face was looking more strained with every word he uttered. "Of course, I know you will miss him terribly, but that's the trial of being a mother, I suspect." He repositioned his glasses on his nose slightly, smiling kindly at Emily once they were settled where he wanted them. "And it does put you in the position of having time for yourself and your own career, perhaps for the first spell since you started your family. It might feel a bit uncomfortable right now, but I think you'll take off as soon as you realize you're truly free."

Emily stared at him, and then drank her last swallow of wine. Her jaw tightened. "Professor, I hadn't planned on losing my children after I worked so hard to get them. You must understand that," she added, but then suddenly realized she knew almost nothing about him or his family and had no right to suggest anything about his feelings where relationships were concerned. "You are married and a father yourself, are you not?" She felt embarrassed now. "Forgive me," she said, looking down at her hands. "I had no right . . . I just assumed . . ."

"You're absolutely correct," he said, seeming totally at ease. "I do have a two-year-old daughter and another child on the way almost literally any minute."

"Good heavens, how exciting," Emily said. "But your wife must find the schedule you keep here starting a new music school and teaching and running the Bach Choir and . . . everything else you do rather wearing for her with all her domestic duties. You can't be much help at home," she added, with a laugh.

"So true!" he responded without hesitation. "But my wife was an opera singer, much to my father's disdain, and so although she gave up her career when we met in Leipzig and married, she understands mine perfectly and supports it completely," he said, raising his head to look at Emily better through his glasses. "You had to deal with much more when you chose both paths, and I know the family must have meant everything to you or you wouldn't have put that weight on top of the one you had to carry for your music." She raised her eyebrows, as if in doubt or simply because she had little memory of that decision made long ago. "I wonder if all that pressure makes for a better artist. It must be hard, as I said, to suddenly realize one of the weights has been lifted from you, tipping you off balance after all these years of struggle."

He looked at her with more sympathy and understanding than she was used to. "This is a good place to get your balance back

again," he said. "We're all family here." She realized she was returning his gaze wide-eyed, as if in disbelief of the possibilities he'd
outlined already. More than the refined, elegant clothing and hands,
the shiny dark hair parted at the side and mustache so becoming it
was hard to imagine he'd ever been without it, the young professor's
face radiated so much pleasure it was hard to imagine him unhappy
with anything.

"And now the climax of this little party!" he exclaimed, picking
up a silver letter opener from his desk and brandishing it above the
chocolate cake. "I have no cake knife, but that shan't stop us. Can I
cut you a piece?"

She shook her head. "Not quite yet," she said, gesturing as if to
include the professor and the entire office as well as the picnic
mementos. "I need to digest . . . all of this first."

"I understand," the professor answered, nodding. "Let's take a
few minutes to talk about what you've experienced at the college so
far. You may have questions I can help you with." Somehow he'd
already collected the plates and forks without her being fully aware
of it, slipping them neatly into the hamper along with the fruit,
cheese, and bread. The chicken had disappeared long before.

"You're very good at the logistics of entertaining," she said,
grinning at him as she settled back in her chair, for the first time
relaxed and without her guard. "How did you learn all of this?" She
suddenly felt completely at ease with this unusual, gifted young man
who seemed to know her better than she knew herself.

"An Irish lad usually spends much growing-up time in the
kitchen," he said, also apparently more relaxed now that his hosting
duties had been almost entirely fulfilled. "I don't think British boys
from affluent families do, but it's different in Ireland. And I like
rituals," he added, thoughtfully. "They make me feel grounded in
much the same way piano practice does."

Emily's eyes lit up and she smiled, so much that a dimple in each
cheek started to show.

"Yes, that's most certainly what practice does. Both grounds you and sets you free at the same time. I've been trying to explain that magic to a couple of my new students here, but I think they may be a little too young to grasp it. Time will take care of that." She suddenly reached for her wine goblet sitting before her, and without saying anything, her host lifted the bottle from its bucket of ice, pouring her another third of a glass.

Nodding slightly, he refilled his own glass and settled back in his seat, as she'd already done in hers. "I agree that an expectation for practice at a very young age is not going to be satisfied. I'm probably a bit sterner with them than you are, but I don't know that it accomplishes much. I just can't stand it when they don't put their music first. It's another reason I'm so happy we have such wonderful world-class female musicians such as you teaching here now. We need that woman's touch to soften what I know is my uncompromising views about music and art."

"Oh, come now, Charles," Emily teased, instantly shocked that she'd dropped all formalities either because of the influence of the wine or the ambiance of the afternoon. "How can you resist those adorable little boys looking so serious in their knicker outfits and button-up boots when they study a score you know is way beyond their emotional maturity? They can't possibly understand your adamant demands for quality and always a full effort."

He pushed his dark hair back off his forehead with a laugh. "Who are you picturing now, so serious in his knickers? Trust a mother to fall for the clothing instead of the student," he chuckled.

Emily smiled as she took another sip of her Chablis. She'd had very few students to discuss with a colleague in the past and found it an unusual pleasure. "That lovely little mulatto boy brought in by his grandfather a few weeks ago. He'd been teaching the child the violin himself and wanted to see if he might be ready for the college. He's much too young of course, only around ten I think, but every little bone in his body is tuned to music. He's adorable, so maybe someday..."

The professor chuckled. "Oh, yes, he's impossible to resist. That's Coleridge-Taylor you met; Samuel," he added. "And there are others in the group. It will be quite a class someday. Vaughan Williams and Gustav Holst, they're all much the same age and all exploding with talent. But do you know what's the most wonderful thing about them?" He leaned forward in his chair, fixing his gaze on Emily's face as if to hold her quite still in her seat. She shook her head. "It's that all their parents, teachers, and mentors brought them to us. Not to Leipzig, Berlin, Vienna, or Paris, but to London and our college. All this future talent will be with us instead of leaving the British Isles for the rest of Europe. That's what we're here to do." His eyes flashed with an intensity she hadn't seen before.

"And we'll make them teachers as well as musicians, Emily. We'll instill the joy of passing their skills on to others right here, and that includes those who can't afford the classes, like Coleridge-Taylor, and many others. That's why we need to raise even more money than we already have. There's so much to be accomplished." He sank back in his chair, finally spent by the excitement of his vision for the future of the Royal College and Emily's role in it, as well. She felt a bit odd to see herself as part of a specific group of performers rather than an individual within an amorphous community.

"And you see me as a part of this . . . team?" she asked, trying hard to understand what it was he was asking her to do.

"No, no, it's not a team!" he exclaimed. "It truly is a family. The members in a team must let go of their individuality and blend seamlessly together. That's not what we do here. Each one of us retains his or her singularity while we offer support and loyalty to the group. We give the best of what a family can offer: allegiance to each other. The Royal College family is already producing results, such as the little ones with giant talents. Do you see?"

Emily nodded her head slowly. "I believe so. But perhaps you rhapsodize about family because of your age. You haven't had time to develop the bitterness that comes with disappointment." She realized suddenly that the strain of the last weeks of dealing with her own family's troubles had left her depleted in an odd way. There'd been too much pain and disappointment and not enough music. "Still, I wonder if I might not moderate the bitterness with a piece of chocolate cake, Charles," she said, in hopes of diverting his attention to give her emotions time to recover. But Charles was not so easily distracted.

"That might be so," he said, thoughtfully, "but I know that as we age, we'll still have our musical family and we'll always be here to support each other. Someday, you and I will be very good, old friends."

"Maybe . . . ," she said, her voice drifting off somewhere else, ". . . but I'll always be older than you."

Watching the smooth, even way her host carved her a slice of cake with his letter opener instead of a cake knife, Emily began to believe anything was possible at this strangest of tea parties. She took a polite forkful of cake and closed her lips around it, letting the rich dark chocolate frosting melt slowly on her tongue. "Oh, my," she exclaimed. "I hadn't realized it would be so good." Charles had also taken a bite at the same time, smiling serenely as he acknowledged his cook had outdone herself again, and that he was not surprised.

"How can you know how good something will be unless you try it?" he asked, innocently. "And by the way, I've enjoyed watching your husband rehearse the chorus for our upcoming concert. It's very decent of him to volunteer to help me right now when I have so many irons in the fire." He took another mouthful of cake and nodded gently, as if acknowledging the fact of its superiority once again. "He's gifted with singers, you know," he added as an aside, as if Emily might have underappreciated her husband's talents. "He certainly could have a place on our staff as well, if it's something you think he might consider."

She shook her head. "I don't think he wants to work full-time but thank you for the compliments. And I'm not sure I would want him working with me, anyway." She'd put the cake down when he'd begun to discuss Corey but picked it up again and ate two more large pieces in succession, hoping to cover what might have appeared a thoughtless remark about Corey's musical abilities. It was not how she'd intended it.

"Ah, well you must be the one to decide what works best for you," Charles said, looking at her without any discomfort or judgment. "I want *you*, and nothing should come in the way of that." Emily put her plate down abruptly with a clash of the plate and fork. "Forgive me," he said. "I didn't mean it as it came out. I only wished to convey that ever since your father sat here in this room and told me about you, I knew I had to have you; for the college, I mean." His usual smooth, unperturbed expression had begun to look a bit strained, and a faint blush spread up to his hairline. He pulled a handkerchief from his inner pocket, wiping his face with it and suggesting perhaps the little office was becoming too "close." "I'll crack the window a bit if you don't mind," he announced, rising from his chair and turning his back on her to open the casement behind him. By the time he'd turned again, he was as calm and easy as he had been at the beginning of their lunch. Emily gave no indication she was uncomfortable with the conversation.

"Charles, the college is going to train orchestral conductors, too, is it not?" she asked as if there had never been a break in their conversation.

"Oh indeed we are," he answered, cheerfully. "It's time we had someone other than a German leading our great symphonies." He smiled at her fully.

"And you yourself are a concert conductor," she added thoughtfully. "Do you find that training helps you in other life challenges? I have a friend who feels we should play the orchestra as Wagner said he did but never people's lives. Would you agree?"

"I would," he said, "although it's not so easily done for some. But it does seem to lead to much happier outcomes for all concerned, including oneself. I remember suggesting that to your father once, but not getting far with it."

"Ah," Emily whispered quietly, almost to herself. "Perhaps that's where I get the tendency . . . but I'm not used to being so idle," she added with a genuine smile. "Would you let me help clean up our delicious banquet and dispose of the ice bucket? I can't just sit and watch you do all the work." She picked up her wineglass, draining the little that was left of her Chablis to indicate she was truly finished with her meal and ready to free her host, and herself, for an afternoon of whatever lay ahead for them both. She'd begun to feel the intensity of the professor's message and needed room to breathe more freely to think more clearly. At that precise moment, a tentative knock on the office door made Emily jump slightly in her seat, but the professor smiled, apologizing for the interruption and explaining his students and staff were used to his perpetually open door.

"Come in," he called out, barely changing his position while Emily found herself swiveling around to see who they'd be dealing with in the professor's close quarters. She smiled inwardly at her discomfort, recognizing immediately that the school environment was quite different from Grosvenor Square. There she knew every possible connection and interruption in advance, mostly in charge of the interactions even in her father's house. But this factor of surprise reminded her more of the de Koningh mansion in America when her children had been small, and almost any possibility had to be expected and adjusted to.

The door inched open slightly, and the coffee-and-cream-colored face of a beautiful mixed-race girl in her late adolescence peered around it. "Oh, Amanda," the professor exclaimed, "come, come in. Have you met Madame de Koningh yet? She's going to be teaching in our violin department—that is, I hope she will be!" he added with much enthusiasm.

"I've seen you occasionally in the halls," Amanda said, gently bowing her head before opening the door any farther. "But we haven't officially met. I know of your reputation, of course. What a pleasure." Moving through the narrow opening in the door a little, she seemed aware of the tight quarters and compensated naturally to take up as little space as possible. And yet, she had the most unusually regal bearing Emily thought she'd ever seen in a girl of that age. "Forgive the intrusion," she said with a slight bow to both Emily and the professor, "but we're starting final rehearsal for the concert at the Gaiety in Dublin now, Professor Stanford, and no one seems to know if we're singing the Schubert or not. Could you clarify?"

"Well of course we are, Amanda." His response was robust. "How could students of mine ever question if we're doing Schubert? Do you need me to come with you now?"

"No, sir, not now. But possibly you could stop in later this afternoon to hear how we're doing. It would be much appreciated." She flashed a beautiful smile at Emily as she started to back through the door again. "Thank you, and I'm sorry for the intrusion." The professor nodded magnanimously, and Amanda was gone as suddenly as she'd arrived, silently shutting the door and leaving Emily in a state of disbelief that she'd been there at all.

"Another mixed-race student," she breathed in wonder. "And another scholarship . . . I had no idea. And she's so . . . noble of manner." She looked to Charles for clarity.

"Coleridge-Taylor will not be our first," he said with a grin. "Yes, Amanda was our first voice pupil of mixed African heritage, and a female musician as well. But she's no scholarship student. Amanda is the youngest daughter of Ira Aldridge, whom you may have seen perform Shakespeare anywhere there's a theater presenting it. He was born in New York, but moved here a long time ago, I suppose aware that he had a better chance of success on the British stage and living here as well." Emily's large dark eyes widened as she nodded, acknowledging her familiarity with the famous actor.

"Amanda was born here," the professor continued. "I do feel her mixed race—her mother is Swedish—plus her family background in the performing arts give her a real advantage in her future career. She's studying with Jenny Lind, fortunate both from the point of view of the quality of a world-class teacher but also with Miss Lind's cultural background. Amanda's mother was only too delighted that we could provide a little of her own culture in her daughter's daily musical training here."

"You're right that she has a much better opportunity here than in America currently. It's something my husband has been upset about ever since the war ended in America. Both the lack of public music education in general, as well as anything of value for the newly freed African population have disturbed him ever since he traveled in the South with his father after the war."

The professor's eyes shone with pleasure. "Well, Corey's working now with Amanda in our chorus group. You should talk with him about her. One could not be anything but inspired by her voice, and she will also make a great teacher someday. She's already working with some of the young ones who want voice lessons, and I can see that spark in her that will benefit us all." He reached over for Emily's glass, carefully wrapping it in one of the napkins with the reverence due its crystal perfection. By the time Emily stood up and brushed her skirt off to be sure no evidence of the picnic or chocolate cake came with her, both hampers were packed and closed with only the remaining ice bucket visible proof of the meal they'd shared.

"Charles, this has been a great pleasure, and I'm more than impressed with your entertainment skills. I can see why you're the ideal choice to run this new college in every way imaginable. And now I must go and give thought to what you've proposed. I promise to get back to you soon when my personal life has settled down a bit and I can see my way better." She held out her glove-less hand, as she always had since she'd passed childhood, and he grasped it securely, apparently used to the more direct human contact women of his profession preferred. She smiled and turned toward the door, sidestepping her chair with some skill in the tight space.

"Ah, your trouser culottes again!" the professor sang out. "You must have ridden your bicycle here."

She turned and flashed her smile at him, but not from embarrassment with his discovery of her skirt separated into trousers at the back. "I did," she said, "but I had to bring it inside the front door as you have no place outside to secure it. That would need to change if I came here to teach."

He nodded with a chuckle. "Rest assured," he said. "I shall have a bicycle pole installed at the side of the building tomorrow." She didn't know quite what to say to the speed of his adaptation, and so left the room without comment, nodding at him again as he accompanied her to the front door and her bicycle, and offering another breath of thanks before leaving through the main entrance. Emily was relieved to realize no one of great importance had come in after her to see the unusual vehicle there, as the image the college presented suddenly mattered to her. She was also thankful that she would have some time to be alone in her head while she rode home in the fresh air. She needed order and understanding for the chaotic jumble of thoughts spinning in different directions since the start of her picnic with the professor of composition and conductor of the new Royal College of Music orchestra.

Professor Robert Haussmann
New York City, New York, USA

Dear Robert: 30 September 1885

I've been thinking about my early lessons on the violin with you
lately . . . you have had the most lasting effect on me, at my
center . . . I'd like to have the same impact, all my personal trials
and triumphs as a violinist turned into assets for another generation of young musicians. This is what families are for, is it not? To
pass on the things that matter from generation to generation. In
this case, the music is everything.

Thank you profoundly,
Emily

17

Epilogue

"It was a lovely funeral. I'm so glad I could get here for it," Emily said, turning to Connie and noting how well the years fell on him. Now that he was in his sixties, his formerly blond head had altered to a frothy gray, as if the luster of his good spirit had found a way to manifest itself in his looks. He never wore hats, as most men did, and so his curly silver head was even more noticeable. The soft yellow silk ascot at his neck spoke to his aversion for ties. His fame as one of the House of Worth's designers was not hidden behind a costume of conventionality, dressed as he was in a dapper light gray three-piece suit at the Westminster Abbey funeral.

"I wish Father had come with you," Connie said, watching his mother closely for signs of exhaustion brought on by the long journey from New York to London, and subsequent emotional stress of the ceremony for one of her dearest friends, Sir Charles Stanford.

She smiled gently. "Your father didn't want to leave the house in New York. He's always felt it was his duty, even as a young boy. I think he was so delighted to get it back after your grandfather died that he doesn't want to miss a moment in it now. We revert to our childhood habits in old age, and he's definitely re-creating his youth."

Connie grinned. "That must be hard on you," he said.

"Not at all," his mother answered quickly, with a flash of the familiar dimples he saw so seldom now. "I preferred him then. He was a lot more fun, and we were much closer." Connie chuckled, unable to hide his pleasure in his mother's free spirit and the picture of his now elderly parents as children frolicking around the de Koningh mansion on upper Fifth Avenue. He'd feared Stanford's funeral might drain her, but her legendary energy was still apparent even though she'd recently traveled from New York and would be returning there not long after the funeral, a lot of effort for someone her age.

Leaving the north choir aisle of the Abbey when the service was over, he'd let his mother linger a bit longer at the nearby grave of Henry Purcell, showing no impatience to get out to the sunshine of the warm April day. "Here lyes Henry Purcell Esqr. who left this life and is gone to that blessed place where only his Harmony can be exceeded," she whispered, reading the shield with his epitaph. Connie knew his mother needed to visit with her musical family. He'd read in *The Times* that morning of Sir Charles's legacy from the world's great musicians who came before him, and that he'd shown how "thoroughly as composer he belonged to their line." Those great musicians who followed him—who hadn't been killed in the Great War—had performed his compositions at the ceremony in his honor. The orchestra of the Royal College of Music, led by his friend Sir Adrian Boult, ended the service with a funeral march Stanford wrote for Tennyson's *Becket* in 1893. Emily remembered the first time she'd heard it played at the college, bringing back vividly those early years of joining the faculty at Professor Stanford's insistence.

"He never got over the loss to the Great War of all those young men he taught," she murmured. "His boys . . ." Connie watched her but said nothing. She needed to talk. "George Butterworth's death almost killed him, but Ivor Gurney's gassing and Arthur Bliss's wounding pushed him further into the abyss. He was too sensitive for war. He never really recovered from the fear of the air raids by the zeppelins." Emily looked distressed by the pain of her old friend's escape from London to Windsor.

"As tough as he could be on his students and colleagues, he had the soul of a romantic, and his exacting habits were about his reverence for the music, in no way affecting his generosity of spirit towards the musicians he loved. They had no trouble adjusting to calling him *Sir* after he was knighted because he'd always been 'Sir' in college. But it was hard for me."

She smiled softly as she gazed out the window of the Grosvenor Square house she'd been born in, cared for now by Connie and his wife and four children. The mews she could see from the window no longer sheltered a horse; an automobile had taken its place. Connie's offspring had once used the extra stable space the groom had lived in to play with the noisy toys their mother found objectionable in the house. It had never been a home to her, nor had her father ever lived in it for very long, so she was at peace now with the fact that it had a family filling it with the spirit and life it deserved. It was ironic how she couldn't imagine William here, or in anyplace else, for that matter. He'd never belonged anywhere, it seemed, which made it easier not to think of him too much at all.

"I heard he had quite a temper—Stanford, I mean—falling out to the point of hostility with his old friend Hubert Parry. And those fights with Elgar . . . ," Connie added, wanting to show his mother he had been engaged in her narrative to bring her back. "May I pour you some sherry?" He raised the decanter on the library bar, poised as he waited for her response.

"Not really," Emily said, still looking out the window toward the mews. "He ended up successfully lobbying for Parry to be buried in St. Paul's Cathedral, and that would not have happened without him." Connie frowned slightly, obviously struggling to follow her conversation having nothing to do with his offer of sherry. "I warned him," she muttered, softly.

"Warned whom, about what?" Connie lowered the decanter while he waited to find out where his mother's thoughts had strayed.

"Charles," she answered forcefully, turning to look Connie in the eye. It reminded him of her challenges leveled at him and William when they were children. "I told him that family can disappoint in the most horrible ways—those we love are not always loyal to us. But Charles was too young to understand and I'm afraid he was often hurt by those he most constantly supported, Edward Elgar being a good example." Connie frowned more deeply, watching his mother, now in her eighties, reviewing memories he didn't even know she had. "Still," she added with a deep sigh, "he always took them back, something I could not bring myself to do. So, perhaps he was right all along."

"I've never known you to hold irrational grudges, Mother," Connie said, pouring a dram of sherry and handing it to her without being asked. She was beginning to look tired. She glanced up at him as she accepted the glass barely touched with sherry and shook her head.

"Have you conveniently forgotten my refusal to attend your brother's funeral?" she asked. "I'd say that qualifies as a grudge of major proportions."

Connie eyed her steadily. His usual cheer had been replaced by a grim expression he made no effort to hide. "A funeral is a sign of respect for the departed soul and for those left behind. Neither one of those held true for you in his case."

"Ah, but they did for you," she said, pulling herself up straighter, "and for your father, and Robert Haussmann, and Johnny Dunne, and I'm sure if John Mackay had been alive, he'd have been there, too." The list of his mother's closest male companions was so familiar to Connie he took no more notice of it than he would of any of his family.

"So, you regret that you didn't . . . adjust your standards?" he asked.

Her jaw tightened and eyes narrowed. "No, never. Some things one can't forgive."

Connie took a large swallow of his own sherry and refilled the glass. "No one thought any less of you for not being there," he said, trying to gently move her thoughts forward.

"But who was I trying to teach with that lesson?" she asked, absentmindedly. "William is the only one who might have benefited, and he was the one not present."

"William would never have learned anything," Connie said, very quietly.

"I know," his mother answered. "*I* learned *that* a long time ago." Her eldest son's untimely death at the hands of a German Nationalist during the Treaty of Versailles had been predictable. He'd always practiced the art of public humiliation, as his brother knew well, which was not a useful trait in a diplomat. The German citizenry who felt betrayed by the "November Criminals" holding Germany solely responsible for starting the war took their frustration out on some of the organizers of the conference, William among them. The metaphorical target on his back had been there all his life, and she knew someone would shoot at it eventually. There was nothing anyone could have done to help him. She'd tried often and failed.

"And did your students, and musical colleagues like Professor Stanford, make up for some of the disappointments you had in William?" Connie asked, watching his mother very carefully. He knew enough not to try to push her away from the thoughts she wanted to complete. "You seemed elated when all those young musicians from the Royal College spoke with you, and Sir Adrian Boult introduced you to the congregation with such respect and warmth. We could feel the admiration for you coming from all that illustrious Royal College crowd. Did that not make you feel fulfilled and proud?" He suddenly dropped to the stool next to her chair to get a better look at her face. Her cheeks appeared to be wet, and her expression was one of profound regret. And yet, her large dark eyes shone with an inner fire suggesting a complete disregard for the years the soft lines in her face endorsed.

"Yes," she said, "I'm proud of us all. And most of all thrilled for Charles's sake that his vision of a self-perpetuating legacy spawned by the college would take on such monumental proportions. I think of my own students who are influencing all the most gifted musicians of their day. I noted Marian Anderson has just been signed by the RCA Victor company as their first African singer. And Paul Robeson is touring and living here now, undoubtedly because he wasn't welcome in America, but that's England's gain—which reminds me that every great singer today has been influenced by Amanda Aldridge. I remember the day I met her at the college. What a present she's given the mixed-race community of artists as well as all the rest of us." Emily's smile seemed lit from within. "And oh, what a voice!" Connie nodded slowly, aware that his mother had touched so much of artistic importance in her life and career.

"What a joy it is to befriend a musical instrument at an early age," she said, looking at Connie directly as if he'd understand perfectly, which he did. His own artistic expression had found him as soon as he could hold a pencil. She nodded, reading his mind. "There were times I thought the trials of my life would consume me, but that magical violin of mine always saved me. I wish every child could have a chance to form such an attachment early in life, as early and as powerfully as you and I did." She rested her head on the chair back, closing her eyes.

"We're the ones," she whispered. "Tried as silver; it's nature's way."

Author's Afterword

It's been almost a decade since I decided to satisfy my curiosity about Emily Alden and Corey de Koningh. As much as we try to convince ourselves our characters arrive by some mysterious divine intervention, they're always iterations of ourselves. There are many elements of me as a child in both Corey and Emily. Researching and writing a story about the themes of the nineteenth century running parallel to those of the twenty-first gave me the chance to let them out to stretch at last.

Emily was lost and alone, suffering from an overwhelming fever in a huge bed in a strange house not her own. Likewise I couldn't shake visions of the visits from Corey during her illness to rescue her from that loneliness and the grown-ups he thought were treating her poorly. And so, I had to write about these two children or be driven mad by them. Of course, the story grew from there, naturally, surprising me as much as anyone else. And the similarities and differences between their time of living and ours were impressed on me with ever increasing power whenever I made a new discovery in my research.

And oh, how that research threatened to take over the story and my sanity at times! As always with history, one thing leads to another, and knowing what to discard and what to keep became the biggest challenge of all. When it wasn't the introduction of the bicycle as the primary advancement to women's social lives, it was the development of a new era of professionalism for every endeavor in Victorian society. The momentum of change took over British life to a dizzying degree, even as the class stratification seemed unshakably in reverse. And when I couldn't find what I needed in the source material I had at hand, I turned to living classical musicians to verify and share their wisdom of the musical arts.

Most unexpected for me was that this adventure with these two children took me with them through to their old age. Between readers who wanted to know "what happened next," to my editor, Walter Bode, who insisted that there was more to be told each time I finished a book, it was impossible to avoid the inevitable. More of their lives needed fleshing out. And so now with this third book in the series, I feel I've gotten to know them as if I lived with them side by side, with people who had real historical presence, helping me to travel back and forth in time. They shared the crucial lessons of their day, and that's all we can ask of the past, because it prepares us for the future as nothing else can.

Acknowledgments

Anyone familiar with my books knows I have an allergy to the standard form of acknowledgments. Pages of names listed with little or no attempt to make them meaningful to a disconnected reader serve no purpose, and are, in fact, an embarrassing dereliction of the author's duty to make sense of the words on the page. Of course there are hundreds if not thousands of people who have affected the product of one's imagination, but as such they need not be noted with any specificity, as it's a natural event occurring to us all.

Where I break with that is to thank the individuals who have joined me as collaborators. And again, with this last book in the Emily Alden Trilogy, they are mostly the same people who started out with Emily and me in the first and second books. My editors, Walter Bode and Dan Janeck, took us all on an adventure this time that greatly affected the book, making it better and more of what I'd intended to begin with. My designer, Katie Holeman, slipped seamlessly into the graphics that represented the book best with a minimum of effort, suggesting the third time might be the charm. And my publishing partner in Momentum Ink Press, Paul Pitcoff, somehow never lost faith that the long delay presented by the pandemic wouldn't sink the book completely. I am so grateful to the entire publishing team for their calm, unwavering belief in my ability to slog through my pandemic artistic inertia.

And then always, I salute the musicians and performers who inspire me as a great collective, along with Sean Lee and Jia Kim, two of the most singularly generous string instrument players who never send me away when I need a musical question answered. Along with those patient inspirers, I must always thank my writing community and all of you in the current workshop around the writers' table who brought me out of the pandemic stupor I found myself in last year. Denise Dailey, Janet Mackin, Kathleen McGraw, Helena Sokoloff, Eric Grossman, and always Paul Pitcoff, whose idea it was to resurrect the workgroup again. Without you all, *Tried as Silver* would never have been finished.

Thank you, and happy creativity to you all,
—*Sidney S. Stark*, 2022

BOOK GROUP QUESTIONS

Designed to start a discussion, not finish one.

1. Is there a sense of change in the music and musicians who write and play it in late-nineteenth-century England? If so, why? What is it and who is bringing it about?

2. What are the existential issues in Victorian society, and how are they dealt with?

3. What are some of the new technologies bringing about change for British society?

4. Why were the Victoria postage stamp and the bicycle considered to be the most important innovations of the era?

5. Did you have a sense of who Charles Worth was before reading the book? Are you curious to know more?

6. How was art changing during this time, and did it mirror the changes in music?

7. How did the gossip of European society of the late nineteenth century mirror the social media of the twenty-first-century world?

8. How had the morality laws changed during the 1800s? Why did some laws not change, even in societies boasting sexual freedom?

9. Why was the reformation of the Royal College of Music so important to the musical legacy of the composers coming from it in the late nineteenth century?

10. Although there were a few people involved with the college's rebirth, why was Sir Charles Stanford considered to be its most important benefactor?

11. Why did Emily finally recognize the importance of teaching to the success of her career?

12. How were Emily and some of the other characters able to find pleasure and fulfillment when their lives at times were not what they'd imagined themselves living?

13. What does acceptance mean, and how does it change Emily's view of the world as some doors were closed to her and others were opened?

ABOUT THE AUTHOR

With *Tried as Silver*, Sidney S. Stark has completed the trilogy of historical novels about a female violinist at the turn of the twentieth century. Her next work will be a book of biographical fiction, moving to the era before and during the French Revolution.

Sidney writes personal essays published on her popular blog, **The Unblocked! Writer**, and is the founder of MOMENTUM INK PRESS, a micro-press cooperative printing the books of writers whose work deserves to be shared with discerning readers. Follow her on Facebook, Instagram, Twitter, and on her blog at https://theunblockedwriter.com.

Momentum Ink Press is a cooperative advancing the work of writers unavailable through traditional commercial publishers. Each book is carefully reviewed by a collection of authors, editors, and designers ensuring an authentic artistic version of the writer's best work. By selecting and reading a Momentum Ink Press book you are joining and supporting a community of readers and writers committed to quality in literature. We hope you appreciate our books as much as we enjoy bringing them to you.

www.ingramcontent.com/pod-product-compliance
Lightning Source LLC
Chambersburg PA
CBHW050408260626
47156CB00003B/925